Paperback/hardcover published in 2019 by
Rouge Planet Publishing.

Illustration by Gerónimo Ribaya.
Editing by Jim Spivey/Working Vacation Studios.

ISBN 978-1-946807-15-1
Fiction / Science Fiction / Post-Apocalyptic / Dystopian
CIP data for this book is available from the
Library of Congress 2019937292.

For
MonkeyBear,
Poppy-Pop,
and Róní.

Inspiring to the end.

WORLDS OF IAIN RICHMOND

Thank you for purchasing this book. Visit
www.iainrichmond.com
and sign up for my spam-free newsletter
and receive a free copy of
BEYOND TERRA, Tales from the Seven Worlds,
an anthology of short stories!

I'll let you know when new releases are in the works, give you sneak peeks at rough drafts and original storyworlds. Free, no spam and a unique view into the worlds of Iain Richmond.

IAIN RICHMOND

BATAL

SPARTAN CHRONICLES

ROGUE PLANET PUBLISHING

If you enjoyed
***Batal, Volume I of the Spartan Chronicles**,*
please leave a review to let the world know.

Independent authors need your voice as much as their own. Thank you for supporting my storyworlds.
Without you, they would not exist.

– Iain Richmond

Min ma jgarrabx il-hazin ma jafx it-tajjeb (THOSE WHO HAVE NO EXPERIENCE WITH EVIL CANNOT KNOW THE VALUE OF WHAT IS GOOD).

— SKYE STONE PROVERB

1

RED, WHITE, & BLUE

Mediterranean Sea
Island State of Malta
The Present

The residents of the ancient walled city of Mdina rose that morning to a clear sky and gentle sun. Beyond the towering walls and rocky hillsides, the sea lay flat with the occasional ripple running from any one of a number of lazy oars pulled by rugged men in colorful fishing boats.

Elias Spartan rowed his boat just far enough that he could easily see the red tile roof and balcony of his family's home. Locking the oars to the boat's gunwale, he reached deep inside his wool coat and produced a two-handed flask filled with bajtra. Not seeing the small form he was waiting for on the distant balcony, he took a heavy swig and savored the magical remnants of fermented prickly pear. *If one sip hit the spot*, Elias thought, *two would finish the job*. So he took another mouth-filling slug. He glanced at his phone, stuck with Velcro to the inside of the hull: 6:20 a.m. He had at least ten minutes before she would shuffle outside, rotate the telescope his way, and wave. A tradition he'd shared with his father from this same spot and now one he played out each morning with his youngest daughter.

He glanced at the fishing nets on the deck and instead grabbed the coffee-stained newspaper that was smaller, thinner, and more expensive than it used to be. Printed words felt right on a fishing boat. Elias stretched out and for the first time read the front-page headline: **North Koreans Militarize Space Lab! USA, China, and Russia Follow**. He scanned the paragraphs and a chill rolled over him. According to the *Maltese National*, the North Koreans had smuggled a dozen nukes into their "space lab" over the past decade. The USA and Russia quickly amassed nukes onto their own space platforms.

"Always finding new ways to threaten the world," Elias mumbled. "Maybe we should talk more and terrorize less." Weathered hands crumpled the pages into a ball and tossed it near the stern just as a figure moved across the distant balcony and traipsed toward the telescope.

Elias rolled on the bench, found his binoculars, sat upright, and focused them. A curly black mop of hair appeared behind the telescope and Lela's small hands rotated the copper cylinder toward the sea. A smile broke across his face as she waved then followed with a spastic throwing of more kisses than Elias could catch while still trying to hold his binoculars. The kisses stopped. Lela spun back toward the house, where a woman ran out, scooped her up, and ran back inside.

The boat's hull rattled and buzzed, the phone rocking back

and forth while its screen flashed red and white with an EMERGENCY ALERT symbol followed by:

BALLISTIC MISSILE THREAT INBOUND TO MALTA & SURROUNDING AREAS. SEEK IMMEDIATE SHELTER. THIS IS NOT A DRILL.

Surely this is a mistake... His wife's image appeared on the phone, and Elias ripped it off the hull, staring up at his home. "What is happening—?"

"ROW ELIAS! ROW FOR YOUR LIF—"

The line went dead and was replaced with a flashing ALERT.

Elias snatched up the oars, dropped them into the locks, spun the boat around with one oar, and then ripped them through the water's placid surface. Other boats small and large raced and rowed all around him. Thunder boomed and echoed above from the cloudless blue sky. As Elias pulled harder, shiny streaks appeared from the west. Reddish, blurry dots that left white trails raced in from the east. "Oh God! No, no, no!" His arms were numb, the oars skipping, losing their rhythm. Directly overhead, a field of white dots erupted.

A bright flash exploded in the north, followed by a towering fireball and the unmistakable shape of a mushroom cloud. *Sicily*, Elias thought; he had friends and family there. More clouds climbed high into the graying-sky from all directions—some close, some distant. Spain, the United Kingdom to the west, and possibly Turkey or Syria to the east? The shapes kept appearing, growing into one another as they reached for the sky.

The sea pulled his fishing boat away from the approaching shoreline. His body spent, chest pounding and lungs burning, Elias dropped the oars. His fishing boat was dragged north. He flipped onto his back, chest heaving, and he spotted the outline of his wife and three children on the fading balcony. He tried to raise an arm, a final farewell, but he could not move.

A shadow covered his boat. The sky darkened and the sound of rushing wind grew to a deafening roar. Elias Spartan's fishing boat disappeared into a fifty-meter wave churning with bodies, boats, and buildings—heading toward Mdina's walls.

2

BATAL & DANU

Skye Stone
Four Hundred Years Later

A gentle knock sounded on the woven grass and hide door.

"Batal, are you awake?"

The thick stone walls of the small room held the early morning heat at bay.

"Yes, Mother." Batal sat up, spun his lean, tanned legs over the straw mattress, and yawned. "Ready in five minutes."

The shadow remained under his door.

"Blessed eighteenth birthday, my son. You are an elder now. I'll leave so you can use the light." Steps echoed down the hallway, and the shadow disappeared.

Batal stood, stretched, dropped his shorts to the limestone

floor, and opened his bedroom door. Natural light and growing heat poured in from the shaft that ran from the roof to the foundation at the center of the structure. Naked, Batal started with his feet, spreading the space between each toe.

"Check," he mumbled and ran his hands up each calf, both thighs, then moved to his man-parts. Relieved, he angled his back, so its reflection was lit on the wall-mounted mirror. Fine, white lines started at his shoulders, cascaded serpentine downward, and ended in a large mottled patch above his ass. "Scars look bright today."

He then squinted at a small dark spot sitting just under his left shoulder blade. "You may be new." He shuffled closer to the wall. "Shit. Almost made it to eighteen without a single one." He raised a hairless eyebrow. "Still, a record."

Batal rotated in the light, looking down at his thin, but muscled chest and found a single hair. "Ha! How you like that!" he exclaimed, fluffing the lone follicle the best he could. Grabbing a small hand mirror and using it in concert with the wall mirror, he checked his smooth scalp, neck, and ears. Batal stared into his own golden eyes. Even your eyes weren't safe; radiation seeped into everything. "Check."

"Breakfast is ready!"

Batal caught the strain in his mother's voice. *She's lifting something heavy. Bread!* he thought; dense, beautiful, and as important as clean air: Birthday Bread. "Coming!" He stretched toward the pile of clothes on the cold floor, sniffed for the cleanest ones, and was on the move, getting dressed as he hopped, stumbled, and bounced toward the kitchen.

Reaching the tall arch that led into the open space with the cob oven in its center, Batal pushed his arm through the shirt's final sleeve and appeared out of the dark corridor. Batal stood wide awake, the scent of bread swirling up into the vaulted beams bracing the stone-slabbed ceiling. He then stared at his mother, a broad shit-eating grin covering his face.

"Birthday Bread!" Batal hugged the small woman, his arms wrapping around her slight frame, which disappeared within his broad embrace.

"Careful, Batal."

"Sorry, Mother." He released her, his gaze falling on the many lesions covering her arms, neck, and smooth scalp. Her skin was much darker than his and hid her wounds from a distance. She was getting old, already in her early forties with a healthy chance to make it to sixty, which was rare these days, but not as rare as it was during the early generations.

No wife or children, Batal was already older than when most healthy fathers had their first child. He had the start of his first radiation lesion at eighteen when average men were covered in them. His family, the Spartans, were the most successful breeders in all of Skye Stone. This also made Batal's pairing crucial to his family's future and that of the island fortress they called home. Skye Stone's vast walls kept the fire and waves at bay, but the radiation continued to flow, silent and deadly. It was carried by the wind, pushed through the ocean currents and filtered by every living creature left on earth.

Batal sat heavy on one of the four small stools set around the wooden table. The grain ran smooth and tight; oil from generations of Spartan hands permeated the table's surface. The scent of fish, herbs, and blood emanating from the table hinted at the skill and trade that kept Batal Spartan, and the ancestors before him, in luxury. Fishers fed the community's survival and provided immense economic might to the island nation of Skye Stone. But Spartans were as much fisherman as warriors.

A mighty loaf of steaming bread thumped on the table before him.

"You're somewhere in that head of yours." His mother sat at the stool next to him. "The bread is cooling, let's eat it before the aroma fades, and the fish no longer swim at the surface." She reached under the table and rested a small earthen container with a shiny lid in front of Batal.

His face lit up. "Is it?"

She laid a small, flat knife next to the container. "Open it and see."

Batal's hands were on the container before she finished. "Butter! Fresh butter!" He tore off a chunk of bread, slathered it on, passed it to his mother, and repeated the action for himself.

"Batal?" She leaned in and kissed his butter-covered cheek. "I love you. Your father would be so proud of who you have become."

His hands stopped, and as chunks of bread fell from his mouth, he ran his arm across his mouth to clear a path. A shine covered his eyes. "I love you, too... I miss Father. I miss them all."

"But we are still here and you, my son, must carry on the Spartan name and improve upon the Spartan family line," she replied. "We only hope to find others that resist the radiation better than those lost to it, with bodies hardened to its effects, and its poison. Your father has given you a longer life, and you must do the same for your children."

Batal stuffed more bread into his face, added more butter, and tore larger-size pieces from the shrinking loaf. "The aroma is fading." Another smile appeared and Batal handed his mother the last piece with extra butter. "First, Mother, I must pull in the nets and deliver the catch to the market"—he pushed the last piece into his mouth—"and then we can speak of finding me a wife without lesions." Cheeks filled, mouth covered in glistening grease, Batal stood, bent down, and hugged her. "I adore you, Mother, and there's no better Birthday Bread than yours."

She looked slyly to her son. "And how would you know I have someone in mind?"

"You are a baker—the best on the island. And you trade with those from beyond the wall. You are also the most cunning of creatures and the smartest person I know." Batal opened the exterior door and turned back toward his mother. "And you always have a plan that begins long before the rest of us learn of its existence."

"You know your mother well," she replied as she tossed him a warm sack. "On your way. Plenty to discuss later."

He smiled, slung the bag over his shoulder, closed the door, and headed toward the outer wall and his fishing boat.

Batal looked skyward. The walls of Skye Stone were legendary long before missiles rained from the sky and changed the Earth forever. Twenty meters tall and twenty meters thick, the original protective barriers crafted of massive blocks of limestone withstood the first nuclear blasts four centuries ago. But that was only the beginning. *The Book* told of winds made of fire turning the island's inhabitants who were living above ground to ash and that the waves that followed washed away the few who still lived as well as the endless corpses of the dead. The ancient island formerly known as Malta was left for those poor souls who toiled in dank basements and cellars. These survivors rose by the hundreds and took control of what was left and called it Skye Stone.

Quickening his pace, Batal still could not fathom the image of the original walls at only twenty meters tall. Generation after generation used those walls as a foundation to build higher and higher until the outer wall now stood at over a hundred meters tall. The entire city was in its shadow. A mirrored tower in the island's center stood at one hundred twenty meters tall and provided fresh air and extra light for the city's five hundred inhabitants.

Batal reached the reinforced Iron Gate and the armored Guardians who controlled it. Two Scottish deerhounds sat at attention; their lean gray forms followed Batal's every move. Curiosity filled their noble gaze and just enough ferocity to remind those that the deerhounds had a purpose to their watch, one that would end badly for anyone that crossed their pack. After the Descent, the deerhounds were the only dogs to survive in Skye Stone and adapted faster than their human companions to the new, harsh environment.

Jenna, the biggest of the four Guardians, leaned down until Batal could smell the homemade wine on her breath and see the patchy stubble on her head. "Leaving late today, aren't we, Batal?"

"Birthday. You know what that means?" He unslung the sack over his shoulder and offered it to the four women who had become his good friends over the years.

"Birthday Bread!" They shouted in unison and tore the loaf into pieces. The gate opened, Batal walked through, then it closed behind him to the ravenous sounds of those hungry but working on being hungry no more.

In the distance, white-topped waves broke on the stone jetty surrounding the deep, small harbor facing the Mediterranean Sea. The sky was hazy but clearer than most days and its pinkish hue appeared a softer shade than usual. Batal glimpsed the towering pinnacle of rock in the distance. The lone remains of

Sicily. Much of the European continent lay covered in water after the land split and collapsed during the quakes, but a piece of Sicily rose to towering heights. When other survivors chose new names for what became new lands, the proud few of Sicily kept its name. They numbered less than one hundred and were renowned for the finest sea salts.

Colorful wooden boats bobbed in the protective zone. Harvest yellow blazed over their gunwales, Skye Stone blue on the first planks, coral orange and sun yellow followed until the final planks of blue disappeared into the sea without showing where the boats stopped and the sea began. Each sail sat rolled at the bottom of a tall wooden mast. A commotion spilled out from around the curving outer wall. A large, drunken man with his back to Batal was kicking at something substantial in the shadows. *There's always one*, Batal thought as he walked away from the brute and toward his fishing boat.

A guttural bark boomed from behind, and then a sickening yipe, followed by a sorrowful howl.

Batal froze, spun back toward the thug, and before he realized it, had covered the twenty meters between them and was standing behind him as the bastard continued to kick the furry mass still snarling and snapping at his boot.

As the bludgeoning boot reloaded for another go, Batal hooked it with his foot, grabbed the back of the man's shirt, and pulled back as hard as he could. The man's lone remaining boot lifted off the ground, his head flung back, and he fell headfirst into the gravel. In dazed amazement, the brute was back on his feet and hammering wild punches in Batal's general direction.

Batal blocked the first few, but one got through and sent him sprawling to the ground. He kicked up hard when he saw the wild-eyed man lunging downward, Batal's foot sinking in the ample fat around the brute's midsection. He was now on top of Batal; the stink of the man was everywhere, the weight crushing the breath out of him. Batal kept up his elbows, hands shielding his face, but he was losing, and it was about to get much worse.

"AAAHHHHH, ya fuck'n bastard!" the brute howled. The punches stopped and the man reached back to seize the neck of the bloodied and matted Scottish deerhound biting his leg. The dog snarled, the man gripping its neck tighter, but the hound didn't let go. Instead it clamped down harder. The man cried again and shifted his weight.

Batal seized the opportunity and thrust up his hips, throwing the man off to the side, then rolled with him until he was now on top, unloading short, powerful punches. One after another, Batal alternated his hands with the shift of his weight until the man was silent, alive, but unconscious. Batal pushed off the man's bouncing belly and staggered a few steps away and dropped to a knee. The deerhound shook its head a few more times and let go of the meaty calf it had shredded.

"It's OK." Batal huffed, blood running from his nose and the corner of his mouth. The dog was tall, its matted silver fur formed twisted lumps, but its eyes were bright. Injured, but alive. "Aren't we a lovely pair? How've you survived without the protection of the wall?"

He stood, put his hands on his knees, and looked again to the brute-size heap of shit that lay in a pool of blood and piss, snoring with frothy red bubbles simmering through broken teeth. Batal moved toward the dog, which stood its ground even now, and kneeled next to it. Keeping his eyes down, Batal offered his hand for it to sniff.

The deerhound limped forward to Batal's extended hand and

clamped its teeth down on it. Batal flinched but did not pull away even as its grip felt close to breaking skin.

"Fair enough." He looked into the hound's eyes. Even up close the majesty of this ancient breed was humbling; its mistreatment infuriated Batal. "I'll never lay a hand on you, and as long as I draw breath, you will have my protection." He saw something else in its stare, too: strength and fearless loyalty. "And I'll have yours?"

The deerhound released his hand and sat, panting, exhausted. Batal caught the hint of steel under its matted neck. He reached for the collar buried in tangled fur. The hound showed its teeth but allowed him to uncover the small piece of scrap-metal shaped like a heart that hung from a threadbare material with a thin piece of wire.

"Danu," Batal read. He then glanced at its belly to check if it had man- or lady-parts. "Hello, girl."

Her ears perked up, back straightened. She was a magnificent creature, and Batal would not forget it. As soon as he pulled in the nets, and if she allowed it, he'd clean her up and offer Danu a new home within the mighty walls of Skye Stone.

3
FIRE & WATER

The Mediterranean Sea was calm today, waves rolled toward the rock foundation of Skye Stone, lapping at Batal's colorful fishing boat before making their way toward the island. Danu sat a hundred meters away on the long and narrow rocky spit. It served as a fishing point for those who couldn't afford a boat or couldn't build their own. Red, yellow, and green dots bobbed in the distance: the fishing boats of brave men and women willing to leave Skye Stone's protection in hopes of a bigger catch.

Batal tried to bribe Danu aboard his boat, but the blood-caked dog watched her potential friend from a safe distance. The Scottish deerhound radiated strength even from there, Batal felt. He threw the hand-knotted net as far as his lean, muscled form would allow, his technique flawless. The net arced, spread into its full circumference, and dropped into the water without a sound. Batal held the rope that allowed him to retrieve it.

Counting to ten, he followed the shadow cast by the mighty outer wall of Skye Stone, a black form moving across the water's surface a few hundred meters away. The wall soared into the low-hanging morning mist, its stone blasted smooth as far up as Batal could see. Hundred-meter waves broke against the fortress often and with little warning. Fire had scorched the stone black in places, and the waves did their best to erase the remnants of the nuclear blasts. The firestorms came and went when the dilapidated and malfunctioning space stations orbiting the Earth discharged their aging missiles. Centuries of random warheads fired from uninhabited orbiting platforms that sooner or later would fall from their deteriorating orbit and unload their remaining munitions on islands below. Until that day, Skye Stone and the remaining inhabited islands played the ultimate game of roulette.

Reaching ten, Batal pulled the line until he reached the net. Looping the edge on a long spindle fastened at the stern of his boat, he turned the wheel fixed to the deck and cranked in the net. The first few meters coiled around the spindle without a single fish. Batal strained and leaned into the wheel. Water vibrated and a mass of floundering anchovies broke the surface.

Danu barked and spun in circles on the spit. Batal cranked the final few meters of net filled with twisting silvery shapes. *How in the hell can she see the net from there?* Batal cranked the catch into the center of the deck and quickly sorted the fish. "Three eyes," he observed and threw the anchovy over the gunwale and back into the sea. "Too many lesions"—back into the sea; "healthy, happy, and two eyes"—into the container fitted at the bow. On and on, Batal sorted the fish into those showing the effects of the poison and those not.

Just like me, Batal pondered. Trying to give the next generation a few more months of life and a healthier existence. An existence bent by the ability to live with radiation and build an immunity to its effects from a three-century-old war that continued to this day. But now the missiles had no targets, no enemy; they fell from the sky without warning.

"Danu?" Batal remained fixed to the deerhound still turning in circles and howling. The net was clean, Batal pulled it up at the center, bunched it and moved to the stern. Danu's barking grew more chaotic and reached a frenetic pace. Batal spun and released the net at the perfect moment. It soared, spread out—she's looking up. He followed the angle of Danu's muzzle into the sky.

"Oh no." Batal let go of the line and the net shot out into the sea.

Behind a thinning layer of clouds, a red ember released a gray streak. *West*, Batal thought. *Toward the Dead Zone.* The line of exhaust stopped, and the fluffy streak was already dissipating. Somewhere within the low-hanging mist, high atop the wall of Skye Stone, a bell sounded; then another joined in until a chorus of clanging copper found a rhythm.

"God, no. It's too close." The words slipped out of his mouth as the red missile dove toward the horizon. "Danu! Come! Swim, girl, swim!"

The deerhound stopped its circles, her bark fell silent and, without hesitation, she jumped into the sea and smoothly paddled her way toward Batal's boat. *She's too far out. She won't make it.*

"Swim, Danu, swim!" he bellowed. He threw anything not fastened down into the water. Within seconds the boat was empty, the anchovies gone along with spare nets, weights, seats—all floating off the starboard side. Batal kept a single line, thick and heavy with a small lead weight stitched into the end. He pulled the mast out of its base, dropped it on the deck, grabbed a dark pair of goggles and slid them over his scalp and began swinging the line in expanding circles.

A bright light bloomed along the horizon line and a mushroom cloud climbed high into the distant sky. The sea remained calm, no wind, just eerily quiet, the only sound was the swinging of the line and Batal's own heaving breaths.

Muscles burning, Batal released the line. It shot out across the sea, the lead weight barely missing a floundering, exhausted Danu, who was within twenty meters of the boat. The deerhound bit down hard on the line and Batal pulled with everything he had. Claws scratched at the hull planks and Batal reached down and lifted the dog into the boat. Batal moved to the mast, released the mainsail and tossed it overboard, then lifted the mast and dropped it back into its base.

"Hold on, Danu," he commanded, and the deerhound wedged herself under the stern bench. Batal held the release line for the emergency sail. It was three times the size of the mainsail and could pull a thirty-foot fishing boat at a sickening pace under heavy wind. Or the sail could just as easily flip the boat. The expanding mushroom cloud eclipsed the horizon. Batal kept his eyes on the water, waiting to release the sail, waiting for the pull or the push.

If the current pushed, he thought, *we may make it back to Skye Stone before the deadly winds hit.* If the sea pulled away from Skye Stone and toward the horizon, a wave was building, and if he was lucky, a powerful wind would charge in front of it. Either way, they had to wait.

Batal's eyes remained locked onto the small, limp embroidered flag attached at the top of the mast. The drooping end stitched in bright blue thread fluttered and fell. Batal pulled the release line taught and waited. A cool gust hit the bow of his boat, almost knocking him off balance and into the sea. Batal widened his stance, leaned toward the bow and into the wind, the flag at the top of his mast blew perpendicular to the wooden post.

He turned his head, found Danu's gaze fixed on him. "It's OK, girl." Like hell it was, but as long as he had the emergency sail, they had a chance. The small boats in the distance had raised their emergency sails early and were being drug toward the horizon—and their doom.

Danu's urgent barks echoed from under the tiller.

"Too soon, Danu! We must wait!" Batal yelled over the rushing wind hammering his chest and face. The mast flag drooped, and silence consumed them. Batal's heart thumped in his chest and ears. The water under his boat pulled, ripping at her sleek wooden hull and dragging her toward the growing wave and away from Skye Stone.

Another bark, even louder.

A second later Batal felt it. The warm breeze at his back. The strengthening wind pushing from the stern and toward Skye Stone, and against the current of the receding sea. He tied off the release line, strapped himself onto the stern bench, and grabbed the tiller. Batal looked to his feet and smiled at the fury face looking up at him, swallowed hard and triggered the emergency sail.

VOOOOMP!

A massive, red expanse of waxed canvas caught the blasting wind. The bow of the fishing boat lifted out of the churning sea and the sail drove it toward the island fortress. Batal clung to the tiller, desperately steering the boat toward the harbor and the lone gate he had left only hours before.

More barks from Danu prompted Batal to glance over his shoulder. A dark mountain of water loomed behind them. A wave like none he had ever seen before blocked out the sky, with only the red heat of the rising mushroom cloud above it. Bodies pinned to the decks of colorful spinning fishing boats dotted the wave's expanding surface. He turned back and the protective rocks around the harbor were closing in. The iron gate beyond was open. Jenna stood next to it, smashing the hilt of her sword into the swinging bell attached to the stone.

"JENNA! Hold the gate!" Batal bellowed and his fishing boat flew toward the stone jetty that now seemed like a fortress of its own.

VOOOOP!!

A gust hit the sail, Batal yelled as he fought with the tiller. His hands were numb, but he held fast, aimed at the harbor's opening, the rocks rushing toward his fragile boat. A shadow raced beyond his boat and up the stone wall. Batal stole another glance behind them.

Rocks gashed the port side, and Danu and Batal flew forward, his back smashing into the mast, Danu crushing into his chest. The fishing boat shot across the harbor, skidded onto the beach and rolled to its side, dumping its passengers onto the sand.

Everything was black, a roaring sound filling Batal's ears. Water dripping down his face, something was biting his neck, he was spinning in darkness... Something growling, the great hunting mountain was upon him, smashing his body into the sand.

"BATAL! Get the fuck up!" The voiced boomed in his aching head. Growling replaced the roaring noise.

His eyes flashed open. Danu was pulling him toward the iron gate, Jenna racing toward them, armored, shouting as each leather soled boot hit the sand. She reached down and ripped Batal to his feet. "Run or we die!"

With Danu leading the way, Batal and Jenna scrambled toward the iron gate, now only partially opened. The other Guardians stood inside, hands gripping the locking mechanisms, ready to close it the second they entered. Batal felt the pull of the coming tsunami at his back, the Guardians at the door were screaming.

Danu shot through the opening, and Jenna threw Batal the last few meters. He crashed into another Guardian, both falling to the floor. Jenna squeezed through, slammed the iron gate shut, spun the locking mechanism, then dropped to her knees exhausted. They all sat, backs pressed against the outer wall, Danu laying across Batal's lap with the other two deerhounds leaning against the Guardians. Jenna reached out to Batal and he quickly took her hand.

"The sea brings life. Each wave a gift. The wall is strong. Each stone placed by an ancestor, each ancestor a stone." They whispered in unison, repeating the prayer as they had many times before, as all around them fell under a growing shadow.

They were beautiful. They were terrifying, Batal thought, fear mixing with the excitement of surviving something others would not. *Regardless of the death toll, Skye Stone could not exist without the replenishing gifts brought by the titans of the sea.*

4

SHE GIVES & SHE TAKES

Shovels scraped across stone on every pathway and rooftop. The fertile soil fell from the tops of every building; even the Guardians shoveled the thick layer off the stone wall. Lines of carts made of reeds, hides, and old fishing nets effortlessly rolled up the narrow lanes in a well-practiced dance. Some pulled by teams of deerhounds, some by groups of goats, and others by the human residents of Skye Stone, but regardless the joyful harvest continued. Every capable soul stopped what they were doing and joined in.

Carts began their journey empty and by the time they reached the farms on the northern end of the island, they were overflowing with the churned sediment of the ocean floor. Each wave that crested the wall brought rich soil for the farms, clay for pottery and water filters, wood for buildings, and weapons and death for those who couldn't find shelter from the ocean's power. Skye Stone celebrated life at every opportunity as death was guaranteed.

Music filled the five boroughs within the walled island, but outside, the fishermen paid homage to their fallen in silence. The sea lay flat, but the water was clouded with a hint of the destruction it carried only hours before. The city's stone wall stood proud, without a trace left on its limestone surface of the biggest wave to break across Skye Stone since the records were first entered into the Book in the year 105.

Batal looked across the glassy expanse toward Sicily and all he could see were the familiar faces of men and women who'd surrendered to the power of the sea, clutching their hounds, knowing what was next. Many of those friends now lay before him, in pieces on the beach. Twenty-five inhabitants of Skye Stone dead, most fishermen and deerhounds caught out on the open sea and a few crushed by logs and debris inside the wall. Survival came first and grieving was short, because life was short.

Danu sat and leaned against Batal's leg. He looked down at the deerhound, her fur brushed, wounds mended and dressed. She had saved his life. If she had gotten into his boat when he had called instead of remaining on the spit, they would have pushed out beyond the shadow of the wall, out where the fish clustered around the patches of thick algae and seaweed. Instead, Danu had spurned his coaxing, waiting for Batal to prove himself worthy of her loyalty and friendship. She had limped out to the end of the rocky spit and watched. *I could not leave you far behind*, Batal thought. *Kept you in sight and stayed close to the safety of the wall.* He scratched Danu's ears, bent down, and kissed her muzzle. "Thank you."

Those gathered outside continued collecting colorful pieces of wood along the beach, placing them inside a fishing boat beached on the sand. Another group of fishermen carefully collected the dead or pieces of the dead and wrapped them in finely embroidered cloth, then laid them in the center of a reed mat laying near the shoreline.

Seeing nothing left on the sand, the fishermen lifted the mat and tenderly placed it into the boat, folding the extra material over its contents. Pushing the boat back into the receding tide, the men and women, now waist deep in water, surrounded the boat. A fat clay-fired jug passed between hands. After every swig, they spoke a name to the sea and then to the sky and passed it to the next waiting hands.

"Kennan..." "Amal..." "Curra..." "Tara..." "Fatima..." "Lia..." On and on the jug moved until the twenty-fifth and final name —"Tassos"—found its peace in the sea and on the wind.

Batal lingered on the last name. *Tassos*, he thought, *you are not the last.* There were twenty-six who died. His eyes looked to where he had left the brute. The beast who'd hurt Danu, the man Batal had left bleeding on the ground. But instead of guilt, his eyes moved to where Danu sat a few meters behind them. He had served justice.

The jug found the rough hands of the eldest fishermen. Holding the jug over the folded reed mat, she poured its remaining contents over the bundle and spoke to the sea.

"To the sea we are born; to the sea we toil; to the sea our ashes return and our souls are free." The others repeated each word as they pushed the boat toward the center of the small harbor. Bells sounded from the top of the wall that was no longer hidden in the mist. Most of the residents of Skye Stone looked down from their perches on the wall above. Harvesting the gifts from the sea ceased, it was time to pay tribute to what the sea had taken.

The bells fell silent, then hundreds of flaming arrows, one after the other, rose into the sky. Dropping with precision, they formed a single glowing trail into the fishing boat. Not a single arrow hit the water, creating a growing melodic hum from flaming shafts with stone tips piercing spruce, again and again. The fishing boat burst into flames.

Hours passed, and the citizens left the wall, returning to the harvest. Batal and Danu remained on the beach, standing in silence. The flames consumed the boat and its contents until the sea's running tide took what was left. The sun hung low in the sky. *Tired and worn like everything else in this world*, Batal thought. His eyes locked onto the northern horizon, the setting sun illuminating a shape on the water. He turned toward the wall and the iron gate. "Jenna!" He yelled over the distance and pointed.

"What is it, Batal?" She took a few paces in his direction, stopped, and ran back. Pulling her sword, Jenna spun the blade and hammered the hilt on the bell.

Far above, shouting echoed from the top of Skye Stone's wall. Bells rang, and Guardians shouting orders massed on the north and western sections.

For the second time in less than a day, another force was rising. Not a mountain of water, but worse: the northern horde was coming. Following the tsunami and hoping it had caused a breach or weaknesses in the stone. The shadow split into a fleet of strange-looking vessels hugging the sea. Batal had never seen boats of this shape. This was something new.

Jenna shouted from the gate as Batal and Danu ran toward her. "You're no longer a fisherman, Batal! Grab your bow, sharpen your sword, and don your armor! You didn't think we all trained for nothing, did you? Hurry!"

5

THE NORTHERN HORDE

Bells hammered and clanged from all directions, but the west wall of Skye Stone was closest to the approaching horde fleet. Batal quickly fastened the last strap of his leather armor, snugging it tight to his chest. Grabbing the hilt of his short sword, he raised it over his head. The blade caught the light. Engraved fishing knots radiated on the cold, gray iron and reminded Batal of what he was fighting for. Artists from the former lands of Scotland, Libya, Russia, Turkey, Greece, Egypt, and many more had made their mark on its blade. People of Skye Stone chose to build, love, learn and stand side-by-side against those who wanted to destroy, control, and bring darkness.

Batal then lowered his sword, spinning the blade point down to slide it into the leather sheath attached to the back of his armor next to a rectangular quiver filled with arrows. Danu sat by his side, watching his every move, her silver fur lending a philosophical depth to her face. She turned toward the corner of his small stone bedroom and stared at the long wooden chest Batal now hastily opened. He grabbed the stout bow and slid his left arm through until the bow rested in a notch molded in the leather at his shoulder. Each of the bow's copper tips was sharp and deadly, unlike the stone tips of the bows used for practice and ceremony. His breathing matched the pace of the clanging bells. He quickly dropped to a knee in front of Danu.

"I'm scared, girl. Never tried to kill anyone before, on purpose at least. Protect Mother, Danu." Batal ran his hands down each side of the hound's face.

She replied with an assertive bark, her eyes never leaving his.

"Good girl. I'll be back when it's over." He sprang to his feet, a layer of sweat already having formed under his leather armor. "I can do this," Batal whispered, and then was on the run. He kissed his mother at the door, knowing she would don her armor and weapons as soon as he left. She was too old to stand on the wall or join the defenders of the five boroughs, but would protect their home if needed.

"I'm coming back. I promise," Batal called out as he ran up the stone path; a promise he hoped he could keep.

Skye Stone was in full defensive mode. Armored citizens joined the Guardians on the wall and within the boroughs. Batal ran through the paths, keeping to the right and passing others moving the opposite direction on his left. Everyone had their place and their duty. Batal's was at the base of the western wall, near the iron gate that led to the harbor. The clanging bells of Skye Stone quickened in unison, a warning of the Horde's fleet closing the distance. Batal reached the base of the outer wall. Ropes with thick wooden slats attached to their ends hung half a meter off the ground, the other end somewhere high above on the wall. They looked like swings for children dangling from a one-hundred-meter rope. Next to each swing was a perfect stack of bricks. In full battle dress, Jenna stood among a dozen other Guardians and moved toward Batal.

"What can I do?" He heard the rattle in his voice.

Jenna placed a hand on his right shoulder, her eyes falling on the gleaming tip of the bow slung on his left. "Take a deep breath, Batal. The first time is always the hardest." She looked up. "And these fucking bells don't help." She smiled and pointed to a nearby wooden slat. "We need good bowmen on top in case they try the old ball-and-chain maneuver again. Besides, you're surprisingly accurate with that short bow of yours. You terrify the target dummies!"

Batal had witnessed the Horde's innovative attempt to climb the wall years ago from the ground. Catapults on the decks of their landers had launched a steel ball over the wall attached to a line, which was then attached to a Horde warrior. One in twenty made it to the top in one piece. That math was tough for the Horde, but most of the lines weren't long enough or the steel balls weighed much less or far more than the warrior attached to it. *Either way*, Batal thought, *innovative*.

"I'm scared, Jenna. I've never actually fought in battle before." Batal swallowed hard, his bow and sword rattling against his armor.

"I am scared, too, and I've fought in many." Again she pointed to the wooden slat. "Stand firm, and when you're ready, tug on the line. Then hold on and don't scream. You can do this, Batal. We need you."

He lifted one shaking foot onto the plank and then the other, took a deep breath, blew it out, and tugged on the line as he gripped it tightly with both hands. Nothing. He looked to

Jenna, who was now standing back a few paces and wearing a shit-eating grin.

"Am I doing it wro—" Then suddenly Batal was flying up the wall, the force pushing him toward the plank, his hands sliding down the rope toward his chest, knees buckling. "HOLY FUCKIN' SHHHHHHIIIIIIIITTTTTTT!"

Fifty meters up, he flashed past a basket full of bricks going down. The sound of bells and voices grew stronger as up and up he went, hands numb, ears popping, the texture of stone and mortar a blur.

"You can stop screaming now!"

A familiar, deep baritone sounded, rattling Batal's head.

"Batal! Shut the fuck up and let go of the rope!"

Batal stood on stone again. He opened his eyes to find a familiar face standing before him. Drago stood in full battle dress. Tiny copper and brass scales in overlapping rows covered his short, powerful frame. The armor was light, effective and stunning in the sunlight and a striking contrast to his ebony skin. "Uncle Drago!" Batal almost broke into tears, but the sight of the rising empty basket once filled with bricks steadied him. "How did you know how many bricks to use?"

Drago laughed. Over his uncle's shoulder, far below, Batal watched the Horde's fleet come into view. "We didn't, which is why you came up much faster than you should have." Drago slapped him on his bicep. "Eighteen and still skinny, but you feel strong and not a single lesion in sight!" He leaned closer. "Call me Drago. No uncles up here, just Guardians."

"Yes, Drago." They walked the ten meters from the inner edge of the wall to the crenellation. At almost two meters tall, Batal could see over the merlons but stood in the open crenel to get a full view of the approaching ships. "What kind of ships are those, and why aren't we attacking them?"

"Too far away." Drago grabbed at his side and handed Batal a worn brass spyglass. "Tell me what you see."

Batal pulled on each end, opening the spyglass to is full length, then peered through. "Fleet of forty. No, forty-one wooden ships, flat with a split mast at midship and no sail. Flat deck, no gunwale or hatch I can see." He continued to move the spyglass from one boat to the next.

Drago grunted. "Hurry, Batal. They'll be within range of our longbows soon. What else to do you see? Look closely."

Batal pressed against the thick stone wall to his left and leaned into the opening, trying to get closer. At slightly over one hundred meters above the sea, he felt little fear of the height, but the incoming fleet terrified him. He would show no fear in front of Uncle Drago, the most magnificent Guardian of Skye Stone, now that his father is dead. "I don't see anything else—wait! There's something under the water behind each ship. Maybe twice the length of the boat, maybe a meter or more underwater." He passed the spyglass back to Drago.

"Well done, Batal. Now only if we knew what they were dragging and where they've hidden their crews." He folded his arms. "Someone is steering these boats, and unless they can smash through a mountain of stone, they must have another purpose." A single, high-pitched bell sounded, and all the others fell silent. "Stand behind the merlon."

Batal moved behind the stone fortification. "Should I ready my bow, Uncle Dra...I mean, Drago?" He hated the waver in his voice, but he couldn't control it.

"No, longbows first. Watch, pay attention, and learn. When

the Horde shows their vile forms, and you can smell their filth on the coming wind, then you may fire your bow. And if need be, you'll rappel back down to the streets, draw your sword, and defend Skye Stone!" Drago spoke like thunder, his eyes bright and full. "You are here because you are a Spartan. You will take your place among your people, a fisherman no more." Drago passed Batal a silver flask decorated with a beautiful engraving of a sword crossed with a bow. "This is yours now. It was your father's, and one day it will be your son's or daughter's. We drink, and then we fight!"

Every man and woman on the western wall raised their own silver flask. "FOR SKYE STONE, FOR THE BOROUGHS, FOR FREEDOM!" The Guardians then tipped back their flasks, emptied the contents in seconds, and returned the empty containers back under their armor.

Drago spread his heavily muscled arms wide and stood in the open space of the crenel. "LET'S SEE IF THEY BURN! FIRE!"

Long, flaming shafts flew from the top of the wall in waves. Each was perfectly weighted to carry a glass cylinder filled with the most exceptional, and combustible, distilled spirit on Skye Stone.

6

SHIFTING POWER

Batal stayed behind the stone wall but peeked out to see the small burning shapes far below. The Northern Horde's fleet sat covered in flame, smoke billowing up high into the pinkish air above Skye Stone.

Drago passed the eyeglass to Batal. "The decks are burning, but the amount of smoke is not right. There is something underneath that protects the vessels. And still no crews."

Smoke and steam mixed and rose in thick clouds. A distant hissing sounded from the sea. Forty-one low-slung ships disappeared under the choppy surface. A cheer erupted, followed by a rhythmic thumping along the top of the wall. Longbows striking the stone floor in unison.

Still, something was wrong. Like a great school of sharks, the shadows of the horde fleet remained just below the surface. Even from a hundred meters above, Batal watched the shapes change. They grew under the sea. Whatever these crafts were, they evolved before the eyes of the Guardians. Now longer, leaner and positioning themselves fifty meters from the base of the wall.

"Ready the stones!" Drago ordered. The thumping bows fell silent. Wooden chutes pushed out, just below the top of the wall, a few meters beneath the Guardians' feet. Workers loaded round rocks at the top of each chute. A simple trigger system would release the rocks, smashing enemy troops landing below. But the Northern Horde's vessels remained a few meters beneath the sea and continued to spread out no closer than fifty meters from the wall—just out of range of the stones.

"They're rising!" Batal shrieked, his voice higher and louder than he intended.

Forty-one elongated vessels broke the surface, each covered in pieces of burnt timber with a dull metallic layer glowing beneath. On each stern, a long iron catapult lay parallel with the surface of the water. The split masts no longer protruded toward the sky, but now lay flat on the starboard and port sides, stabilizing the boats.

Drago spun left and yelled to the Guardians on the wall. "Take cover! Prepare to return fire." He then turned to his right and repeated the command.

Each Guardian moved out of their open notches and behind the stone merlons and waited to see if the catapults could reach their lofty perches. A single round, wooden sphere ran down the arm of the center ship's catapult and came to rest in the bucket at the end. Batal watched in terrified fascination. A snapping sounded, followed by a splash off the bow of the ship as the arm flashed up with tremendous force, stopped, released the sphere, then snapped back into the water. Similar spheres ran down the catapult arms of every ship, coming to rest and waiting.

Up the orb flew, rising hundreds of meters in seconds. The

sphere was high above the wall but looked to fall far short of entering the town. It reached its zenith, then split into pieces like a protective shell and released an object.

A sail, Batal thought as the mottled material spread and filled with air, a humanoid form dangling below it. It was flailing its arms like a marionette from the weekly Saturday morning show put on near Skye Stone's market. *It's controlling it from below. Incredible.* A shaft then whistled downward from the descending figure, and a Guardian fell from the wall.

"Short bows! Fire!" Drago roared. Arrows released, turning the airborne Horde soldier into a bloody pincushion that drifted toward the cobbled pathways below.

The crack of wood hitting steel filled the air. A wave of spheres flew from the sea and climbed high above the wall. Batal unslung his bow, nocked an arrow, and waited for the nearest shell to release its contents. Before the first wave of orbs reached its maximum height, the catapults launched another. Pieces of wooden spheres dropped from the sky and patchwork materials unrolled then filled with air or fell like stone. But alive or dead, the Northern Horde was clearing the walls of Skye Stone and descending into the streets.

A projectile hammered the stone next to Batal's face, splinters gouging his neck above his leather armor. He raised his bow toward the sky, anger taking his fear, then loosed his arrow. The tip entered his target's and exited the other side of the man's head. A small crossbow fell from the sky and clanked off the stone near Batal's feet.

Drago slapped him on the back. "See, your last name is Spartan!" He then twisted around, gutted a dark form landing behind him, and turned back to Batal. "It's in your blood!" Drago pointed to the rope leading to streets of Skye Stone. "Go help my sister!"

With only the slightest hesitation, Batal shot another of the Northern Horde from the sky, tore off two strips of cloth from the dead Guardian near him, wrapped his hands, and grabbed the rope. As he repelled down the wall, the snapping of cloths as they filled with wind continued to sound in the sky above. The bloodthirsty horde of the north was raining down upon the people of Skye Stone. Guardians, bakers, farmers, sons, daughters, and fishermen all unsheathed their short swords or leveled their bows.

Once Batal's boots hit the ground, the stench of the Horde overpowered him. He dry-heaved, steadied himself, then drew his sword. A shadow appeared by his feet, and he dove to the other side of the path. An armored sack of flesh exploded on the stone—its fluids splashing across Batal's chest—a second before a waxed cloth filled with holes settled over the mess. In moments, Batal was up and running toward his home, his mother, and Danu.

Barking sounded from the smashed doorway to his home. Ten meters ahead on the pathway, two of the Horde appeared from around a corner and leveled their crossbows. The skin around the invaders' necks hung in layered folds, resting on some kind of leathery chest plate. Batal fought the need to release his bladder as they fired their crossbows. A bolt sliced across his left forearm, opening a flowing wound. He moved left, another bolt skidding off the wall to his right. A guttural roar came from the doorway followed by more barking, as the rotting figures worked to reload their crossbows.

Batal's blade moved across the neck of the man on his left and the head tipped backward, attached only by loose skin.

Following his momentum, he spun and drove the blade down, cutting through the thin leather on the back of the other man's legs. Steel hit bone and stuck. A terrible bellow erupted, and the man fell. Before the invader hit the cobblestones, Batal drove the point of his bow through his back.

Unable to pry his sword from the dead man's leg, Batal ripped his bow from the corpse's back and raced into his home through the shredded doorframe. There was no barking, no screams, just silence. "Mother!"

Streaks of blood covered the floor, leading down the hall and toward their bedrooms. Batal crept forward, holding the point of his bow like a spear. "Mother?" There was no response. He stepped through the hallway, following the bloody trail that stopped at the door to his bedroom. Pushing the door open with the point of his bow, the light from the hallway illuminating his back, he whispered: "Mother?"

In the corner a shadow loomed, the light from the door showing a bloodied face and a raised sword. In front of his mother, covered in gore, stood Danu—her head lowered, hackles up, growling like a crazed beast, and her eyes glowing red in the filtered light. At the deerhound's feet lay a gutted creature that held only the vaguest resemblance to a human, its damaged armor holding its remains together. Fractured bones, ruptured organs, and sinewy white strands glowed in the light and layers of muscle flayed open dripped blood into a growing pool beneath the body.

Bells sounded from the wall and the boroughs. *We've beaten the Northern Horde*, Batal thought. Danu's growl deepened, her stance lowered.

"Danu, it's Batal." He laid his bow on the floor and went down to his knees. "It's OK, girl." The scent of the Horde, their blood mixed with his own, permeated the air. "Mother, are you injured?" She shook her from side to side, lowered her sword, but remained silent, the shine of her eyes resting on the silhouette of the dog.

Batal opened his bedroom door the rest of the way, letting the light shine in. He then turned sideways, vomited, and sat on the floor. Danu sprang forward and rubbed her wet muzzle against the side of Batal's face. He put his arm around the deerhound, and his mother joined them. Like a dam bursting, Batal wept as his mother comforted him.

"AMIRA!" The voice boomed from the front of the house. "BATAL!"

"We are alive, little brother. We're back here. Your nephew and his dog were very brave."

Footfalls echoed on the stone. Batal wiped his eyes. "Careful, Uncle Drago. My deerhound doesn't like surprises." His hand rubbed the side of Danu's muzzle.

A thick hand wrapped around the door frame, then Drago's broad face appeared from the side of the opening. "Is it safe?" A blinding white smile appeared from the outline of his head.

Danu remained alert but laid her head in Batal's lap, his mother's hand resting on the dog's side.

"She likes you, Uncle." Batal fought to keep the tears from starting again. "I am happy you are alive."

Drago slid to the floor next to them. Blood ran from multiple wounds. "Your arm looks in need of attention, nephew, and your neck has a splinter the size—"

"As does your side, shoulder, and head, Uncle."

Drago leaned in until his forehead touched Batal's. Amira leaned in to join them, while Danu rested in the center. "We lost many to the Horde." His arms squeezed Batal tight. "We need to replace them, otherwise we are vulnerable."

Batal swallowed hard. "Mother has a plan. There is a strong woman who may join me."

Amira leaned back, still stroking Danu's sticky fur. "The Akiro clan in the Hiroshima Archipelago has sent word through the spice traders. They have a twenty-year-old daughter without a single lesion."

"Twenty?" Drago sat up straight. "She is older and healthy? How is she not partnered yet?"

"She has favored the life of a warrior and the path of choice. She is the Akiro clan's greatest fighter and there are others who will come with her." Batal's mother then fell silent.

Drago looked to Batal, back to his mother, and nodded. "Then how, older sister, is Batal to gain the union of this fearsome warrior and why would the Akiro clan send others?"

His mother brushed Batal's cheek. "The Akiros want the firstborn...and our blacksmith—"

Drago stood. "We can't give them the best weapons-maker in all the isles!"

"Easy, brother. Skye Stone's apprentices are ready to take over and we'll double the size of the smithy. Their training is complete, and they'll step up. As is our way."

"But why'd this woman think of joining me, Mother?" Batal asked.

"You know her, my son, at least you did when you were a boy. And she has asked for you—"

Batal sat up straight. Danu's tail wagged, her eyes moving from Spartan to Spartan. "Kaminari..." Batal said. "Yes, it must be Kaminari."

Drago exhaled. "But this Kaminari is a warrior. Tradition will be followed."

"Yes, Kaminari must submit to Batal in combat." Batal's mother extended a hand, and Drago pulled her to her feet. "Let's mend our wounds and clean up." She reached down to pet Danu. "That includes the bravest Spartan of us all. Then we'll prepare for the coming journey."

Batal got up, and both he and Drago began to speak—

"Shh, my family." She looked at their puzzled faces. "Drago, you must go with Batal to the Hiroshima Archipelago. Continue to train him on the journey as you have done since his birth and make sure he can best her."

"You are my elder sister, Amira. I will do as you say. What happens if this warrior of the Akiro Clan defeats my nephew?" Drago stated with a wide-eyed Batal nodding next to him.

"Yes, Mother, what if I lose this challenge? I am a fisherman after all."

"You have never been only a fisherman, Batal. You chose that path when your father died." She held his stare until he looked away. "But your last name is Spartan. You are many things at different times, but in your heart, you will always be a Guardian. If you lose, then it will not matter. You will be dead. Now, let's mend our wounds and help the others." She headed toward the kitchen and the medical kit.

Drago turned and faced Batal. "We will continue your training. I'll do my best to make you a deadly Guardian. Your skill with the bow and sword-work saved your life today." A smile appeared as he put a hand on each hip. "I may also bring the finest thespian in all of Skye Stone. The one you loved as a boy, Batal—the puppet master—to train you to plead for your life. Just in case." He then marched toward the kitchen.

Batal looked down to Danu, who was leaning against his leg. "They're marionettes, not puppets. And what's a 'thespian'? We've much to learn." He ruffled her ears. "Mother's right. You're the bravest Spartan, and I know what you're thinking, Danu. But, Kaminari would never hurt me... Right?"

7
A MOTHER'S LOVE

Skye Stone fell into shadow and a brisk evening breeze cooled the heated, rock-lined paths and the surrounding buildings. Only a few scattered wet patches darkened the ground where the remnants of blood and other fluids required an extra scrubbing session to remove them from the porous stone. The Spartan home glowed with the soft light from the shifting flames of a fire in the hearth, and shadows danced on the face of the common room's stone and plaster. Batal rounded up the oil lamps and carried them into the kitchen to make sure there was plenty of light for stitching wounds and making plans. His mother dropped the last of the needles and blades into the dish. She grabbed a copper flask off the counter, took a drink, then poured the clear spirit over the tools to ensure they were sterilized.

"Batal, please light the lamps and place them around the chair."

He cleared his throat. "Yes, Mother," then came out in a

forced baritone that squeaked at the end, prompting a chuckle from his mother. "Why are you laughing?"

"Don't be so sensitive. You have always feared the business end of a needle. Did you rinse out your wound?" she asked as she dried her hands, reached for the copper tray laden with shiny blades, needles, and silky thread, and walked to her son.

"Yes, the wound is clean. I am lucky to be alive." Even Batal couldn't hold back his nervous laughter at that. "More of a deep scratch, really."

She held the needle with its dangling thread shinning in the light. "Did you drink the cup I gave you?"

"I did. It burns on the way down, and I feel funny. My brain is slow. I now see how it cleans your tools and needles and feeds fire, but why in the gods would the Guardians drink it?" The last few words slurred into one big one.

"You are ready, my son, but this will hurt." Amira pinched the skin together, and the seeping wound ran clear.

Batal grunted during the first stitch but soon it fell into a painful, but peaceful rhythm, stitch after stitch. "They terrified me, Mother. I killed…'men' today. I almost soiled myself—felt I would run if I had a place to go. But the wall would not allow it." He sniffed. "So afraid for you, me, and Danu. I know they are men, but not as I imagined from Father's and Uncle Drago's stories. There was something missing, something wrong with them."

His mother stitched, tied off the thread, and applied a cloth damp with spirits. Batal shuttered, his teeth grinding, and lapsed into relief.

"I cried the first time I reached the top," she replied. "My first three arrows missed the heads climbing the ladders below my feet."

Batal leaned forward, swayed, and stared at his mother. "You fought on top of the wall?"

"I did. It was a third its current height in those days, smaller waves, less stone masons with apprentices, but I am a Spartan, I am of Skye Stone. We all fight when our time comes." Her work finished, she pulled up a chair next to her drunken son and sat, admiring the clean, tight red line on his arm. "You would not be the first to shit themselves in battle."

"No, no, no. I said I *almost* soiled myself. It was only the potential of pissing my pants, but I kept the spring at bay." Batal leaned back and rested his head against the stone behind him, a trail of slobber running from the corner of his mouth.

"Next time, I will only give you half a cup." Her striking smile returned, the wrinkles on her face and scalp hiding the lesions in their depths. "I will share one story of great young warriors that may help. A story that takes place when they were less than twenty and new to death, before they proved their valor and skill on the wall and in the streets of Skye Stone."

"This is a tale I must hear, Mother. Of my father, I hope!" Batal adjusted his chair, leaned forward, and ran his arm across his drooling mouth.

She lowered the wicks on the oil lamps until only one gave light. The lone lamp and the fireplace lit her face but cast the rest of the dwelling in darkness. "The Horde came in vast numbers after a tsunami broke against our wall, just as they did today. It was as if they rode the wave itself, arriving the moment it parted the northern point. There was no time to prepare, and no time to amass the Guardians at the point of attack. The Horde scaled the wall using large crossbows that fired hooks and rope before we could respond, taking control of a piece of the wall and raining bolts down on the people below."

Batal rubbed his hands together. "How of I never heard this tale? The Horde on the wall! What happened—"

"In time...in time," his mother admonished. "Three of Skye Stone's youth donned their swords and bows and jumped onto the 'screamers'—an apt name, don't you think, based on your reaction to riding one today?—flying up the wall toward the handful of the enemy still alive. They were shielded from the Guardians on each side by their dwindling forces, but they continued to fire their crossbows."

"Father? One was Father! It had to be!" Batal belted.

"One was your father." His mother took a deep breath. "Yes, one was your father. The three reached the top and gutted the Hordes' warriors moments before the Guardians broke through from each side and finished the job."

Batal raised his arms in the air. "Spartans!"

She waved, urging her son to calm himself. "OK, Batal, let me finish. The three were of our family—Spartans. The Guardians surrounded them, chanting the young warriors' names until laughter broke out among them."

"Why laugh at the fearless men who killed the Horde warriors? Why?!" Batal cried, still not in control of his volume or balance.

"Because"—Uncle Drago's deep voice boomed from the shadows of the doorway—"first off, one of the three is the woman who mends your wounds and tells you stories she shouldn't. Second, they laughed because I had shit and pissed myself on the screamer halfway up the wall and continued to do so while I fought the Horde on top."

Batal's mother snorted between cackles, slapping her knees and throwing her head back. "Your uncle smelled far worse than any of the Horde ever could."

"It was all part of a brilliant and cunning defense!" Drago walked in with a handful of rolled-up charts and papers and set them on the table next to his kin. "And it worked, by the gods! It worked!" He was now laughing harder than his sister.

Batal cried, tears streaming down his face, laughing so hard his recently stitched wound throbbed. "I think I may piss myself." He stood and swallowed hard. "Or throw up. It is time for me to join Danu and sleep like the dead."

"Yes, time for you to sleep, my nephew, and forget about this terrible nightmare that includes your uncle and his stained pants. You did well today, and I am proud of you."

"We all are," his Mother added. "Sleep well."

Batal paused in the hallway. "Mother?"

"Yes?"

"You were in your youth when you brought me into Skye Stone." He turned to face her. "Was I small? And if I was, who watched after me during this time? How—"

"On her back," Drago stated. "Wrapped in the armor of a carrier. Today was the second time you rode the screamers to the top of the wall."

Batal used the wall for support. "You fought the Horde with a baby on your back?"

His mother nodded. "There were only a few hundred of us then. We could not leave our children behind unattended, and the deerhounds were far less numerous than today and already with the Guardians. So yes, we fought with our children on our backs, mothers and fathers. You were quiet. You did not stir." She stood. "You are a Spartan."

Batal stared, taking in the small woman in front of him who continued to astound with newly told feats of bravery. "I love you, Mother." He then belched and groaned. "Proud to be your son." Liquid bubbled with the last word. Batal then swayed down the hallway, disappearing into the shadows.

Drago unrolled the charts and rested a small piece of iron on each end. "You have done well, Sister. He is a good young man. Much like his father, but there is a softness in him."

"That softness you speak of is part of his strength," Amira replied. "It's why he survived the wave that killed everyone else outside the wall and why he found a deerhound that saved my life today. So yes, Brother, he has the warrior genes of his father and uncle"—she fixed Drago with a look of pride—"and his mother. He also has empathy. He has exactly what makes this"—she pointed toward the roof and made a circular gesture—"community of ours worth fighting for. Our only hope is for the islands to come together beyond trade, but as one people willing to fight for one another or we are all lost. The Northern Horde is growing in numbers, and based on today, their warcraft is surpassing our own—"

"You can't tell me these mindless, half-rotting beasts are smarter than we are. They are lucky to live beyond thirty, and we have yet to see or find a single female among them. They create nothing and only seek to destroy. How can their numbers grow while living as wild animals without mothers?" Drago dropped to a stool at the table.

"And yet today we fought the Horde as they fell from the sky to land within our walls. You burned their ships and still they launched their warriors far above the Guardians. They floated into our boroughs, protected by armored wooden cocoons, killing as they descended. How many fell of our five hundred?" Amira touched Drago's hand.

"At least fifty." His head drooped. "By the next sun, maybe sixty. Most were townsfolk—strong fighters, of course, but their first duties were as carpenters, farmers..."

She nodded. "Then over ten percent of Skye Stone's population. If the Horde did not make these new ships, as well as the shells they sprang from and the cloth that slowed their fall from the sky, someone or something did. We need to unite the islands, and we need the Akiro Clan."

Drago placed his face in his hands.

"What is it, Brother?" Amira asked.

"The Horde. They targeted women with child," he whispered. "They knew exactly where to find them. We found maps of the boroughs on the dead Horde-men. Maps for the purpose of culling our next generation." Drago looked up. "We have spies among us."

A knock sounded on the front door.

Amira's head rocked back and forth. "The elders are here. We have much to discuss, much to plan and little time to do it."

Drago moved to the front door while Amira lit the lamps and filled a large jug of wine.

He reached for the handle. "Spies come in all forms," he reminded, then opened the door.

8

KEEPER OF THE WINDS

Batal stood in the shadows of Skye Stone's vast wall with a travel bag slung over his shoulder. Thirty stitches closed the wound on his arm, but the lingering ache constantly reminded him of what a crossbow could do and how lucky he was it had missed—mostly. He dropped the sack onto the sand. The early morning light poured in from the east, and the glassy Mediterranean Sea melted into the horizon.

The citizens of Skye Stone had remained secure behind their wall for a full day as the Guardians hunted for stragglers from the Horde's attack. So this was the first time Batal had been outside the city since he and Danu had escaped the bomb blast. "It's all the same," Batal whispered. "The harbor shows no sign of their ships, the death, or the wave that blocked out the sky." He shook his head, turned toward the distant spot where he had left the brute, lying in his piss and blood. The body now mercifully taken by the sea. This was Batal's secret to bear, his shame to hide.

The surviving fishing boats bobbed peacefully, unaware of the past or what might again breach the stone jetty that protected them.

He filled his lungs and exhaled. “Fresh air. Not even a hint of the stench the rotting clans of the north brought with them.” And that was the world surrounding the wall of Skye Stone. Something or someone, always scratching around the edges, trying to dig, pry, or bore its way to the souls living inside. Batal pondered the potential simplicity of it all. Good versus evil, light against dark? No, it was far more complicated.

Deep into the night, by the light of oil lamps and aided by Skye Stone’s most exceptional wine, his mother, uncle, and the highest elders hashed out the plan that would take Batal far from his home. Five thousand four hundred nautical miles from his fishing grounds and everything he knew. The path of the vessel he’d be on would pass through dangerous waters and near shores thick with monsters and darkness. They would leave the lands of the Northern Horde behind—

Screeching steel hinges broke his train of thought. Then excited paws thumped on the gravel and sand behind Batal.

“Danu! Clean, bandaged, and fed I see.” He bent down and kissed her muzzle, a wet tongue with the hint of sardines lapped across his face in reply. “I have something for you.”

Danu sat flat on her butt, hind legs spread under her with each rear paw splayed outside of her front legs. Batal loved this position, it looked as close to human as her nobility allowed.

“What do you think?” A strip of hide unrolled from his hand with a chunk of steel dangling on one end. “DANU SPARTAN! Etched it myself and mother traded for the leather.”

Danu stood, raised her head, and locked onto Batal’s gaze.

“I knew you’d love it.” Removing the old collar, Batal reached around the deerhound's neck. "Perfect." He locked the closure. Danu turned toward the wall but remained quiet.

Four shadows moved out from the iron gate, each laden with travel bags and gear. Uncle Drago's silhouette was unmistakable, a walking brick wall. Batal smiled when he came into the light. Jenna appeared next, and Batal froze. She was older than he was, nearing thirty maybe, but always a Guardian in manner and dress. Her six-foot-two height was accentuated by her lack of armor. Thick muscle flowed from her shoulders and back. Lesions spotted every uncovered portion of her frame except her ample and magnificent breasts, which lay beneath a gauzy, billowing tunic. In all their years, Batal had never seen his friend in this light.

"What? It can't be that you've never seen me without my armor." She shimmied her broad shoulders. "Ah, it must be these big tits that have caught your eye."

Batal looked to the ground, feet sliding over the gravel, and cleared his throat. "No, Jenna, I've just never seen you without your helmet. Your stubble is the brightest of reds." He continued to shuffle, hands finding pockets. "And yes, your breasts are quite...prominent."

"Dreaming about me, aye?" She dropped her bag next to his and took him by the shoulders. "Surely you didn't think I'd let you go by yourself?" She scanned the beach, hands set on her wide hips. "Where's my boat? Can't be a captain without it." She marched toward the water.

"It's coming 'round," Drago replied. "Stored in the protected float under the eastern wall."

Two young men with stuffed packs proudly strode up to Drago, exchanged a nod with him, then turned to Batal. The soft, light-skinned boy with only a few visible lesions held out his hand. "Good to see you again, my friend."

"Stefan?" Batal asked. "Why are you and Vlad here?"

"Thanks for the welcome!" Vlad, Stefan's tall, dark fraternal twin, stated. "Good to see you, too."

"Sorry." Batal took Vlad's offered hand, only to be caught in the other boy's iron-handed grip. "OK, you win." With a grin, Vlad released Batal, who rubbed his hand. "Are you coming with us?"

Drago moved closer to the group of reunited friends. "These fine young lads are part of the deal we hope to make on the way."

"Hope?" Stefan demanded. "How could the Akiro Clan pass on this?" He patted his soft, extended belly.

Jenna spun around from the edge of the water. "Thank the goddess you are the best bladesmith in Skye Stone, Stefan. We should get at least five farmers for you." She then raised an eyebrow. "Maybe six." She rubbed her chin, nodded in agreement with her assessment, then turned back to the sea.

Vlad put his arm around Stefan. "Everyone has their strengths, Brother."

"Yes, yes we do, Vlad, and yours is beating the shit out of people." Stefan put up his hands in an awkward fighting stance and lunged toward Vlad, who seemed to move before his brother's pathetic attempt at roughhousing and pushed him to the ground.

"OK, boys, let's move our gear to the dock. She's here." Drago pointed to the approaching forty-meter oak mast towering high above the stone jetty.

Jenna inhaled deeply and exhaled powerfully as the bow of the twin wooden-hulled boat pushed beyond the stones.

"Twenty-six meters of pure speed, the fastest vessel in all the islands!"

Batal swallowed hard. The smooth wooden catamaran used a small sail fastened to the base of her majestic mast to give her enough wind to glide into the deep, protected harbor and drop anchor only twenty meters offshore. Carved on the port and starboard of her twin hull was AEOLUS. Layers of burnished wax glowed on her hull. The sleek cabin bridging the twin hulls hung above the water and the mast grew from its center, reaching toward the heavens. Batal looked to Drago. "The ship that killed my father?"

"Don't you mean the vessel your father designed? And she didn't kill him, Batal; the Northern Horde did." Drago moved closer but kept his distance. "The *Aeolus* is the only hope we have of reaching the Hiroshima Archipelago in time and in one piece. Jenna knows every meter of this boat. Can get her to run twice the speed of the prevailing wind. There is nothing made with two hands that can catch her."

Batal moved a step closer.

"This...vessel left my father in the sea and never looked back, even while the Horde hooked him through the gut, pulled him aboard their foul ship while his entrails spilled out and the sharks circled." Batal's shoulders slumped, his head hung, and his travel bag hit the sand. "Sorry Uncle. I miss him terribly."

Drago's face softened, the Guardian morphing into the devoted uncle. He wrapped his arms around Batal. "He was the best of us, and I know he's proud of the man you are becoming."

Danu wedged her snout between their legs and wiggled in until she was in the middle, part of the pack and comforting as best she could.

"I loved your father." Drago gently let his nephew go. "A day does not pass that I don't think about him in the water, the Horde's fleet scooping him up like a fish while we escaped with our lives and little else." His eyes grew shiny. "If we had turned back, we would all have died, and Skye Stone would have lost all of their best warriors—and their fastest ship. And still it may have been worth it."

"No, Uncle, you were right, and Father would have done the same." Batal straightened. "Spartans look to the greater good, even if it means our end." He reached down and grabbed his bag and moved toward the arriving pack boat. Batal studied the ancient man rowing from the anchored *Aeolus.* Elder García had the thickest gray beard Batal had ever seen—possibly the only one. He knew the elder from the fishing grounds, and it lifted his spirits to know he had survived the tsunami and the battle with the Horde that followed.

The boat slid up onto the beach and Elder García jumped out. "Good to see you standing, young Spartan." He extended a weathered hand.

"And you, Elder García." Batal took his hand. "I didn't see you at the ceremony for the lost. I feared you might have been caught out near the shoals." A smile broke wide across his face. "But so happy you weren't."

"Even the big waves lose power at the edges. It did take a while to find one, but like your father always said, 'You can't outrun the power of the sea, but you can find her soft spots.'" He then whispered, "Lucky as hell." Elder García nodded to the others and walked a few paces with Drago. A small sack was exchanged with a handshake and a pat on the back. "Take good care of our lady *Aeolus* and she will take care of you," the elder said to the group as he took his leave.

Batal and Danu hopped into the boat, followed by Vlad,

Stefan, and Jenna. Drago handed Jenna his things and looked back at the city's iron gate, his leather boots submerged, hand holding the bow.

A small figure then appeared out from the shadow of the wall.

"Glad you waited. I thought I would have to eat all this bread by myself." Batal's mother yelled as she jogged with her gear.

She tossed her bags toward the stern of the pack boat. Batal snatched the lumpy sack out of the air while Jenna caught the others. She swung up and over the side, quickly found a little room next to her son, who was already tearing a piece off a loaf and passing it on.

Drago pushed out the pack boat, climbed in, grabbed the oars, and rowed toward the *Aeolus*. "Keeper of the Winds," he whispered. "The fastest vessel made by two hands and, hopefully, fast enough."

9

A TRITON THIS WAY COMES

The black, moonless night was split by the blade of the coming dawn. Pulled behind the vast sail branded with a head from Danu's lineage, Batal stood at the wheel of the *Aeolus* as she cut through the swells, holding a southeast course. Years ago, women of Skye Stone had crafted the sail from coatings of wax rubbed between layers of hemp cloth until a stiff, sturdy, and effective wind-catching tool emerged. They had painted the outline of the deerhound using wax infused with charcoal. From the stern, every part of the *Aeolus* reflected its surroundings in a natural tone. The sun warmed the deck, and the sea reflected off her hull. The *Aeolus* was stunning, crafted of laminated wood, cloth, and wax, then rubbed and polished by loving hands.

Not a single hard edge existed on the *Aeolus*. Every line of the catamaran ran smooth and seamless. Hatches merged into the deck that curved into the twin hulls and wrapped around the cabin floating between them. Batal thought it was more a sculpture carved from a vast block of ash and lovingly accented with olive. Running his hands over the area surrounding the wheelhouse, he never found a single standing seam under the endless coats of wax protecting her form.

Batal was a fisherman who had sailed boats of simplicity, but the *Aeolus* was different. Those whose lives depended on her loved her. Malice had no place here. His father had died at the hands of the Horde, neither this boat nor his Uncle was to blame. The *Aeolus* was more than a vessel or even an extension of Skye Stone. *No*, Batal thought, *she* is *Skye Stone*. She is home.

Jenna spoke earlier of the wax layers as if they were tree rings from centuries-old oak. *"Hard times shown in dark, thin bands and light, thick rings were years of prosperity and peace,"* she'd said while pointing to a few spots where end grain was visible.

The sun soon rose above the horizon, blazing on the rolling waves and casting shadows in all directions. Batal grabbed Drago's spyglass and spun it toward the north where a distant shadow hung. His breath quickened, and he reached for the clapper on the warning bell fixed to the bulkhead above the wheel.

"It's OK, Batal." The voice closed in from the bow. "No need to wake the others. They've been following us for two days," Jenna said.

Even without her armor, she was imposing. *Fuck that*, Batal thought; she was downright intimidating, and he loved her for it. "Two days. From Skye Stone?"

She opened her hand and Batal placed the eyeglass in it. Jenna focused the end with a single turn. "How many shadows do you see?" She handed it back.

Batal placed a foot on the rail and leaned over the sea as he took another look. "One. It plays in the horizon's mist, but one shadow."

"Move to the bow, look again, and come tell me what you see." Jenna said as she took the wheel.

A few moments passed, the sun gained a strip of sky beneath it, transitioning from red to orange, then Batal appeared again at the wheelhouse and raised the eyeglass.

"It's looks slightly bigger from the bow than it does here?" Batal shook his head, still aiming the spyglass at the distant dark spot. "I think it does. Shit, I don't...tricky bastards!" He sat down on the bench behind Jenna, placing the eyeglass at his side. "The Horde's ships are bow to stern. A single line to hide their numbers."

Jenna smiled. "You're smarter than you look, I don't care what they say. If I liked men"—she released the wheel and bent down, coming face-to-face with Batal—"YOU, Batal Spartan, would be first on my list." She kissed his cheek and stood back at the wheel. "But I don't." She laughed. "They can't catch us, and we are putting distance between us and them. The Horde may wait and try to intercept us on our return."

Batal remained silent, red brushing his olive cheeks, and a smile plastered ear-to-ear. "I love you, Jenna. You are the best of family, the family one can choose."

She straightened at the wheel. "I know." She then swept something off her cheek.

An uneven padding sounded, and Danu appeared. Her eyes half open with the chunk of iron swinging on her collar to match her winding gate. Batal slid over to the far end of the bench. Danu jumped up to take up the rest, laying her head in his lap.

"Getting the hang of this whole boat thing, aye, girl?" He moved his hand through her fur and rubbed her ears. "Haven't puked once in over a day." The deerhound raised her head and gave Batal the look she saved for less noble creatures and laid her head back on his lap.

"She was out there for months, you know," Jenna said.

"Danu?" Batal kept rubbing her ears. "I went out every dawn, never saw her until..."

"Every Guardian on the gate has tried to coax her inside at some point. I even tried a bowl of fried eggs and beer! Never saw a deerhound turn that down. But"—Jenna shook her head—"I ended up pushing it outside the gate and the bowl was empty by morning."

Batal stared at the rolling waves.

"You were right in beating the shit out of him." Jenna continued. "One of the Guardians heard the commotion, but I saw you running toward it."

Batal glared at Jenna. "You let me kill a man? What if he'd beat me senseless and left me to die in the wave?"

Jenna locked the wheel in place and turned around. "You did just fine, Batal. I had two jugs of Skye Stone's finest spirits on the line—"

"You bet on me?" Batal tried to stand, but Danu refused to move from his lap. "A man died, Jenna! And what of Danu?"

"Whoa now." She took a knee. "First off, no one died. After you took your boat out, we drug Farouk's drunken ass through the gate and tossed him in a holding cell to sober up." She paused. "And to get medical attention, champ. Farouk's stumbled around the marina a hundred times. No one knew what the hell he was doing and had no idea there was a deerhound involved." She stood. "But you, Batal. You had a Spartan moment. Yes, Guardian blood courses through your veins."

Batal let out a breath, closed his eyes, and leaned back. Danu snuggled her head into his lap. "I thought I'd killed him by leaving him on the beach. The wave was the biggest I've ever seen. Oh, thank the gods." He opened his eyes, looked down on Danu. "He deserved it, though."

"Yes, he did. Deserved an ass-kicking, that is." Spotting something on the horizon, Jenna picked up the eyeglass, and raised for a clearer view. "There they are: The Spice Islands. The Horde fears them. As should we all. Each is governed by a different tribe, and those tribes will either trade with you—or kill you. They are a fickle bunch at home, but much more pleasant abroad."

"Why not head straight for the Hiroshima Archipelago instead of wasting time with merchants no one trusts?" Batal asked.

"Your mother has a plan," Jenna stated. "And the plan involves the Spice Islands. That's all I know."

"Danu, breakfast!" The voice of Batal's mother came from the cabin's open hatch.

The deerhound rolled off Batal's lap and stumbled off before he could ask his mother if there was food for everyone else. Danu and she now shared a blood-bond. Nothing could connect the living like fighting side-by-side against those who wanted you dead. Batal stood and followed Danu toward his mother and her tray laden with food.

"I'll set the bread and fruit on the bow storage locker," she hollered over the wind and balanced the tray through the rolling swell, her sandals keeping a straight line across the deck.

Drago and Stefan staggered to their feet from their mats on the forward hulls, each suffering after a night of wine and playing Crown and Anchor. Based on Stefan's grin, the dice had rolled his way. Each of their bald heads was dusted with salty brine churned up by the *Aeolus*. Drago dislodged a small die from behind his ear. On the opposite hull, Stefan tried to squeeze by Vlad, who wanted another hour of sleep. Stefan crawled on top of his brother and within seconds found himself on the wrong end of a headlock.

"Vlad, please stop choking your brother," Drago suggested as he stretched. "His brain needs all the air it can get, and if you two fall overboard...well, we are not fishing you—"

A towering black dorsal fin rose next to the *Aeolus*. A meter down its length, a missing chunk with what looked to be teeth marks around the ragged edge—a wound that had since healed but was still noticeable. The twins froze in place, eyes wide, and mouths open. A silhouette twice the length of the boat and matching its pace appeared just below the surface. Drago moved down the railing toward the locker where Batal's mother had just placed breakfast. He disengaged a razor-sharp harpoon from the bulkhead and crept toward the twins, who were now crawling in the direction of the cabin.

"Wait!" Batal yelled as he moved toward the starboard bow. "I think it's a triton!"

Drago cocked the harpoon with Vlad and Stefan hiding behind him.

"Put that down or you'll scare her!" Batal grabbed the rail and pointed toward the dorsal fin. "See that notch a few meters from the tip? Not the bite-mark, the natural one. Mark of a female."

Drago nodded.

"And see how it's swimming next to us?" Batal edged closer. "Nice and peaceful like."

"It's twice the size of the *Aeolus*, Batal, and keeping pace with the fastest boat—"

"'Built with two hands.' I know, Uncle. Please put down the

harpoon and I'll prove it's a triton shark. We see them fishing when we go far beyond Skye Stone's shadow." Batal found the bow warning bell. "Hold on to the rail, everyone." He then looked to Drago. "If you don't put that away, she'll stay below the surface."

Drago glanced at the harpoon and lowered it, shaking his head. "You're fucking crazy." He then locked it back onto the bulkhead. "You'd better be right."

"Come now, my fearless uncle. It's just a big fish, more like a ray." Batal reached for the bell's clapper. "Last chance to grab the railing!" He then rang the bell.

The dorsal fin disappeared below the surface, and he kept ringing the bell. A massive tooth-filled mouth erupted from the sea, followed by an eye and an arching shiny-black muscular form twice the size of the *Aeolus*.

"Wooooo-hooo! Yah!" screamed Batal.

The triton splashed back into the sea, drenching Drago, Vlad, and Stefan. Batal kept ringing the bell, and the shark again erupted out of the waves and crashed back into the sea next to the boat.

"OK, Batal! You've had your fun!" Jenna hollered from the stern. "If that shark gets too friendly, it could clip us."

The bell fell silent. The triton came to the surface a final time and thrashed its caudal fin, soaking Jenna and the wheelhouse before it disappeared.

Batal slid to the deck laughing. He reached up to the tray on the locker behind him and grabbed a hunk of soggy bread and a few pieces of wet fruit. To his left—dry, stretched out, and snoring under the portside bench—was Danu. *Full, happy, and fearless*, Batal thought.

A drenched, but laughing crew joined him at the front of the cabin with Jenna walking up the deck with a scowl that evaporated when Batal handed her some "bread pudding."

"Salty, but hits the spot!" she claimed and smacked him on the back. "Love those damn behemoths. Scary-looking beyond a bloated Horde corpse, but sweet as can be." Jenna turned to Drago. "I get why these two land-rats"—she pointed at Vlad and Stefan—"have never seen a triton, but you've been out here."

"Obviously not enough," Drago stammered. "I may have shit myself a little." He laughed.

"Again, Uncle?"

"Easy, Batal. I'd hate for you to have a long visit with your shark friend." Drago stuffed another wet ball of bread in his mouth.

Batal's mother moved toward the bow and pointed. "You may want to get to the wheelhouse, Jenna. We've crossed into the territory of the Spice Islands." She scanned the deck of the *Aeolus*. "No armor, no weapons, and for the love of the Goddess, Drago, please try to look harmless."

Drago folded his massive arms, tilted his head to the side, raised his heavily scared eyebrows, and fashioned his best smile, one that said, "I won't fucking kill you, this time...I think."

"Goddess help us. That will have to do," she said, shaking her head. "Welcome to the Spice Islands. If we hold our course, look friendly"—she shot a glance toward Drago then Jenna—"we should live."

Three vessels then unfurled their brilliant yellow sails, which caught wind and drew the ships toward the *Aeolus*.

10
QUEENDOM OF SPICE

The *Aeolus* neared the dock. Her escorts, the copper-clad ships with the bright yellow sails, turned toward the horizon. Ten warriors the likes of which Batal had never seen before stood in a perfect line, awaiting the ship's arrival at the dock. More statues than human. *Each is the color of twilight*, he thought. Black, yet blue. They had the high cheekbones of Uncle Drago but were tall and lean like..."Father," he whispered. Batal stood a little taller, straightened his back, and pulled his shoulders square. The soldiers were fierce in their aged copper armor formed to each muscle and body part. The cloth beneath the plating was the same as the color and texture of the sails guarding the waters beyond.

Drago appeared at Batal's side. "See those blades they carry?" He crossed his thick arms.

Batal looked at the hooked, sickle-shaped swords dandling at the warriors' sides. "What are they?"

"Khopesh." Drago stated as the *Aeolus* slid against the edge of the dock only a few meters from the motionless warriors. “Good for slashing in close quarters.”

Batal took a step back. “Strangely beautiful.” He looked toward the end of the dock. A stone path led to a polished wooden barrier at least ten meters tall that ended in a mountainous rock on each side. “They too have a wall to hide behind. A wall of wood protecting a village of stone?” His eyes climbed the mountain peak beyond. *They're watching us*, he thought.

“More a big wooden gate, I'd say.” Drago shrugged. “The Horde is not the only thing to keep out in these parts.”

Vlad tossed a line from the stern and Stefan tossed another from the bow on the starboard hull, and the rest of the crew joined Batal and Drago. The warriors stared ahead, the lines the twins had thrown lying untouched on the dock's smooth planks, the heartbeat-like thumping of the hull tapping against the dock the only sound above the wind.

Jenna brushed against Batal's side. “They gonna let us float off or give a girl a hand?”

Danu appeared from behind and squeezed herself between Batal's legs to then sit down with her head wedged under his crotch. Her eyes ignored the warriors and instead were trained on the wooden wall.

Batal's mother moved past them, to stand at the front of the crew. “Remain silent and still,” she urged. Then, staring at Vlad and Stefan, repeated, “Silent and still.” The twins nodded. Amira moved to the rail.

The two warriors at the ends of their formation grabbed the boat's lines and secured them to the dock, then moved back in position. The squeal of wood on wood sounded from behind the wall. A seam appeared in the center and another a few meters to the right. A door swung open on massive copper hinges.

The slab of wood was at least two meters thick and cut at a bevel, making it invisible when closed, which impressed Batal. Danu shifted underneath him, hackles up and growling. He reached down and touched her head. "What is it, girl?"

Drago and Jenna straightened, feet spreading into a fighting stance, and moved in front of Batal.

A low-hanging shadow bolted out of the opening and raced down the path, followed by another and another. Each was a meter off the ground and covered in thick, shaggy fur. Batal swallowed hard. Ten beasts charged up the dock, their striped lupine legs and dark shaggy fur making each a powerful blur baring white teeth.

Batal's mother stood with her hands to her sides as the beasts—which Batal now recognized as strandwolves—approached the stoic warriors.

Claws scraped and tore at the planks as each strandwolf slid to a halt in front of a warrior until all ten were in place. They arched their backs and bristled the long hairs covering their necks and shoulders. Danu pressed forward, her growl growing deeper and louder. Batal pressed his legs around her and held her shoulders in each hand.

He had heard of these legendary wolves of the sand, but fisherman tales contained a thread of truth. Like deerhounds, they were immune to the radiation—but were they? The creatures standing before them were far bigger than he imagined. At least a meter at their muscled shoulders with long, pointed ears and a toothy smirk that gave Batal the feeling that, if they were given the command, he would die painfully, but quickly. Danu pushed forward again and showed her own teeth.

Batal's mother held out an open hand to the deerhound behind her, and Danu fell silent.

"I am here to see Zasar," she stated to the wall of fur, fangs, copper, and blades. "With news of the Horde, to offer trade, and enter a Spartan in the Trials."

"What news does Amira of Skye Stone bring to the Kingdom of Zaeafran?" asked a voice from behind the warriors. "And why would we trust those who stood by and watched my brother die?"

Ten hands found the hilts of their weapons and the strandwolves in front of the warriors leaned toward the *Aeolus*.

"Enough!" cried the voice.

The warriors and beasts parted, and a lean, elegant form brushed past. She wore a gown crafted of tiny spheres of copper that chimed with each move. Her braided hair swirled up from her face and ended with a striking yellow cloth tied in an intricate knot. Even with her towering hairstyle, the knot only reached the shoulders of the warriors behind her. She placed a hand on each of the strandwolves at her sides.

"Down," she commanded.

All of the wolves laid down on the dock, still staring at the visiting crew. The warriors' hands left the grips of their khopeshes.

The woman, who Batal assumed was Zasar, moved to the *Aeolus*, placed a hand on the ship's smooth hull and walked with her hand gliding along its surface until she stood below Batal's mother. They locked eyes. "I am Queen Zasar."

Batal's mother looked over her shoulder at Drago, eyes wide, then turned back around and dropped to a knee. Drago, Jenna, Vlad, and Stefan echoed the gesture.

Batal just stared at the queen, transfixed by something he could not explain. Familiarity. He knew her face, her ebony skin and the shape of her eyes. *I know you. I was a child—*

"Batal!" his mother hissed, looking behind her. "Kneel!"

Zasar gazed up at Batal. Starting with his face, she scanned his form, then went back to his eyes. "You must be Amira's son?" she asked, followed by a knowing nod and a slight grin.

Batal tried to kneel, but Danu wouldn't budge. So he bowed at the waist and made a strange hand gesture while looking at Danu, who was now staring up at him. *What the fuck am I doing?* he thought, staring at the furry gray face below. "It's your fault," he mumbled.

He returned his attention to Zasar. "Yes, I am her son. Your graceness."

Drago and his mother shook their heads.

"Doing great. Keep it up," Jenna whispered.

"Come forward, Batal, and leave your deerhound," Zasar said. She looked to her resting strandwolves. "Assuming you can control it?"

"Stay, Danu," Batal stated with as much authority as he sensed the hound would put up with. He then muttered, "Please stay," rubbed her head, and moved between Drago and Jenna and around his mother.

Queen Zasar nodded to her warriors. Two strode to the edge of the dock, lifted a gangplank, and placed it on the hull of the *Aeolus*. "Come closer," she said to Batal.

"I don't think so," growled Jenna as she stood, rising to her friend's defense.

Drago and Vlad were next to their feet.

The warriors' weapons were drawn before the crew moved another step forward and the strandwolves were back on all fours and snarling.

"This will not help him," his mother said, catching the queen's eye. "For the love of the Goddess, tell him."

Zasar held up a hand. Her warriors and wolves took two paces back, the warriors' blades again at their sides and the wolves sitting on their haunches.

"I am Queen Zasar..." A bright smile then appeared.

Then Batal knew. The smile.

"...Spartan," she finished. "I am your aunt, Batal, and we have much to discuss about your Trials, but first a simple test to see where you stand." She spun and walked toward the gate, disappearing into the protective sphere of warriors and wolves. "Sons and daughters of Skye Stone!" she hollered from within the armored mass's nucleus. "The gate will not wait!"

Danu was at Batal's side with Drago and Jenna flanking him. His mother was behind him, and the twins brought up the rear.

Batal turned. "What trade have we to offer, Mother, and what 'Trials' am I to be a part of?"

"We trade teachers in the arts of steel and combat for farmers and craftsman." His mother paused. "The 'Trials' make one a Guardian or kill the pupil. The coming days will not be pleasant, my son. It is time for you to rise or to fall and there is nothing we can do but watch. Your time is now, and I am sorry. You are a Spartan, so we expect you to rise." She moved around Drago, wiping her eyes as she passed.

Batal slowed his pace, Jenna and Drago matching it at his sides.

I'm not ready, he thought. No one spoke of the Trials, as the subject was forbidden. Not even Drago hinted to his own experience in the Trials. But what little Batal had heard was brutal and frightening. Days and weeks of physical, emotional, and mental torment until the acolyte could take no more—then they were tossed in a ring to fight to the death. If they walked or even crawled out, they became a Guardian, a Warrior, or a Senshi.

“I didn’t know this was part of Amira’s plan,” Drago confessed. “But this is the way, and no one is ever ready for it. Remember what you’ve learned and do whatever is necessary, Batal. There is only life or death once the Trials begin.”

“I knew it would come, knew time was short.” Batal’s voice was barely audible as he caught Jenna’s stoic gaze, “I may not leave this place.”

Jenna kept her focus on the approaching gate. “Discard your humanity like a splintered shield and reclaim it on your way out. That is how you survive the Trials. You will leave...this place.”

“But first, the test,” Drago said. “The fight which determines your course.”

They then stepped through the thick wooden opening, the scent of saffron so intense Batal could taste the honey-like musk as the gate screeched closed behind them.

Batal stood in the open ring with the wooden wall at his back. He gripped a pine staff with blunt ends and more dents up and down its length than he could count. Batal imagined each dent matched a scar on someone’s head, or worse. Ten meters away, another staff stood upright in the ground. Even from this distance, Batal knew by its even cinnamon tone and lack of any darker knots that the other staff was crafted of hardwood. If there was a single dent, he couldn’t tell and didn’t want to find out.

Beyond that, onlookers sat at stone slab tables that surrounded the yellow earthen-ring and positioned themselves for the best viewing angle. His mother and uncle were seated at the largest table, where they were offered what Batal guessed was one of the Kingdom of Zaeafran's finest fermented drinks. They clanked their copper goblets with Queen Zasar and her advisors, who were seated beside his family.

His mother spoke to Drago. He then stood, said something to Queen Zasar, who nodded and gave what Batal assumed was a wave of allowance, and Drago walked toward him.

"You look good in a diaper. Scariest baby-fighter from all of Skye Stone," his uncle stated with no hint of sarcasm.

Batal looked down to the bunching yellow fabric. "This big-ass stick helps." He spun the staff in front of Drago's face and in a single motion, spun it behind his back, flipped it over his shoulder, and then caught it with his left hand.

Drago awarded Batal's performance with a yawn and a roll of his eyes. "Yes, we have worked often with a staff, but I don't think spinning it around will help."

Two men, one holding a silver horn and the other a copper one, which Drago said were called "shenebs," stood at each end of the queen's table, pointed the long, tampered instruments toward the sky, and trumpeted.

"I think it's time." Drago glanced over at Batal. "Remember our training. You are a Spartan, and this is but a test to show your progress—and will determine your path through the Trials." He pointed to the reddish orange powder under their feet. "Use the saffron to your advantage. Ice and smoke."

"I'm ready, Uncle," Batal snarled. He flexed his lean, ropey muscles, then did his best to lengthen his already tall frame and struck the staff against his chest multiple times.

Drago smiled. "You think you are." He then slapped the boy's shoulder. "Keep getting up, they'll respect that." And he walked off to rejoin his sister at the head table.

"Wait," Batal mumbled. "Ice and what? What the hell does that mean?"

The men holding the shenebs sounded their horns again. A tall warrior entered the room, walking through the standing crowd and between the tables. It was one of the warriors from the dock, but the armor was different. The copper helmet blazed in the sunlight, the chest plate was equally blinding, and the yellow cloth under the plating radiated upon the warrior's ebony skin. The soldier stopped in front of the other staff and stared across the ring at Batal. The shenebs fell silent and Queen Zasar stood.

"Batal of Skye Stone has chosen the Trials!" She raised her arms, laden with copper rings, and the crowd cheered. Those around the stone slabs tapped their goblets until the sounds mixed into a rhythmic chaos. "Zaeafranian rules!" The cheers consumed the clanging goblets. "This is only the 'test,' life will be preserved, but...last warrior standing!"

Batal watched Jenna and the twins advance toward a small table closer to the wooden wall at his back. Jenna made fists and shook them in his direction and mouthed a few words.

Fuck, Jenna, did you just 'good luck' me? Batal thought. *Show nothing and as Uncle said, keep getting up.*

He watched her grab a massive goblet, clank hers with ones the twins had picked up, then drink.

"Take off the armor!" Batal yelled across the ring. "Make this a fair fight!"

The warrior turned toward Queen Zasar, who nodded.

The helmet came off first, revealing a smooth scalp with a handful of lesions. Next came the armor and the yellow tunic beneath, revealing a woman's curves. The warrior stood a bit taller than Batal with generous shoulders and muscled arms. She left a tight yellow band around her chest to flatten her breasts. The crowd chanted as she removed the armor from her thighs.

Batal began spinning the staff again, feet apart, knees bent.

The shenebs released a long trumpet followed by a shorter sound. The warrior ripped her staff from the ground and charged at Batal, who waited to strike.

His breath quickened. *Too easy*, he thought as he stopped the rotation of his staff, cocked it, and brought it down in a perfectly timed...

She slid. Batal watched his staff pass over her face, spotting her smile right before wood hammered into the back of his ankles, sending him cartwheeling through the air. Then she was gone.

"Ice," he rasped on his back, trying to suck air back into his deflated lungs. A yellow cloud of saffron hung on the breeze. A blur streaked past his side. Above Batal's head, through the saffron haze smelling of honey and musk, appeared the business end of a falling staff covered in dents.

"Smoke."

11
THIRTY-EIGHT DAYS

A shaft of light appeared in the center of the tiny dark cell. Batal rolled off his straw mattress, pushed into the corner of the stone room, and crawled out of the shadows toward the warm glow. The stench from the bucket in the opposite corner was fading, or his shit had less of a smell with each passing day. Reaching the light, Batal laid on his back and centered his face under the warm glow.

Pus ran down his side from one of the many wounds on his torso. Most of them seemed superficial, and he continued to use water captured from the weeping stones with a torn piece from his loincloth. It wasn't clean, but it was the best he could do. Someone hammered on the cell's small wooden door, which was barely large enough to stuff Batal through after they were finished with him each evening. *But they do*, he thought, *and they fucking enjoy it*.

He heard someone clear their throat and spit out something heavy and wet. A thin copper tray then shot under the door, slamming into Batal's side, slop splattering on his arm and spilling onto the floor. Batal gazed at the spit in his tray, knowing it had been put there by the biggest of the Zaeafranian warriors —Talin. The one who was taking great pride in inflicting the most suffering.

Soon the door would open, and Uncle Drago would appear with something he'd snuck past the guards any way he could. Batal had been surprised on numerous occasions with what the man could fit in to "places" that showed no sign of the treasures within. Even better was the exchange necessary to toss them into Batal's cell without notice.

Batal rolled toward his morning slop and licked up every bit of it, and then did the same to the filthy stone beneath the tray until he was satisfied nothing was left as waste. "Anything to survive." He growled the mantra as he got to his feet, crept back to his straw mat, and pulled it from the corner.

"Where are you?" His hands searched the crease in the rock where the floor turned to wall. "There you are." He held tight the stone shard he found there. With the sunlight from the overhead hole providing just enough illumination to find his marks hidden behind his mat, he added this morning's hash mark. *Twenty-three days*, he thought. *Well past the halfway point*.

Footsteps echoed down the corridor, and Batal pushed the mat back into the corner and prepared for whatever form his uncle's version of "help" would take this morning. Drago had a part to play in the Trials as the eldest of the capable Spartans: sparring and the morning wranglings.

"UP!" Drago yelled from the other side of the door. "In the light until I say otherwise!"

Batal did as his uncle bid. "As you say."

Keys jingled, and the door swung out into the corridor. The

bottom of a leather kilt filled the top of the opening with two stout calves and broad feet in leather sandals below it. Drago was dressed for sparring. He went down to a knee and his head peered in. Batal slowly rotated in the light, giving his uncle the opportunity to see his wounds, bruises, and anything else that might need attention during this morning's visit. Drago had set up the system on the first day, as Batal's grandfather had done for him. As long as the Zaeafranian warriors heard and watched his uncle dole out the abuse, they paid little attention to anything else.

"Out, lazy whelp!" Drago disappeared from the opening.

Batal crawled out through the door and was met with open slaps to his face, his side, and his back before he could stand. Drago finished by putting him in a headlock. A group of Zaeafranian warriors laughed, then turned to march down the corridor, allowing Drago to continue his lesson.

"Healing salve. Rub it anywhere there's blood or pain," Drago said as he pretended to tighten his chokehold while dragging Batal toward the sunlight and the practice rings beyond. "I slapped it where it looked the worst. Stand in the sunlight of your cell whenever you can. It will aid in healing your wounds." He walked him closer to the light, wiping extra salve off his own hands and onto Batal's face and shoulder. "Our sparring is finished. You'll face Zaeafran's finest until the end. You won't see me again until the end. Each day from now on will be worse than the one before, until the thirty-ninth—the day of death for your tormentors. The day of your rebirth." They reached the end of the corridor and Drago released the headlock, spinning Batal out of the shadows and into the sun of the practice rings.

"That all you have, old man?!" Batal screamed toward Drago as he wiped the salve over his body, the action hidden as hand gestures that looked to be luring back his uncle for another go. "Your strength but a fly to a horse!" He continued the show as best he could, but the Trials were winning, his spirit close to breaking and his body not far behind.

"Enjoy your next beating." Drago then walked back the way they had come, his head down.

Stone walls and buildings rose on all sides of the tiny courtyard. Some had been carved out of the mountain and others built from its quarried stone, but all looked out over the sea from one window or another. Outside their simple accommodations, the crew of the *Aeolus* sat around a weathered wooden table, waiting for Drago. They were less than a few hundred meters from the practice rings and could hear the occasional clash of steel or faint cry for mercy from within.

Drago appeared in the narrow pathway leading to the courtyard from the cobbled walkways. "Wine, please," he requested as he sat in the empty chair next to Amira.

Stefan looked to Amira, who gave a simple nod. "Morning wine for all of us, please." She placed a hand on her brother's shoulder after Stefan left the table.

Drago leaned down.

Moments later, Stefan returned with a large clay pitcher that he strained to carry in one hand while he held a stack of earthen cups in the other. He filled the cups, passing each one around until all of them had wine. They remained quiet, all eyes on Drago.

Finally, Amira broke the silence. "You return early, without a scratch and clean." She let out a deep breath and leaned back in her chair. "Batal's elder and guide is no longer allowed."

Drago straightened, grabbed the cup in front of him, emptied it, then tapped it on the table and waited until Stefan refilled it before he spoke. "This was the last time I'll see him if —" He clenched his fists. "When he sees the thirty-ninth day." He drank more wine. "He looks bad, Sister. Taking a lot of beatings, and Zasar's champion, Talin, has taken a personal interest in delivering them."

Jenna's elbows hit the table as she leaned across it. "I'll kill that fucking bitch with my own hands—"

"Only if you get to her before I do," Vlad said.

Stefan kept his eyes down and everyone's cups filled.

"Batal is far stronger than any of us know," Amira said. "Jenna, Drago, and even I went through the Trials, and here we all sit."

"No, Sister, this is different." Drago slid back in his chair, "Each of our Trials were based on the initial test, judged by a fair ruler who then determined our path and what we would face. My Trials—"

"You must not speak of it," Jenna warned, looking to the windows and balconies facing the courtyard above. "Silence is part of the Code."

"Let anyone with issue, come tell me now or tomorrow!" Drago stated with an echo. "My Trials"—he started again, and this time, they all listened—"consisted of forced containment. In boxes and crates, even just sitting in the cell for a week straight. They threw me in the practice rings for hand-to-hand combat. The worst I got was being knocked unconscious a few times. I faced my first death match on the thirty-seventh day, and that was the only one until the day of blood two days later." His fist hammered the table. "And you Jenna, how many?"

"One." She looked to Amira. "The day of blood."

"Three. One on each of the last three days," Amira added.

"But I thought the day of blood was the only time life or death was the result, the final trial." Jenna grabbed the edge of the tabletop. "Drago, we've broken our vows and spoken of our Trials, so tell us the rest. How many death matches has Batal taken part in? This is only his twenty-third day."

Drago finished another cup of wine. "Five. He spars for four days, and the fifth is a death match against fighters I have never seen before. The last was a Horde prisoner. Each match is progressively harder."

"What have I done?" Amira raised her glass.

"What was needed," Drago replied. "There's nothing we can do but pray to the gods Batal learns to be become the version of himself that is necessary in the moment. That is what being a Guardian means. At our core we are peaceful, but we will fight to the death to defend what we love at a moment's notice."

"Discard your humanity as a splintered shield and reclaim it on your way out," Jenna stated. "That's the last thing I said to Batal. What will we do if he can't reclaim it?"

"Yes, Jenna, that's a danger for anyone surviving the Trials. But your words were true," Amira said. "I will gladly embrace whatever form of Batal leaves this island. It means my son lives and there is hope for Skye Stone and the rest of the new world."

12
DAY OF BLOOD

Batal's lean, muscled form stood once more in the ring of warriors with the wooden wall at his back. *Here again,* he thought, scanning the crowd. *You'll all remember this day.* He smeared the reddish-orange powder from the floor over every visible part of his body and even what was beneath his brilliant yellow loincloth. It helped slow the seeping, fresh wounds that still oozed through it and formed an orangish tar that eventually would harden and aid in their healing. *At least that's worked over the past thirty-eight days.* A wooden staff with blunt ends and covered with more dents than anyone could count stood planted in the saffron-dusted soil a pace in front of him. *As it should be. The Trials are but a circular path, the only true change is in the one who has taken it and now wields the staff once again.*

Ten meters away loomed Talin, the Kingdom of Zaeafran's greatest warrior, this time in full battle dress, the hooked blade of her khopesh hanging from her armored side. Batal had used a similar blade multiple times to permanently silence his opponents. *Seven? No, eight death matches. And this will be nine.* Silent onlookers sat around stone slabs surrounding the colorful ring. Behind them stood a legion of weaponless warriors wearing bright tunics. *They've all gone through their own Trials,* he realized. *They must be trying to calculate the dead they left behind when it was their turn.* At the largest table sat Queen Zasar and his mother. Drago and Jenna sat at the table next to them with Stefan and Vlad, all of whom looked somber and none met his gaze.

Batal pictured himself an arrow drawn back in the stoutest of bows. *So much deadly force waiting to be released. Release it I will—not wild and unfocused, but exact and calculated. Nothing wasted, as death is coming on this thirty-ninth day, when my humanity is discarded as a shattered shield.*

~

Drago leaned toward Jenna. "How long are they going to stand there?" he whispered.

Danu's gray muzzle appeared from under the table. Jenna grabbed her collar and gently pulled her back. "We've been here for thirty-nine days. What's another hour?"

One of the strandwolves sharing Danu's table cave flipped Drago's hand in the air with its muzzle.

"OK, Shitsnack, one more rub." He ruffled its thick mane and "Shitsnack" laid down near Danu, who placed her muzzle on top of the strandwolf's head.

"You have the sweetest names for your friends," Jenna stated. She then glanced behind Drago at the endless muzzles protruding between warriors. "Who'd have thought such fright-ful-looking creatures could be so gentle?"

Drago looked to the saffron-crusted figure of Batal standing in front of the wall. "But harder is the turn of the gentle soul embracing the warrior."

"Your training and the thirty-eight days of the Trials have honed him. He's still in there, I know it. Under the extra muscle, the scars, the pain, Batal is there. We need the Guardian, not the fisherman for what is next, and I don't mean the warrior in front of him." Jenna then eased back, keeping a hand on Danu beneath her.

"What if the Trials took away what was best in him? Broke what can't be mended?"

"Ah, and there we disagree. You have always seen a fisherman who must be forced to raise a sword and draw a bow." Jenna tipped her head toward the motionless Batal. "I've always seen a Guardian, disguised as a fisherman."

"Thank you for coming, Jenna. I couldn't have done this on my own."

"None of us ever do anything alone."

"Agreed," Drago said.

Amira looked over at Drago and Jenna. Her brother's intensity was softened only by the occasional smile—or was it a grimace?

"They speak of the training and its result," Queen Zasar said. "My nephew has evolved into his true self. Like his father, he has reached the end of his path and stands on the brink of life or death."

"Again, you mean," Amira corrected. "You mean, Batal stands again on the brink of life or death. This is the seventh or eighth time you've chosen to place him in a death match."

"Careful, Amira. My brother is gone, and you are not blood." Queen Zasar let the words hang for a moment. "Batal has his own path that required the Trials to place him in harm's way. He needed to learn the value of a good soul versus a rotten one."

Amira turned toward the queen. "Who determined the level of rot, Zasar? Batal killed to save his own life, nothing more." *Where is the lesson in that?* she thought, *You sit here in your copper-scaled costume and play queen behind your gate, but you know little of the Trials as you've never faced them and know even less about family*.

"Regardless," Zasar said, "the man who entered the Trials is gone." She pointed toward the Batal standing in the champion's ring, "Let us pray I know more about what Batal needed to become a Guardian than you, or he will die before us."

"Batal has always been like his father. Gentle by nature and possessing a great potential for focused violence under certain circumstance."

"Yes, we have witnessed this firsthand," Zasar agreed.

"No," Amira replied. "You have not."

"Then what 'circumstances' do you speak of?"

"Those who place his loved ones in harm's way. Those who threaten his mother, his family." Amira sat up straight, her eyes never leaving the Zaeafranian warrior who loomed large in front of her son. Batal's saffron-colored form looked foreign in the distance. "My son has been beaten and bloodied for thirty-eight days. Batal will not forget this...'training' nor those who forced it upon him."

Queen Zasar reached down and placed a hand over Amira's. "You and Drago did what was needed. Batal will know this in time. Know that without the Trials, he could not achieve what all the Clans must have. Our survival rests with him. The Horde presses farther south with each sunrise. Your account of their attack on Skye Stone is unprecedented."

"Every word is true." Amira's haunted eyes found Zasar's. "But I wish they weren't. The Horde is evolving. They have designed vessels of war to breach or fly over any wall. They will die for the slightest chance of killing any of us. How do we combat such evil, such hate?"

"I don't know, but Batal plays a role. We are no longer safe. If we want to live, we need the Archipelago to join us. Their Senshi are fearsome. Their numbers are rumored to be in the thousands. No greater fighters in all the isles. Without them we will fall."

"And my son dies if he fails."

"Kaminari Akiro chose Batal, and yes, if he fails, he dies." The queen's hands found the arms of her throne and she stood.

"Our gods speak of the thirty-nine!" she declared to all watching. "Thousands survived the winds of fire! Hundreds clawed out of the rubble after the earth shook and the mountains fell, then reached into the sky and fell again! Towering waves broke across the remnants of this land! Over and over the churning waters hid the sun and carried away our people. Until only thirty-nine remained!" She moved from behind the stone slab table, the copper spheres of her raiment catching the sun and glowing with each step until she stood in the center of the ring.

She then raised her left hand high above her head. "Anku!" A warrior in full battle dress carrying a spear passed through the sea of yellow tunics and into the ring, coming to stand in front of the warrior facing Batal. "Tatara!" she continued as she raised her right hand, and another armored warrior, this one carrying a rectangular shield and crescent-headed cutting ax, pushed through the crowd until she stood in front of the first.

Amira had seen this ceremony before, and so turned her gaze to Batal. Stone-still, the whites of her son's eyes were bright behind the red-crusted soil. *Goddess help us all. Please forgive me, my son, but show no mercy on this day.*

Without moving his feet, Batal knew the layer of crushed saffron beneath him and his opponent was slick, damp, and leveled by hand. The breeze shifted and blew across his face. The pungent scent of the herb no longer overwhelming his senses. He filled his lungs. Fear. The two newest warriors closest to him shook, each breath uneven. *And they should quake where they stand*, Batal thought. They had taken part in his Trials. Taken pleasure in his beatings when he was bound and helpless. Talin, the tallest, waiting at the back, gave away nothing. After all, she was Zaeafran's most ruthless soldier and enjoyed inflicting pain and terror. *Terror has no power over these eyes anymore. This body accepts pain—and returns it.*

The glittering shape of the queen strode into the center of the arena and turned. Her back radiated as Batal's mind raged. *Those ridiculous copper beads—or are they bronze spheres, or fucking scales like Uncle Drago's armor?—whatever they are, I want to tear them off and add a few dents to my staff. Queen, aunt, and tormentor—how can this be our line, our heritage? Why keep this truth from me, Father? But death keeps one's truth from everyone.*

Batal's attention shifted beyond the queen with her arms in the air, past the three warriors in full battle dress, and to...

Mother. Amira. You stare at your creation and wonder who or what stares back. You brought me here, always scheming, always planning every detail, and yet, for thirty-eight days your son has been beaten, bloodied, and starved. You wanted the Guardian and thought it worth the death of your son to bring it out?

Amira then became a blur. Jenna and Drago vanished with the crowd. All that remained was Queen Zasar and the column of three warriors behind her.

Just drop your fucking arms and let this begin. One or all, matters little. Just let the blood flow.

Batal pushed out a breath, reddish-orange snot shooting from his nostrils, and still he remained a statue. Caked soil and crushed saffron cracked around each defined muscle with no noticeable movement.

The queen glanced over her shoulder, eyes wide. While keeping her arms raised, she scurried out of the center. Her mouth continued to move, then her arms fell and she disappeared into the visual blur.

The first warrior released a shriek and charged. Shield up, an ax cocked.

Beautiful craftsmanship. The incoming crescent head warmed by the sun. Almost as good as Stefan's work, Batal thought. *You're holding your shield close to your armor and your stride is heavy on the back foot. A shield-heavy slide and that ax will find my spine as soon as I am upended.*

Batal pulled his staff from the ground and shifted his weight to his back foot, keeping the blunt end of his staff pointed at the charging warrior. A few meters from contact, she brought her shield into her chest with the ax hidden beneath it and slid at Batal—a gliding battering ram.

At that same moment, Batal hammered the staff back into the ground directly in the path of her slide, pulling back on the top and widening his stance.

The warrior's foot slid into the base of the planted staff, flipping her upward and launching her over him. She cartwheeled into the red dust, coming to rest in a stunned heap. Batal had the staff out of the ground, in the air, and arcing downward with all his strength before he knew what he was doing. Her neck snapped on impact. Blood pooled around the protruding bones.

Batal reached down toward the dispatched warrior, disappearing into the saffron-red cloud created by her landing.

The wind swirled and carried away the dust. He stood with his opponent's shield and ax in his possession, a statue once more. The warrior's lifeless form lay in a heap behind him next to his bloodied staff.

The second warrior moved behind Talin, using her as a shield while wrapping something around the base of her long spear.

"You sneaky fu—" Batal began.

The shiny point of a spear tore across his cheek, a thin hide line attached to the weapon's tailing shaft. Batal raised his shield and stumbled to the side, blood flowing along the cracks of caked saffron dripping from his jaw.

The line was yanked away, pulled by the warrior behind Talin, the still unflinching human shield. Batal stomped down on the passing shaft and regretted it. The spear was smooth except for a single palm-sized grip in the center. Before he could shift his weight, the sliding shaft gave way to the razor edge of the tip, which slashed the bottom of his foot.

The red dust grew wet. "Think, you fool," Batal muttered, "Rage is a tool—use it as a dagger, not a club." Crouching behind his shield, he hobbled toward the back of the earthen ring, dug the shield into the loose soil at an angle, and crouched behind it. *Even the fucking Zaeafranians have a code of combat*, he thought as he tore off a piece of his loincloth and wrapped his bleeding foot. It throbbed and his cheek stung, but the limp was for show.

From behind his shield, Batal gazed upon the great and unflinching warrior of Zaeafran. Behind Talin was a spear and a coward. And a long fucking rope. *Who's really the coward, though? I'm hiding behind a shield in the dirt*. A smile appeared on his face, only to fade as the spear tip clanked as it glanced up and over his shield. The hide line followed. Batal raised his ax blade and cut it.

The blur surrounding the ring pulsed, the faces of the crowd coming and going, sounds ebbing and flowing.

Stay focused. Your life depends on it.

Batal emerged from behind his shield, dropping it and his ax as he picked up the spear. Talin still stood there—hands at her side, her hook-shaped khopesh hanging from her armor, its blade playing in the sunlight. No sign of the other one. Batal sprinted to the side, slid to a stop, released the spear, and was already moving back to the shield and ax when a body dropped behind Talin, a spear imbedded through its side.

With a single motion, Talin flung the body out of the ring with her foot. She raised her khopesh toward Batal, pointed it at the dead warrior in a heap, and then to the stone wall behind him. Holding the shield and ax handle in one hand, Batal reached under the armor plating at the neck of the fallen warrior and dragged the body to the edge of the ring. With haste, he stripped it and donned the armor, then pushed the dead warrior outside of the ring, crossing her hands over her chest.

Tight, but better than a loincloth. Then he thought, *Fuck it*, and tossed the shield toward wooden gate. "Sword and ax!" he growled and charged, holding the ax out front in both hands.

The giant Zaeafranian assumed a wide stance—both hands out, the one with her khopesh raised to her side.

The "Iron Cross." Batal had witnessed Talin use it many times over the past thirty-eight days, slashing down from above in devastating fashion, her victims then sliding beneath her, missing their heads and arms. *You have broken me, beaten me, and bloodied much of my body and it ends now.* Batal closed in, moved his right hand down the ax's handle until it met his left and raised the weapon over his head, and continued his charge. *There!* The shift of weight toward the balls of her feet, bracing for the hammer of an armored slide, a slight turn of the wielding shoulder preparing for the death strike.

Batal cut his stride, slid upright only meters away, and used his momentum to hurl the ax forward, end over end with a deafening roar. The handle spun twice, and the crescent head disappeared in the center of Talin's chest, lifting the great warrior off her feet. Bloodied armor slid to a stop.

The background blur came into focus, but Batal stood a statue once more and stared ahead. Talin lay next to a table with clouds of saffron dust sifting through the air. The air cleared. Beyond the body, Queen Zasar and Amira sat at their table, stunned.

He stood rigid, the tight armor increasing the blood flow through the caked, cracked saffron that dripped and ran. *Yes*, Batal thought, *what a stunning sight to see and the culmination of all your plans and work, Mother. On the thirty-ninth day a Guardian stands before you.*

Amira met his stare, eyes wide, then his mother covered her face and wept.

Drago and Jenna moved toward him, but it was how Danu crept out from under the table, head lowered, teeth showing and growling in Batal's direction that brought him back. It was the way Danu had looked at the brute Farouk on the beach of Skye Stone as he kicked and attacked her. Batal dropped to his knees shaking. "What have I done? What have you done to me?"

Drago knelt and pulled a sobbing Batal into his chest. "Thirty-nine days are complete. Like your mother and father before you, like me and Jenna, you are now a Guardian."

Jenna wrapped her arms around them. "Batal," she whispered, "you've made it. Many don't. Find the best of yourself and fuse it with the warrior. Become the Guardian. We need you."

Four more arms wrapped around them, adding another layer. "This Batal scares the shit out of me," stated Vlad.

"That means a lot coming from you," Batal replied, with the beginning of a laugh. "What is that smell?"

"Sorry," said Stefan. "It was very scary watching. You know my stomach."

A furry face followed by a long tongue pushed inside the circle and lapped at Batal's tears.

"Thank you, Danu. You are my core and see the best in me. I will strive to be that Guardian." Batal then raised his head. "The fisherman is dead."

A distant and chaotic trumpeting carried from the mountain tops of the island. The warriors and strandwolves ran for the armory. Queen Zasar turned toward the group. "To the armory, then meet me on the wall."

Drago spoke to Jenna, who nodded and ran to Amira. They then both headed in the opposite direction.

Batal watched them heading toward the wooden gate. “Where are they going, Uncle?”

“To ready the *Aeolus*, but we go to the armory. You are about to see a Spartan general firsthand. And call me Drago.”

13
QUEEN & GENERAL

Batal climbed the stone steps etched into the mountainside. His bow and sword were fastened to new and better fitting copper armor, each plate of which was rubbed in ash and mud the color of the surrounding rock. Most of Zaeafran's warriors blended into the wall and all carried the longest bows and tallest shields Batal had ever seen. Each set of eyes carried hatred or respect. Batal cared little of what the warriors harbored toward him, the Guardian who had killed the best of them, as long as fear was part of it. He reached the two-meter-wide ledge hewn from the rock over the past centuries. A meter and a half of the wall protected the ledge from the sea and enemies beyond. Rich, yellow flags hung limp and high on the posts embedded up and down the ledge's path. The Zaeafran crest emblazoned on the flags was distorted in the bunched material.

Batal stared at the horizon and the line of Northern Horde

ships approaching the island. "How is this possible? There are so many."

Drago appeared, his armor smeared with ash and his face painted to match. "Ten times as many as we faced at Skye Stone. The Horde is growing and remains unchallenged."

"What does that tell you, young Guardian?" a voice behind the two men asked.

Batal turned to see his aunt, who was wearing the same ash-smeared armor as the rest of her warriors. The only difference in hers was the symbol etched in the copper breastplate: a pair of crossed khopeshes.

"Queen Zasar." Batal half bowed, then gave up. "The other nations of the Spice Islands are likely dead, or worse, they have made an alliance with the Horde."

"Maybe." Her hand pointed to the horizon. "The Horde are not men. Those choosing the North lost that distinction long ago." She opened a hand toward Drago—"Your spyglass."—who placed it in her hand. She passed it to Batal. "Which is it? Dead or an alliance?"

Batal leaned into the wall and scanned the endless ships covering the horizon. "Dead."

Zasar nodded. "Even from here, I can see there are many vessels from the nations of the Spice Islands floating among the Horde's ships."

"Yes, there are many," Batal confirmed. "But the decks are filled with the radiation-rotting beasts of the North." He handed the spyglass back to Drago. "They are closing in and they have the catapult ships with them."

No longer trying to hide their numbers, the ships in the Horde's fleet now spread out in an endless row across the sea. *Two-hundred twenty*, Batal counted. At least twenty bore the hull design of the catapult ships that had launched their warriors into Skye Stone.

A lone vessel hung back. It was three times the size of the next largest ship, a vast catapult built off-center into its deck so its catapult arm could clear the mainmast that was also part of the frame. The ship's metallic hull reflected in the sunlight. *She is beautiful*, Batal thought, *and a destroyer of walls. How could beasts design such a thing?*

The flags on the wall fluttered southward and drooped. It would not be long before the winds decided what happened next. Batal prayed that Boreas, god of the north wind, would spare the nation of Zaeafran and his family and not fill the sails of the Horde. *So...the Trials of the Guardian have not taken everything from me. I am afraid for those I love. That is something.*

A girl then filled his thoughts. Bright green eyes with braided hair the color of silver and sunlight with the pale skin of a northern clan from a faraway nation. A land destroyed by volcanic eruptions and consumed by the sea. *Why choose me, Kaminari? Why choose a boy you tormented with insults and laughter? One who now has his first lesion and has not avoided the radiation's grasp. I am like everyone else, slowly being consumed by the legacy of our ancestor's creations.* He looked to the sky, waiting to see the next streak from those dying weapons spinning around the earth. *We have fallen so far. Or have we?*

"She would not stay with the strandwolves!" A voice called from below.

"Vlad?" Batal asked, looking over the edge. "What are you doing down there?"

"Stefan and I are doormen or door openers for dogs, or something. Good luck! We'll see you when it's over!" He then disappeared.

Danu raced up the stairs and slid to a halt at Batal's side. She wore embossed leather armor that covered her back and chest. The designs reminded him of those from Skye Stone. He ran his hand down her neck and patted her armored side. "No, she doesn't wait. Danu the brave," he said. "The bravest." He leaned toward her muzzle. "I am sorry, girl. I will not lose myself again. I can't bear to see that look in your eyes one more time."

Danu's tongue found his face, her eyes never leaving his.

A gust ripped the flags above the ledge and held them steady, pointing south, toward the wooden wall.

"Fucking, Boreas!" Drago spat. "God of wind? Fuck the northern bastard!"

"Here they come," Queen Zasar said.

A deep bellow of a horn rumbled from the encroaching fleet. Dirty white sails dropped from the masts of the Horde's vessels and black ones rose from the captured Spice Islands ships. The massive vessel's sail filled first, hiding the rest of the ship. A blood-red circle with an hourglass inside it was painted on the sail. Batal's breathing shortened, his throat dry, but he still stood. The symbol of mass extinction was closing in. A hand rested on his shoulder.

"Do not fear, Batal." The queen's voice grew louder like a pounding drum. "They approach a nest of vipers." She then turned to address the gathered army. "Warriors of Zaeafran!"

The Zaeafranians roared back in reply.

Drago readied his bow and Batal followed. Danu placed her paws on the top of the wall and stood on her hind legs, eyes following the approaching ships. Her nose raised, puffing and snorting.

"If they smell this bad to us from so far away," Drago said with a laugh, "I feel sorry for the hound!"

Shadows appeared and grew larger near the shoreline. A hundred wooden decks broke the surface, their catapults already in motion toward the wall. The Horde had shown their fleet with intended arrogance while the bulk of their catapult ships crept in from below. The sky filled with armored orbs and not a single arrow flew in their direction.

"Behind your shields!" commanded the queen, now their general, too. "Let them open! Let the Horde spill from their cocoons!"

Batal followed the spheres' descent as another wave filled the sky, and another. *It's happening again. No one is safe.* Once the ships' supplies of orbs were spent, their catapults stilled. The first shells split. Patchwork sails opened and muscled men, rotting and stinking of death, dangled from ropes, twisting and turning as they fired their crossbows at any target they could spot. Batal shifted to the side of his shield and started to draw his bow, but bolts shattered on stone all around him and clanked off his shield. He moved back under its protection.

The grunting, brawny forms descended behind the Zaeafranian wall, unmolested, drifting on the cool breeze, sending bolt after bolt, until landing in the killing ground of the strandwolves.

"The doors!" Zasar commanded, and hundreds of armored wolves erupted from the walls, charging out of wooden doors, perfectly set into the stone and covered with mud and ash.

Those invaders still in the air began firing at the strand-wolves, and the Zaeafranian warriors left their shields to loose arrows at a sickening pace. Wolves died, but only a few, and the killing field soon became a feeding bowl. Batal drew his bow multiple times only to find his target riddled with arrows and falling from the sky. Danu did not join the feast and instead remained at Batal's back, adjusting her position as he spun, searching for living targets.

"They are escaping! The Horde's ships are fleeing!" sounded all along the wall.

"Arrows!" the queen-general commanded. "Before they submerge!"

There was something about Queen Zasar's order that puzzled Batal. Arrows against hardened hulls? Pointless. Her gaze fell on him for a moment. Was that a smile? But then it was gone, and he continued searching for targets.

The sea resounded with the *thunk* of arrow points penetrating wood and the slice of shafts entering water. The Horde's catapult ships disappeared beneath the surface. A sheneb blew and the strandwolves, now covered in gore, stopped feeding and disappeared into the mountain sides once again, the doors closing behind them and fading into the rock.

Drago turned to Batal. "If Jenna had seen that, she would not think these wolves so gentle."

"But the ships got away," Batal replied. "We had them and let them go. We could have filled the bay with spirits and turned it all to flame. Why—?"

"You've done nothing but twirl with your dog and watch," the queen stated. "Why not watch a bit longer, YOUNG Guardian. The Horde doesn't engage a strong enemy, and fleets don't fear bows and arrows."

The massive Horde ship moved ahead of the remaining ships in the fleet, dropped her sail, and four anchors splashed into the sea. The sound of a chain rattling over steel filled the air then stopped. A glow appeared from the deck. The fleet stretched out at the lead ship's flanks, and then each sail fell slack and limp.

"Wall!" ordered the queen.

Every warrior dropped to their knees and pressed their bodies against the stone. Drago and Danu followed, but Batal stood long enough to see the ball of flame launch from the Horde ship, the force driving the towering bow into the sea while the stern anchor snapped with a metallic *twang*.

Drago pulled him down. "What the fuck are you—?"

Fire hammered the wall, and the impact flung warriors off the far ledge to the ground below. Some stood dazed, others lay dead or unconscious. Outside, the stone burned with a black tar, the heat traveling through the rock.

"Incoming!"

Another ball of flame exploded a meter above the last, and a crack appeared in the wall. Another impact. The crack grew, and fractured stone slid off the wall's face.

"Hold!" the queen ordered as two more projectiles slammed into the wall, one after the other. She peeked over the stone; most of the fleet's sails had been raised again and were filled with wind, moving the ships beyond the anchored monstrosity that continued its siege. "Let them come," she whispered before crawling toward a shaking Batal, Drago, and Danu. "Only a few minutes more, Spartans," she said with a wicked smile as she crawled past. Below in the killing field, strandwolves and their handlers burst through doors beneath the cracked end of the wall, seconds before it shook from another impact and the section collapsed.

Batal raised his head just enough to see the Horde's fleet racing toward the shoreline and the opening in the wall beyond. Their decks filled with fighters. The siege vessel, protected by a handful of ships, launched a final few salvos of smaller projectiles that thudded against the stone and rolled along the sand. Hundreds of heads with wide eyes.

What was left of the other Spice Islands nations? Batal wondered.

A flaming arrow rose into the sky above the wall. Queen Zasar was loosing them at a methodical pace. On each side of the wall facing the sea, ash-and-mud-covered doors dropped open.

Batal watched as strange rods resting on heavy wooden guides slid out of the mountain, then pointed at the bottle-necked Horde fleet. Crews attached ceramic vessels on the front of the rods and lit a fine piece of cloth on the tail ends. Each bolt was at least four meters long and thick like an oak branch. "Ballista," he murmured. He couldn't take his eyes off the huge crossbows.

"FIRE!" Zasar roared, a banshee warning of death's arrival.

Rods flew from their cradles, were reloaded in seconds, and fired again. Smoke trailed from behind. The first volley exploded across the rear ships of the fleet, turning their decks and hulls into raging infernos, which blocked the retreat of the rest. Burning bodies collapsed whole or in pieces as the ballistae kept firing, wave after wave, until they engulfed the bay in rolling flames that leaped from ship to ship.

Another flaming arrow rose into the sky. Yellow sails appeared from the west, the ships tacking to keep their sails full. The Horde's siege ship rocked as her crew worked to pull up the four anchors. The protecting Horde vessels headed toward the small Zaeafranian flotilla, but they were too late and the wind was against them.

Smoke-trailing rods flew from the sides of the main sails and the five Horde vessels erupted in flame. The yellow sails tacked around the burning hulls, a smattering of desperate arrows thumping into their sides. The siege ship's mainsail filled, and she ran for the open sea until her sail faltered. Then she again tacked toward the wind. The Zaeafranian ships cut off their chase, and with the aid of the wind, raced toward the safety of Zaeafran's wall and the ballistae.

Another fleet then appeared on the horizon—this one filled with the Horde's massive siege ships.

"Go!" Queen Zasar yelled toward Batal and Drago. "Go while you can. The wind is with you! There is nothing you can do here." She hugged Batal, then pressed her lips to his ear. "The Trials are over, leave them behind. You carry your father within you. He was our king before he chose Amira and Skye Stone. You must unite with the Akiro Clan, or we all fall."

A small group of Horde vessels broke off in the distance, tacking east.

"They're trying to cut us off." Batal looked to Drago. "They know why we're here? Where we're going?"

"Trust no one," the queen insisted. "Leave now or all will be for nothing. The *Aeolus* was the finest ship your father designed, and she will fly with Jenna's hand." Queen Zasar then moved back to the wall.

"We will hold!" she yelled. "We are Zaeafran! We are warriors!"

The roar of her warriors faded with each step as Batal, Drago, and Danu entered the gore of the pit. Vlad and Stephan exited from one of the wooden doors, and the five ran toward the dock, passing men pulling catapults toward the wall. Warriors and strandwolves jogged up mountain trails to man additional posts and weaponry.

The Zaeafranians are ready for this day, Batal thought as they passed wagons full of ceramic spheres. "It would take decades to create these fortifications and weapons," Batal stated.

"Your father started it, and his sister, Queen Zasar, continued the work," Drago huffed.

A shadow passed overhead and a body thumped to the ground, riddled with arrows.

"We must close the gate!" a warrior hollered from a ledge above, and the hinges screeched as the wooden slab began to close.

Danu jumped through the gap with Batal and the rest spilling out after her. A few Horde boats sailed into the protected harbor. Jenna and Amira were on the *Aeolus*, crouching behind the cabin and popping up to fire well-timed shafts.

"Run for fuck's sake!" Jenna screamed as arrows and small stones skipped off the deck. "It will only get worse!"

Batal and Danu flew across the dock and slid up to the hull with Vlad, Stephan, and Drago right behind them.

A stone grazed Batal's chest plate, and he ducked down again. "We can't get out of the harbor with those—shit!"

A handful of wooden doors covered in ash and stone swung down, clapping off the stone below, and ballistae appeared on the hillside above the gate. Thick bolts tipped with ceramic heads flew toward the Horde's ships, and within seconds, fire consumed them. Screams followed, and the *Aeolus* now had a clear path to open seas.

"Siege ships are coming from the north!" cried a voice from one of the warriors operating a ballista. "The queen sends her love, Batal. Zaeafran's survival rests with you. Go! And may the gods be with you!"

14
THE WEST WIND DECIDES

The *Aeolus* rested on the placid surface of Zaeafran's protected harbor. Her lines clean and beautiful with only a few scratches where arrowheads and stones had skipped off her hull. The small and agile sail used to pull her from her confines lay slack and uninspired. Around her, the world was chaos. Zaeafran's lethal ballistae launched their stout shafts toward a distant Horde fleet, which was using its oars to push out of range.

Drago looked around the deck. "Gonna hit the rack for as long as I can." Before anyone could answer, he descended into the cabin.

Stefan and Vlad sat near single oarlocks on each side of the twin hulls and each pulled a single, long-handled oar in unison to Jenna's cadence from the wheelhouse. Batal sat on top of the cabin, near the mast, with a thick line gripped in both hands. The main sail waited on the deck like a coiled snake, waiting to spring toward the sky and capture the wind.

"If she blows west, we have a good chance," stated Amira, as she watched the Horde fleet from the deck.

"A west wind carries us east, toward the Akiro Clan," Batal said as he kept an eye on the flag on top of the mast. It raised, spun, and drooped. "But an east wind just means we tack our way west while the Horde brightens our nights with fireballs and flaming shit-filled sacs." His eyes fell hard on his mother. "Or do you have another torture excursion planned?" He regretted the jab before he finished it. *Sorry, Mother.* To her credit, she let it pass. She was as much to blame for the Trials as Batal was for agreeing to begin them. Both knew it simply had to be done.

The swirling breeze grew to a gust and was gone. A small fleet with drooping yellow-and-orange sails appeared from the east, rowing their way toward the harbor. The sky filled with streaking flame and half the fleet of Zaeafranian clippers exploded and were taken by the sea.

Shenebs trumpeted from the wall and the gate opened. Muscled men dragging small ballistae, ceramic spheres, and bundled shafts grunted as they went to the dock to refit and reload the boats.

Amira sat on the bench next to the cabin door and continued to focus on the horizon and the waiting Horde fleet. "We have until the wind decides our fate." She then glanced up at her son. "And to answer your question, yes, I needed to know how deep your strength runs. I needed to know if you carry your father's spirit, Batal, his fearlessness, his courage, and most of all his compassion."

The oars slapped at the sea a final time, then Vlad and Stefan pulled them in on Jenna's order and waited for her next command. The flag fluttered at the top of the mast and fell slack once more.

"After a month of being beaten, starved, and forced to fight with my hands, feet, and even my teeth, your son butchered Zaeafran's three greatest warriors." Batal fell silent, the images rushing in. "All I know, Mother, is I once fished for the people of Skye Stone. Now I am a murderer, a butcher, and a Guardian." He swallowed hard. *I will not cry, I will not give in to the boy I was*, Batal admonished himself. "Oh and, Mother, I am not 'untouched.' I found my first lesion on my back before the rogue wave hit Skye Stone."

Amira stood, faced her son. "I love you. You will come to understand your path in time." She moved through the door and stopped. "You do not have a lesion on your back. It's a tiny birthmark tucked under your shoulder blade. Your father had one just like it, and it grows darker with age. You are the first to be free of the radiation's effects, and Kaminari Akiro of the Hiroshima Archipelago is the second. The wind is here. I'll wake Drago." She disappeared into the cabin as the flag at the top of the mast pointed east.

Danu popped her head out from below, assessed the situation, and padded back down the steps following Amira.

Not long after, Drago stumbled up from below. "What's the plan, captain?

Jenna followed the flag atop the mast. "If the west wind holds, we row out of the harbor, wait for the siege ships to fire"—her eyes fell to Batal at the base of the mast still holding the line—"and we raise the main."

"Fucking brilliant." Drago folded his arms. "The plan is to raise the sail?"

The wind died down.

"Ever been aboard the *Aeolus* when she catches a full sail from a standstill?"

"No."

"You soon will. Now reset the sail while Batal climbs the mast. We're gonna need a faster method to raise the main." Jenna turned the wheel. "Stephan, Vlad, on me. Pull...pull...pull."

"You want me"—with his eyes, Batal followed the thick base to its lean point forty meters above, a resting crossbar big enough for a leg on each side stood a meter from the point—"to go up there?"

In between cadence calls, Jenna hollered while pointing at the deck. "Hatch—pull!—gloves—pull!—thigh bands—pull! —now!"

Black sails grew in the distance.

Batal threw open a small hatch near the base of the mast, put on the waxed-palmed gloves he found inside, then wrapped and snapped a resin-soaked cloth around each thigh. It felt strange to be wearing his leather pants again, no armor or loincloth; he could be fishing. *You can do this*. He then took a deep breath and up he went.

"By the gods, boy, you've gained a few stone of muscle!" Drago growled as he refolded the sail to ensure a quick rise. "I'd give you a proper beating, if I thought I could. Still much to teach you."

"I'm still hoping you'll try, Uncle." Batal smiled from above, hearing the relief in his uncle's words and still a fading guilt. *He feels it, too,* he thought. *Just like mother*. Batal's arms burned, and the skin on his hands stretched and pulled under the sticky gloves. He timed each lunge, reaching up with his hands until the stick of wax on wood held, then he released his thighs and pulled himself upward, over and over, the line dangling from the top of the mast playing off his back. He eventually reached the short crossbar, wrapped a leg around one side, then the other, and grabbed the line, giving it a quick tug.

"He's in position," Drago called out from the deck.

More words muffled by the wind rose from below as the flag above Batal's head whipped and snapped due east. The mast rolled starboard, and he tightened his grip on the line and locked his legs. His ass hurt and muscles burned, but Batal was not afraid of the height nor what was about to happen, it felt good to be alive, free of combat rings and cells.

"I am a Guardian," he whispered, "like my father, my uncle, my mother," while his head followed the arc of dozens of flaming spheres streaming tar-like smoke across the sky.

"Hold, Batal!" Jenna yelled from behind the wheel.

"Be bold," he spoke to the rushing wind. "Just a little fear keeping me focused." The image of blurred stone while riding the screamers to the top of Skye Stone filled him with confidence. Somewhat. *Nice try, Batal. Just don't piss yourself or worse. Uncle Drago would never let up.*

The *Aeolus* moved beyond the calm waters and rocky walls of the breakwater and into the swell of the sea. Fireballs splashed off her port side, with one sphere striking the water meters from the hull. Queen Zasar and her warriors launched a barrage from their ballistae in response.

"Vlad, pull, pull, pull!"

The *Aeolus* spun starboard and aligned with the wind. She sat rolling with the sea as the sun, unaware of the coming destruction, lit her hull.

Jenna turned her head, locking on to the Horde fleet to the northwest. "Oars up!"

Batal's heart drummed. Another volley from Zaeafran sliced overhead. The Horde's fleet began its charge. *Control your breath*, he thought as he looked down at the sail resting near Drago's feet. *He looks terrified. For me.* Batal then subtracted the distance from the deck to where the sail attached to the mast and adjusted his grip on the line. A gust ripped the flag overhead. Batal flew backward, dangling upside-down, his legs losing their grip.

More balls of fire filled the sky.

Jenna leaned into the wheel. "Brace yourselves. Now, Batal!"

Blood rushing to his head, he straightened his legs. The deck rushed to meet him. Screams sounded, or maybe it was the wind. The golden planks. The tight grain—

WOOMP! SNAP!

Batal skidded on his side, cartwheeling each time the resin on his legs or the palm of his hand caught the deck. His stomach dropped and rose into a darkening sky. Carried on the wings of a…my wings. Heat and…hells! Tar and smoke. Cold, rushing cold, down into the abyss.

"Hold on, Batal!"

"Tie it down!"

So cold. Ice formed around his feet and filled his veins, crawling up and up. *Hold on to what, gods of the darkness? Is this hell?* Tar and smoke and a sucking cold, so cold. Screams turned to whispers. His arm stretched, ached, he was back in the Trials. His shoulder clicked and snapped. Cold attacked, was inside of him, flowing and freezing. His skin fell loose and something wet and heavy slid down his chest and legs. *Sorry, Mother.*

"I'm losing him! By the gods, boy, help me!"

Even here, my uncle's voice follows.

A silver-haired girl appeared, extending a hand toward a beaten and bloodied boy. Green eyes and pale skin with the grin of a wicked kindness. Other boys lay sprawled or heaped in pairs. Her leg flashed backward, another boy rolled away, groaning. And still the outreached hand remained as her leg returned to the ground.

"Not this time!" Drago yelled. "You can't take him!"

Naked, Batal rose out of the water, the wind lifting him off a cresting wave. A vise-like ebony hand was attached to his. A black sail followed, an hourglass within a circle emblazoned upon it. The shimmer of steel flashed and tore into the water near Batal's chest.

"Take the wheel!"

Jenna hooked her foot on a cleat. "Reach up, Batal. Do it now or we die with you!"

Another harpoon hit the water near Batal's feet. He reached up with what he hoped was his other arm. Nothing worked, just numb—

Barking cut through the fog. He was on the deck looking up at Danu and, behind her, the head of a giant deerhound on the biggest sail he had ever seen. Jenna and Drago, sat on each side of him, huffing, disheveled, staring at the Horde ship as it lost ground behind them.

Batal raised his head and turned to Jenna. "I'm naked."

"And freezing by the looks of it." She pushed up to stand and returned to the wheel where Vlad and Stefan kept the *Aeolus* on course.

Batal attempted a smile. "Thank you. All of you. I will not forget."

A blanket spread out and Amira tucked the edges underneath him. "Do it now, before he feels it."

"Do what? Fuck!"

The *snap* and *pop* was followed by relief. Batal reached up to his right shoulder.

Drago patted his chest and stood up. "Won't be the last time your shoulder gets dislocated, I'm sure."

The *Aeolus* tilted to the starboard, her sail stretching to hold the wind. "They're falling farther back," Batal said, no longer able to make out the symbols on the larger black sails. There were so many of them. The smaller boats continued the chase as the siege ships dropped their sails.

"There're going to try one last volley!" Jenna hollered over the wind. "Can't do it under sail with any accuracy."

Flaming spheres launched into the sky from the bobbing siege ships and plunked behind the *Aeolus*.

"Mother?"

"Let's get you to the cabin to rest." Amira offered her hand. "We can talk later."

"I saw her," Batal continued. "Kaminari. At least a vision of when we first met." He sat up and rearranged the blanket around his waist, held it with his right hand, and grimaced. "We were children. Why would she ask for me now after so many years? Does she want to kill me or love me? I was just a boy she knew while he was being bullied." Batal took his mother's hand and stood.

Her eyes softened. "Some see immediately what others take a lifetime to understand."

They eased down the steps and ducked into the cabin.

Drago joined Jenna at the pilot's wheel.

"Those harpoons didn't have points," he stated, staring back at the fading Horde fleet. "Just blunt hooks on a line. They wanted to capture him, just like his fath—"

"I know," Jenna replied. "Batal has enough to worry about." Her biceps flexed, fingers gripping then releasing the wheel. "We must get him to the Archipelago and the Akiro Clan, even if we forfeit our lives."

"Not today, though." Drago ran a hand across jaw. "Maybe tomorrow?"

SEA SHANTY (SONG & PRAYER)

Oh, we'd be all right if the wind was in our sails
We'd be all right if the wind was in our sails
We'd be all right if the wind was in our sails
And we'll all hang on behind...

And we'll ro-o-oll the old Aeolus *along!*
We'll ro-o-oll the old Aeolus *along!*
We'll ro-o-oll the old Aeolus *along!*
And we'll all hang on behind!

Oh, we'd be all right if we make it out the bay
We'd be all right if we make it out the bay
We'd be all right if we make it out the bay
And we'll all hang on behind...

And we'll ro-o-oll the old Aeolus *along!*
We'll ro-o-oll the old Aeolus *along!*

We'll ro-o-oll the old Aeolus *along!*
And we'll all hang on behind!

Now, another cup of wine wouldn't do us any harm
Oh, another cup of wine wouldn't do us any harm
Woah, another cup of wine wouldn't do us any harm
And we'll all hang on behind...

And we'll ro-o-oll the old Aeolus *along!*
We'll ro-o-oll the old Aeolus *along!*
We'll ro-o-oll the old Aeolus *along!*
And we'll all hang on behind!

Oh, we'd be all right if the wind was in our sails
We'd be all right if the wind was in our sails
We'd be all right if the wind was in our sails
And we'll all hang on behind...

And we'll ro-o-oll the old Aeolus *along!*
We'll ro-o-oll the old Aeolus *along!*
We'll ro-o-oll the old Aeolus *along!*
And we'll all hang on behind!

And we'll ro-o-oll the old Aeolus *along!*
We'll ro-o-oll the old Aeolus *along!*
We'll ro-o-oll the old Aeolus *along!*
And we'll all hang on behind!

15

LUSCA!

The *Aeolus* chased, caught, and flew by the rolling swell as they ran from the west wind. *By the gods, she's fast!* Batal rested on top of the cabin, the line round his waist tied off on a cleat toward the stern. "If you're gonna go for a bit of a swim again," Jenna had said, "better to go off the stern so the *Aeolus* doesn't cut you in two. One Batal is plenty to keep track of, but if you don't holler real loud, you may skip around for a while back there."

He managed a laugh, and Danu's head perked up, her flaring snout facing west, into the wind. Her ears then laid flat, nostrils relaxed, and she wedged her head back under Batal's good shoulder. She was already at home on the *Aeolus*, shifting in time with the boat's movements, but always alert for the Horde's return. Always sniffing the air and scanning the horizon for any sign of the beasts hunting them.

Three times the sun had come and gone since their escape, and the west wind filled the towering sail. Jenna, Amira, Drago,

Vlad, and even Stefan shared duty at the ship's wheel and felt her power cutting through the seas with only the three hydrofoils keeping her from flying away. Batal listened more than he spoke, letting the hushed words of others inform him on things left unsaid.

Much of it revolved around a man he knew little. A man who had created, loved, and was then left behind by the boat he'd designed and by the Guardians he'd led. Batal's father had been the King of Zaeafran until a siren named Amira tempted him to Skye Stone. Batal ached from within. Beyond the torn muscles and dislocated limbs, a part he'd kept for himself had been ripped out. The Horde, the Trials, finally the death of the boy fisherman. His moral compass was damaged, not gone, but now possessed a different north. It had kept the Guardian within him at bay, suppressed the anger. *No*, he realized. *The rage.*

A growl vibrated under his shoulder. *Danu always knows.* She slid out, legs flailed to the side, and she rested her muzzle on his chest, eyes locking onto his. Another growl followed by a deep puff.

"I know." Batal rubbed her ears and ran his finger down the space between her eyes. "You are my moral compass now."

Below his feet, Drago's head appeared from the cabin door. "Ready to get back to it?"

Batal nodded. Danu got up and headed below for lunch.

"Jenna?" Drago yelled to the stern. "Can Vlad and Stefan take over? We need to talk."

She handed off the wheel to Stefan, who held it for a moment before Vlad punched him in the shoulder and took it over.

"Brothers never make it past five years old," Jenna stated

when she met Batal at the cabin door. “Shoulder looks good. Clothes are a nice touch.”

“Thank you, Jenna. I thought I was dead.”

She placed an arm around his shoulder. “So did I. Your uncle is the one who did all the work, though.” She leaned in and rested her head against Batal’s. “How he held on to you? No fucking clue.”

“Act of the gods,” Batal replied.

“No. Love.” She released him and entered the cabin.

Batal lingered at the door. He scanned the rolling seas, searching their tops. Stefan and Vlad laughed and argued a few meters away, still fighting over the wheel and who was the greatest captain the *Aeolus* had ever known. A slight pull on the hydrofoils. He repositioned his bare feet, so the bottoms were flat on the deck. The orangish stain of saffron still clung between his toes. There it was—a slight hiccup. Batal looked to stern, beyond the bobbing heads of the twins. A shadow flashed under the *Aeolus*, the hiccup timed with its departure. He rubbed his eyes.

“Did you feel that?” Batal hollered over the wind.

Vlad cupped his hand around his mouth. “What?”

Batal took a few paces toward them. “A drag on the boat. Did you feel it?”

Stefan and Vlad exchanged a look, shrugged, and pointed toward the rushing sea under the catamaran.

“Not a lot of drag on those sticks! Hull’s out of the water!” Vlad said, passing the wheel to his brother. “Jenna estimated the wind at twenty knots. If she’s right, the *Aeolus* is pushing thirty-five to forty!”

“She’s right. Jenna’s always right about boats.” Batal gave a final nod and moved back toward the door, where Amira was now waiting. *What could keep up at that speed? Nothing made by human hands.* Batal shook his head. *Too many days staring at the water.* He then ducked into the calm of the cabin.

Around the central table sat Drago and Amira on padded benches. Jenna stood, leaning across a chart held down by four smooth stones. Like the decks and hull outside, wood curved and rolled from deck to table and even into the eight bunks placed in the bow. Every hatch was locked and not a single item was without a home that kept it snug. *My father designed and built this.* The *Aeolus* had won over Batal, and his father was part of her, his touch and pride showing in every detail.

Amira slid over and patted a spot on the bench next to her. Batal sat down, maneuvering his feet around a sleeping Danu, who woke, readjusted, and laid down on his feet. He reached under the slab of wood and rubbed the deerhound's ears as Jenna adjusted the chart so the others could see.

"We're making excellent time. Three days out from Zaeafran and the Spice Islands"—she placed a small coin on the chart —"and we are here."

Batal examined the chart. Even the newest charts started by tracing one of the old world and then erasing most of the landmasses now covered in water or raised by earthquakes. There was even the occasional volcanic birth of a new island. And how many of those still wait to be found? *Most*, Batal assumed. Accuracy was relative, but he was seeing a new world with every passing second.

"The Bern." He looked to Jenna. "We've traveled five thousand kilometers? In three day's time?" A boyish smile appeared, and Batal looked to his mother and uncle. "Five thousand!"

"Give or take a few hundred, but yes, we're nearing the southern isle of the Bern." Jenna used a straight edge and a sharp black stone to mark the course. “We could continue there and resupply from the Sherpas.”

Amira exhaled. “They have treated us fairly in the past. My grandmother traded with them last, but no one since her passing.”

“Don’t forget Seb. He took the *Aeolus* there many times to read their manuscripts and share design ideas,” Drago said. “They will know of his wife and son. Surely they must have heard of Amira and Batal?”

Seb. Seb. Batal looped the name over and over inside his head, and still it sounded foreign. The little history he had of his father never seemed attached to his given name, Seb. This man traveled the world, was born of spice and kingship, designed and built beautiful and deadly things. This was Seb and what little Batal knew of his father. Seb was a stranger. *Mother is unaware*, he thought. Her eyes hardened as her head tilted to the side. She did not understand his father had traveled to the Bern, perhaps to trade and scheme?

Drago fell silent, eyes still locked with his sister’s.

Jenna then followed suit, and all eyes were one Amira, who folded her arms and looked at the coin that sat on the farthest southern island of the Bern.

“We go to the Bern and resupply. There is also a teacher I would like Batal to spend a day with, if she is willing.”

Batal sat up straight. “Another—”

Amira closed her eyes, exhaled, and turned toward her son. “This is a different lesson, one that will help you replace what the Trials have taken.”

“There’s another choice to be made.” Jenna added another coin to the chart between their current position and the Bern. “We can save a day’s sail if—”

"You're mad if you think we can pass through the Emerald Towers!" Drago's hands gripped the table. "The whirlpools alone are not worth the risk. What of the Varghori Monks?" He leaned back hard. "They eat people!"

Amira held up her hands. "They only eat their own creation, and that 'source' is barely human anymore." She looked around the table. "At least that's what I've heard. It's worth the risk and the Horde will not follow. Even they fear the Towers."

"Like they feared the clans of the Spice Islands?" Jenna asked, looking to Drago. "If Queen Zasar and her people still draw breath."

Batal's jaw dropped. "Mother? You speak of people like the cattle of the old world. How could you?"

"Are we not of greater importance?" She moved her fingers over the faded, erased text that had once read *Mumbai*. Now it was just a few dozen green rectangles in the great sea. "Cattle did not hurt the world—their keepers did."

"We go in daylight," Jenna said. "The Varghori are nocturnal, so it's our best chance."

The coins slid on the chart as Danu scrambled out from under the table. She was growling, pacing up and down the center of the cabin's deck. Batal felt it, too. A drag on the *Aeolus*, a force flowing against her momentum.

"Help!!! Help! Something has—" Stefan bellowed over the rushing wind.

Batal slid out and quickly reached the first step leading out of the cabin. The *Aeolus* had lost her wind, the sail flapping above, and Batal held tight to the rail with Danu sliding up behind him. The hull met the swell, the boat rising and falling with the sea. Jeanna and Drago exited the cabin one after the other, while Amira remained below.

Stefan stood at the stern, the limp line from the mainsail in one hand. He was ghostly white and stared out over the rolling waves. "He was there and then he wasn't." His voice could barely be heard over the sound of the crashing waves.

"Where is Vlad?" Batal demanded. "Stefan!" He slapped his friend's soft face. "Where the fuck is—"

A rising shadow appeared beneath the *Aeolus*. Jenna sprinted to a locker at the bow. Batal stared at the growing blackness.

It's gotta be forty meters across, maybe sixty, he thought. *A shape like a rotating star, getting closer, closer. Five points, no seven...* Bubbles broke the surface off the starboard side. Batal moved to rail. More bubbles and—

"Leather trousers?" The water grew pink around them. They bobbed in the sea with the unmistakable black boots of Vlad attached. "NO!" Batal screamed as the current pulled a handful of ragged entrails from what was left of Vlad's waist.

Jenna slid to a stop, longbow ready, and waited for whatever was below to surface. Drago followed and tossed a short bow and quiver to Batal, who snatched them out of the air, mouth open, but silent. He notched an arrow as tears streamed down his cheeks. The shadow hovered meters below the boat, the gray sky hiding its features and the deep sea nothing but a dark canvas below it.

Then two tentacles broke the surface. Each towering appendage reached high above the *Aeolus*, two rows of suckers that ended a few meters from the tips covering their fleshy underside.

"They're real," Batal stated. "Luscas are real."

Jenna loosed a thick bolt that passed through one tentacle. "There are no fucking monsters! Just a hungry, gigantic octopus living in radiation like the rest of us! That's all! Kill it!"

The sun found an opening in the clouds and the surrounding sea turned a translucent turquoise. The octopus was on its back. A brilliant red underside with a gaping mouth at its center. A beak appeared from within, growing and snapping.

Batal pushed Stefan out of the way and loosed two arrows. The first bouncing off the creature's underside. The second hit near the beak, and a trickle of blood mixed with the sea.

Drago fired his crossbow, reloaded, and fired again before a tentacle slammed down, sending him skidding into the gunwale.

Six more tentacles broke the surface and wrapped around the *Aeolus*. Danu barked from the cabin, but Batal held up a hand and she remained with Amira.

"It's too big! We're not doing enough damage!" Batal continued loosing arrows into tentacles without effect, but Jenna's longbow was making progress.

Another thick shaft tore into the octopus's underbelly and the tentacles shook the *Aeolus*, thrashing the boat from side to side. Batal dropped his bow and grabbed the rail. His quiver followed, and both slid toward the gunwale where Drago lay bleeding and unconscious. Jenna sent another shaft hammering near the octopus's beak and it released the ship. The red underbelly rotated toward the boat. A vast black head the size of a rowboat rose from the turning mountain of flesh with two intelligent eyes sitting low on its extended mantle. The fluttering form covered an area three times the size of the *Aeolus*.

Stefan then appeared, holding the harpoon from the bulkhead and screaming at the octopus, with the harpoon's razor point cocked behind his ear.

Jenna nocked two shafts at once and pulled back hard, then held and—

The octopus lifted the stern using three of its tentacles.

Jenna's arrows flew wide and over its head. Another tentacle swept in from the side, wrapping around her and pulling her off the deck.

"Batal!" she screamed as she disappeared beneath the surface. Then the rest of the octopus's tentacles and its head plunged into the sea.

Jenna was gone.

Batal threw open the stern compartment, lifted the spare anchor, and grunted as he pulled it to his chest. He held out his other arm, hand open. "Stefan! I can still see the shadow!"

Stefan tossed Batal the harpoon. He caught it, sucked in a deep breath, and jumped. The surface was warm. He relaxed and let the anchor tow him down, dragging him behind it. He held the harpoon tight to his body, its point a meter above his head. Pressure built, and the temperature dropped with every fathom. Batal released the air from his lungs. *Just like diving for abalone, slow and steady*, he thought. *Lose your shit, you die.*

He caught sight of Jenna below him. Bubbles streamed from Jenna's shaking face, arms thrashing, her eyes white and wild as a sucker-covered arm that was wrapped around her legs pulled her deeper into the darkness.

Just a big fucking octopus, that's all. It hasn't seen me yet. One chance, Batal. You have one chance to save your friend.

The octopus slowed its descent and flattened out into a vast fleshy disk with snaking arms. The one holding Jenna curled toward its mouth. The tip of the beak appeared and grew until it extended meters from the creature's underside. The beak opened and snapped over and over as it pulled in Jenna's flailing body. But its eyes and head were on the other side, still unaware of the plummeting Guardian.

Batal fixed the base of the harpoon's shaft into his side then slid his hand down before shifting the harpoon as far above his head as he could. His lungs burned, eyes bulged, and needles stabbed at his eardrums. Batal hammered the two-meter harpoon into the open beak and buried it inside the octopus. Blood clouded the murky sea. Jenna floated free, and the octopus released a cloud of bloody ink before disappearing into the pitch-blackness below with the spare anchor.

Batal grabbed Jenna's hand and kicked toward the faint glow of sunlight far above. He released his final breath, lungs tight, and kicked again in the direction of the rising bubbles. Brighter. *Kick, Batal, kick.* Jenna shook and jerked in his grasp, and Batal kicked and clawed toward the light. An angel appeared from above, holding a ray of sunshine and moving closer with an outstretched arm.

Jenna fell loose in his grip and, for the second time in as many days, Batal gave in to the sea.

16
ROAST PORK

Batal spun the wheel, and the *Aeolus* cut across the headwind and continued its tack. Since the octopus attack, the west wind had fled and left them no choice but to cut through the Emerald Towers to keep their distance from the trailing Horde. He wouldn't admit it, but Batal kind of wanted to see the Varghori Monks of legend. He spun the wheel the opposite direction and checked the heading. Drago's spyglass hung around his neck and he extended it toward the glowing northeast and spotted the first shadowy glimpse of the Emerald Towers lit from the side by the rising sun.

An amber streak caught Batal's attention. He looked to the southeast and dialed the end of the spyglass. "Another aimless missile falls from the heavens. The game of chance continues," he whispered and followed the exhaust trail until it disappeared beyond the horizon, somewhere deep in the Great Unknown. *How can things so old still burn so bright? Then ancients were as brilliant as they were flawed, and how little we've changed.*

The spice traders often spoke of the endless sea that had once cradled the Australian landmass. Now it seemed a magnet for the missiles. The Great Unknown would remain lore and myth as long as the missiles continued to fall there more than any other reachable area. Batal assumed it would one day be another dead zone like the lands west of Skye Stone. *One day I will cross the dark ocean with the* Aeolus *and see this dead zone with my own eyes*, Batal decided. It, too, had collected a great share of the missiles for decades and then they stopped falling. *What a world Earth must have been four, maybe five, centuries ago.*

He looked to the deerhound sleeping on his feet. Danu rolled off and wedged her long body into the bulkhead behind the wheel, her legs moving in midair, a low growl coinciding with the chase. Her legs dropped to the deck, eyes opened for a brief glimpse at Batal, and then back to sleep she went. He spun the wheel and the *Aeolus* cut toward the port side. Jenna's snoring ratcheted up a few notches and Drago pushed until she flopped over onto her stomach. The top of the cabin was the fresh air recovery area and seemed to always have a patient or two strapped or leashed to it.

Tears threatened and Batal forced them back. Jenna's safe and only a bit banged up, but the thought of losing her pulled at last night's dinner and he swallowed hard to keep it down. How Amira and Stefan had dragged them out of the sea was another tale sure to turn into myth with each new Skye Stone generation. *Yes*, he thought, *Skye Stone will go on. Somehow, we will continue to carve out an existence.* His mother and Stefan slept below in the cabin. Stefan was lost without Vlad, and Amira was being consumed by radiation. The longer one lived, the more the radiation took hold. New lesions were appearing every few days, but his mother was strong. Spartan tough.

A soft light spread over the deck. The sun was close to whole, only its bottom clipped by the horizon. Batal checked the compass a final time, but the Emerald Towers were in sight and he lashed the wheel in place. Danu was up and the two of them eased past Jenna and Drago to head toward the port hull of the bow. Batal tucked his feet under the bottom rail and Danu wedged herself between his legs, her long snout testing the headwind.

Two heavy breaths on the spyglass's lens, then rubbing it in his shirt, and Batal had the spyglass clean. He dialed in the focus by twisting its brass base. "Beautiful. I've never seen anything like it, Danu."

A dozen human-made rectangles rose from the sea, each covered in vines and some bright green plant. *Moss maybe, sea moss?* He raised the spyglass again, scanning the towers to their tops. Green shaggy growth covered every square meter. "Except"—he lowered the spyglass to where the towers met the rolling sea—"the bottom, Danu. Orange, blue, and some pink? How 'bout that, girl?"

Danu's nose twitched, muzzle pointed up with her mouth open and tasting the wind.

"Coral," explained a raspy voice from behind.

Batal dropped the spyglass, its leather cord snapping at the back of his neck. He turned and wrapped his arms around Jenna, who had a thin horsehair blanket around her shoulders. Though a few inches taller and at least two stone heavier, she felt small in his embrace, weak. That would soon change, and thank the gods for it. Batal held tight and did his best to wipe his tears on the blanket before she noticed.

"I know that move, Batal. Wipe your tears and be done with them." Jenna squeezed the air out of his lungs then pushed him back. "Thank you." She wadded up the blanket and tossed it toward the cabin. "Now I will not forget."

Batal held her gaze, nodded. "Coral?"

"For hundreds of meters. All the way to sea floor, I'm told." Jenna stretched her arms, twisted her back, her neck. "Maybe that was a fucking lusca." She chuckled. "Sure could take a beating. You know, I have no idea what the hell that is. Lusca? Sounds like something a sailor would spit over the side."

"Sea monster, something like a giant octopus crossed with a triton." Batal shrugged. "An octo-shark."

Jenna shook her head. "Or, just a big-ass octopus with a bigger fucking beak."

"You remember the beak?" Batal shivered. "Good place to store a harpoon. I thought you were dead."

"So did I." This time Jenna wrapped her arms around him. "Sure of it, until this back-lit bastard, dragged down by my favorite anchor and bearing harpoon gifts, appeared." She released Batal again, wiped at her eyes. "That'll be the fuck'n' end of it."

A low growl followed by snorts and puffing sounded from between Batal's legs. Danu pushed forward, her body half in and half beyond the rail, her snout sifting through the coming breeze. She growled again.

"Easy, girl." Batal sniffed the air, licked his lips. The hint of sweetness and musky aroma tickled his nose. Rotten eggs, the metallic scent of copper, sewage came next, growing stronger with each passing second. His stomach turned sour, the taste of bile tickling the back of his throat. The Emerald Towers now loomed high in the sky.

"That's smoke." Jenna probed the approaching structures. "Leftover stench from centuries of roasting humans."

Batal dropped to his knees, pushed Danu to the side, and purged himself into the rolling swell. He spat a few times and got to his feet, clutching the top rail. "I thought it would smell like pig." He brought his shirt up to cover his nose and mouth. "It does. A little." He then dry-wretched, coughed. "But there's something..."

"Blood and shit." Jenna looked over her shoulder toward the wheelhouse. "We should wake the others. Be passing through the towers in an hour. We'll need help."

"OK, but what do you mean blood?" Batal asked through his shirt.

"Do you remember how to dress a stag? Though it's been many years since we had something to hunt."

"Sure. We used everything: organs, bone. Even blood as a base for paint and dyes."

Jenna nodded. "We hung and bled the stag, composted its entrails, and processed the organs." She pointed toward the bright green towers. Visible vines hung between them, connecting them to one another. "The Varghori Monks cook men whole and alive. Fear and duress of the 'animal' spoils the meat, blood burns and carries the stink of copper, and the shit-filled intestines follow."

Batal was pale, shivers radiated from his stomach. "Why? Why would you treat anything that way?"

Jenna took a few steps toward the stern. "I'm told the monks believe eating that which fears them, that it somehow strengthens them."

Batal let his disgust turn to anger, and hatred of what the smell and the towers represented. "Or the evil fucks feed off being cruel. Parasites sucking off fear in those who can't fight back. We're talking about people. They eat their own."

"We don't know what they eat." Jenna stated. "Just like your fish-topus, they're nothing but myth and legend, until they're not... Now wake up the others." She headed to the wheel.

"It's a lusca," he mumbled as he neared the cabin steps. "A fearsome sea monster, not a fish-topus." He knocked on the door.

"Come in, Batal."

She always knows. Amira's voice was clear, bright, and calming. *She's feeling better*, he thought as the changing wind brought a new scent. Batal's stomach tightened, he took a deep breath, letting it all in without a fight. It was better to get used to now, so he took another breath. *Fuck if it don't smell like roasting pig this time without the "other" aromas.* Maybe it is all myth and legend, but there was something mixed or carried with the scent that reminded him of the Horde. An unmistakable rot hiding within.

"For all the gods! Away, fishy-face, away... Not in the mouth!" Drago complained as Danu used her tongue to wake Batal's slumbering uncle.

Batal laughed as he watched Drago and Danu rolling around overhead for a moment, then he ducked and entered the cabin. Amira and Stefan sat on the bunks together, embracing while she quietly spoke. Stefan nodded, wiped his eyes, and walked past Batal and out of the cabin.

Amira looked to the ceiling, then back to Batal. "You enjoy your deerhound's methods far too much, my son."

"Please, no more, devil-hound! I'm up, I'm up!" came Drago's voice from overhead. He finished his plea with a deep bellowing laugh, as he always did when Danu made the morning rounds.

"Everyone loves Danu. You and Uncle Drago the most." Batal sat next to his mother, who was suited up in her leather armor. "I've always felt safe when you wear your armor."

"And now I'll feel safe when you wear yours." Amira leaned against him. "The monks are a brutal clan. Far worse than the Horde. Thank the gods they are few."

Batal wrapped his arm around her shoulder. "I was hoping for a false myth or fisherman tales, but the smell is pure evil."

She pointed under the far bunk where a lone set of leather armor lay rolled up and tied next to a short bow and sword.

Batal made his way to the bulkhead, knelt and pulled out the bundle of leather. Bumps ran up and down his arms, death carried on a swirling wind filled the cabin. Batal unrolled the chest piece, a black symbol embossed in its center. "The deer-hound of Skye Stone. Father's armor." He reached down, grabbed the short bow and ran his fingers over the symbols carved into it. "Great grandfather, grandmother, father." At the base of each end, before it turned into a point, was a fish. "And me."

"Vlad carved each fish at night while you were sleeping." A shine found her eyes. "He wanted to surprise you."

Batal let his tears flow. It honored his friend and he couldn't stop them anyway. He set the bow on top of the body armor and found the grip of the short sword. "No." He then spun on his knee toward his mother, holding the leather scabbard with a pommel made of ivory with carvings that depicted beautiful pregnant women. "I cannot accept this."

"The Mother Warrior has served me well." Amira stood and walked over to her son. "It's too heavy for these arms. My bow and dagger are all I need. That sword has been in my family since the Fall." She pushed the sword toward him. "And it will stay that way. Put on your armor. Based on the smell, we've only a few minutes before Jenna—"

Stefan popped his head through the open doorway. He now

wore a tight-fitting leather chest piece with seams straining at the sides. "We're approaching the first of the towers."

Batal finished putting on his body armor and Amira held out her hand. He took it and stood. "We're coming," she said to Stefan, but he was already gone.

She then moved to the far bulkhead, opened one of the small hatches built into it, grabbed another roll of leather, and tossed it to Batal. "Queen Zasar had this made."

Batal unrolled the long leather piece. It looked like a big cross with straps, with a flap on each side embossed with the same black symbol as on his armor. A grin spread wide on his face. "She's gonna love this."

"All Guardians need armor," Amira replied. "It'll protect Danu's back and sides without limiting her movement."

"Thank you, Mother. It's beautiful. Danu thanks you."

"Thank your aunt—"

"Whirlpools!" Drago hollered from outside.

"Keep Danu here, Mother." Batal then burst from the cabin, moved to the port side, sat on the deck, dropped the long oar in the lock, and wedged his feet under a cleat. His chest thumped, legs tightened as he focused on his breathing, doing his best to block out the sweet scent of roasting flesh...and something else. He caught sight of the edge of the whirlpool ahead of the Emerald Towers. Lazy currents turned counterclockwise, running around a still center—a forty-meter wheel of water imprisoning a bed of kelp that reached for the bow.

"Batal, port! Stefan, starboard! Grab the oars!" Jenna called from the pilot's wheel. "The whirlpools are farther out than I thought." She loosened the line to the sail, releasing the wind and reducing the *Aeolus*'s speed. "The only safe passage is through the center of the Towers. Drago, call out the whirlpools. We need to enter at the edge of each, moving with the whirlpool's current. Batal, Stefan, be ready if we need an extra push or pull. On me!"

"Starboard!" Drago yelled.

Jenna spun the pilot's wheel, the line to the sail kept from sliding by two blocks of wood shaped like a *V*. "Stefan, push! Batal, pull!"

The *Aeolus* cut to the starboard and entered the edge of the whirlpool, the pull of the sea changing her course. Batal leaned over the port hull. Beneath the calm center, a massive rectangle of coral loomed where the sunlight fell to shadow. Rails protruded from the edges and slender towers grew from its top, trying to reach the surface.

"Sail!" Jenna yelled.

Batal pressed his feet against the cleat and raised his oar from the water. *WOOMP.* The sail filled and pulled the *Aeolus* out the far side of the whirlpool. The Emerald Towers approached and pools of various sizes spun fast and slow between them, some churning and crushing the logs and debris captured over the decades and centuries. Beyond the moat of whirlpools, calm water flowed around and through the Emerald Towers—a gentle current meandering through the center like a path through a sleepy town.

The sail fell slack, and Jenna placed the line back in its vise. Batal looked through the cabin porthole to see Amira and Danu sitting on the forward bunk staring out another porthole that faced the coming towers. Batal relaxed his feet, wiggled his toes, and rotated his ankles. A red mark shone bright on the top of his foot, one that was the exact width of the cleat.

"Port!"

His feet wrapped around the cleat once more and the *Aeolus* cut across the swell.

"Batal, pull! Stefan, push!" came the familiar command from the pilot's wheelhouse.

Holy shit! Batal thought as the *Aeolus* tilted toward her starboard hull and was dragged toward the center. The swell vanished as the boat swung wide and descended into its vacuous depths. Wind howled in Batal's ears, his body pulled back and forth as the spiral tightened its grip.

"Push, Batal, push!"

He tucked his thumbs under the shaft, then dipped the oar blade and pushed with everything he had. Meters in front of him, Drago strained to hold on to the rail.

"Sail!"

WOOMP.

The *Aeolus* rose toward the far edge of the spinning sea, her bow hammering through the water. Batal's feet released, and he tumbled backward. A snap sounded as a piece of the oar handle struck his back. His arms flailed as he slid down the deck. He grabbed for the rail above the gunwale but was ripped away by his momentum. The cabin flew by. A hand appeared and grabbed the strap of his leather armor, then pulled him toward the pilot's wheel.

Jenna looked down at Batal. "Going for a swim again?"

He sprang up from the deck and lunged toward the starboard hull. Stefan's outstretched arms passed by, followed by his screaming face. Batal snatched his friend's boot, grasped the rail with his free hand, and swung Stefan into the pilot's area. The *Aeolus* continued her steep ascent. Jenna clung to the wheel as Batal and Stefan tried to pull themselves up.

"Anyone else—" Jenna ducked.

Drago slid across the cabin's roof, followed by a wave of seawater. Batal and Stefan caught him and then they all crashed into the stern rail, a heap of arms and legs clinging to anything attached to the boat. The bow of the dual hulls raised out of the water, and Jenna's feet slid back toward the others as she gripped to the wheel. The boat climbed higher and then fell, skating down the back side of the whirlpool and into the calm current that ran through the center of the Emerald Towers.

17
COCKLESS MONKS

The *Aeolus*'s sleek, twin wooden hulls skimmed the water's surface. Her mast stood bare, the sail with its mighty head of a deerhound folded, rolled, and stored at her base. Vines clung to every vertical surface of the towers surrounding the ship. The coral gave up a few meters above the waterline, where the vines took over, many growing into the seawater without success, but still alive. The water was like a sheet with no break, change, or visible current; just a glassy mass flowing through what Amira had told him was once a great city of the Indian Empire. Each tower was once filled with the ancient ones.

Batal rested on his knees and elbows, studying the chart that lay on the deck of the wheelhouse. The Emerald Towers were clustered in the chart's center. Batal erased a few lines and rectangles and redrew them as accurately as he could.

"The Arabian Sea?" he asked Jenna, who was manning the wheel above him.

"Old names without a namesake." Her eyes darted left, right, then up as they passed the first two towers.

Batal tracked the tower off the port side. It rose hundreds of meters above them and disappeared into a light mist. Empty squares surrounded by thick green vines watched with empty sockets as the *Aeolus* and her crew floated by. *What would people do in these structures?* he wondered. *Work, live, and surely die*. They were depressing, dark, and dank-looking as far as he could see inside the square openings that were once fitted with glass and steel.

"Long ago, merchants like those of the Spice Islands sailed and traded throughout this area. They were Arabians, and their sea is all that remains, as their vast peninsula is no more." Jenna motioned for Batal to roll up the chart. "The monks are clearing the openings." She pointed to the tower off the portside. "See, the lower ones are free of vines."

Batal gazed up the tower and into the sky. Fifty meters up a thick group of braided vines crossed over the water and into the tower off their starboard side. It sloped at an angle, disappearing into an opening. Similar vine groupings went back and forth as high as Batal could see until the buildings faded into the shifting mist.

"Where are the monks?" Batal then coughed. The hanging stench of rotting manure and only the gods knew what else, worsened with each passing second.

"Watching," Jenna whispered without moving. The first towers were now behind them. "The vines." She moved her head to her right.

Rising to his feet, Batal turned halfway then glanced over his shoulder. Painted white figures flew from the Towers. Each wore a green harness with a shiny rope that linked them to the vine above. *There must be twenty or more*, he thought.

"They're not nocturnal," Jenna continued. "And there sure as fuck are a lot of them. Something to add to your chart." She adjusted the longbow fastened to the bulkhead above the wheel.

Farther up the deck, Drago lay on his stomach in full battle dress. He had painted his once-shimmering scale body armor with a black clay paste that almost matched the color of his skin, but he stood out against the wooden deck. His bow was in one hand, quiver in the other. Amira lay next to him, blending in with her leather armor, her bow also at the ready.

"She won't stay down here with me," Stefan said from inside the cabin as Danu appeared, leather on her back and sides. *A fucking Guardian like no other*, Batal thought. He was proud of her unwillingness to stay below, while Stefan would require a pry bar or jug of wine to get him to come out.

The Emerald Towers were beautiful with their rich, green coverings and pink-and-yellow coral foundations. But the stench that swirled around them was evil and menacing.

A group of three towers on the starboard side caught Batal's attention. There was movement at the lower level openings. The stench was now unbearable. Drago retched, liquid appearing in viscous pools near his face. Batal reached for the spyglass, which was hanging near the wheel, and moved to Jenna's side.

"They're in the bottom floors. Covered in white mud." Batal's breathing quickened. "I see filthy crates everywhere." He refocused the spyglass, moving to another opening. Hollow eyes stared back. Big, bloodshot eyes surrounded by cracked white mud watched the *Aeolus*.

"What else?" Jenna demanded. "What are they doing?"

White faces appeared in the lower levels of all three buildings. Patchy heads with random dreadlocks pushed through the square openings. With the spyglass, Batal saw the outlines of radiation lesions under the white mud; they looked far worse off than any from the other island nations Batal had been. Eyes swollen shut, mouths drooling and crooked. Hands hung out the openings or supported resting faces. Varying numbers of fingers, webbed, swollen, and bloody.

"Abominations," Batal reported as he scanned the towers floor by floor. "All of them, abominations."

"We're almost through," Jenna stated. "Only two towers left and we're out. Then we can make for the Bern, where we can rest and get supplies." Her hands were white, knuckles red, as she clamped onto the wheel.

A few hundred meters ahead, two towers remained, one on each opposite side of the calm channel. Behind them, a blurring mist descended, hung above the water and in the air. A whirring sound grew louder as they approached.

"Sounds like a swarm of locusts." Batal leaned forward. "Underwater."

Jenna grabbed the spyglass from him. "Take the helm. Keep us in the middle." She rested an elbow on the top of the cabin as she peered into the water below. "That's not good."

Amira and Drago crawled toward the helm and dropped into the wheelhouse.

"Look," Jenna said as she passed the spyglass to Drago.

"Current?" he asked.

"No, look left and right. The mist is moving toward the center."

"That's impossible. It would be over one hundred meters. A whirlpool that big doesn't exist." Drago passed the spyglass to Amira.

She rotated the end. "And yet there it is. The buildings beneath the surface could create it by altering the currents. They surround the Emerald Towers, probably hundreds of them below us."

"It's a vortex or a maelstrom," Batal stated from behind the wheel. "If it's powerful enough to churn and create a mist in the air around its edges and pull it toward its center—"

"You've been reading the books I gave you!" Jenna slapped him on the back. "And we're fucked if we don't find a breeze and a new course to—"

Danu sprang out from under the bench, barking and sniffing at the deck before trotting toward the bow with Drago close behind. Jenna nodded toward Batal and took back the helm. Batal then followed his uncle. Danu stopped at the bow on the port side, growling as she hung her head over the hull. Drago laid on the deck next to the deerhound and looked out into the sea.

"Shadows!" Batal pointed off the port side. "Moving aft!"

Drago was up and met his nephew back at the stern with Danu arriving first, barking at the water behind the *Aeolus*. Ten meters behind them, five dark shadows broke the surface, white mud clouding the water around them as the distance grew.

Batal watched the water moving around the figures. "They're stationary. Anchored to something."

The bow of the *Aeolus* then angled to the port side.

"It's not me!" Jenna yelled as the towers closed in.

Batal moved back to the bow, lying on the deck, and positioned himself between the two hulls. Snapping and crunching came from the mist ahead. The maelstrom was chewing and spitting out anything it could suck into its swirling mouth. *There!* Batal focused on the edge of the port side interior hull.

The outline of a thick line just beneath the surface appeared. *No*, he thought, *a fucking vine.* He rolled onto his side, his leather armor already soaked in sweat and sea water. "They've attached a vine to the hull!" He drew his short sword and rolled back, grabbed the bottom rail with his left hand, and raised his sword.

"STOP!" Drago slid up to Batal. "Sheathe your blade." Drago puffed, hands on his knees, "They pull us in"—his chin lifted toward the port side where dozens of men caked in white mud stood on a narrow dock fixed to the bottom of the tower—"or we are torn apart"—his eyes moved beyond the bow.

Batal let go of the cleat and got to his feet. The mist had thinned beyond the towers and a swirling hole lay only thirty meters away; the engine of the gentle pull that had taken many ships to their destruction. Centuries of wreckage spun round and round, grinding against one another like a massive grain mill. The braided vine emerged from the sea, all slack removed, like a giant snake dragging its helpless prey toward its den. The breeze shifted and the smell of fire, flesh, and shit was back.

The vine ran from the bow of the *Aeolus* to an opening in the nearest tower. Batal pictured what lay beyond the dark opening —another giant octopus sucking the vine into its beak, a meter at a time. Buzzing clouds shifted in the air near the Varghori Monks.

"Flies." Batal looked to Drago. "Flies pouring from the towers' openings."

Jenna walked up behind them. "No need for the wheel."

"The Monks are worse than I imagined," Amira said when she joined them.

"Stefan?" Batal asked.

His mother shook her head. "He's been through much pain

on this voyage. He is not Vlad, not a warrior spirit. For the moment, his fear controls him."

Details of the monks were now clear as the *Aeolus* was dragged closer to the tower. The mud covering their naked bodies was a grayish white—bone white. Some type of loincloth was wrapped below their waists. A slight-framed man appeared from the hole where the vine disappeared and slithered his way toward the *Aeolus*, the braided vine passing through the grip of his hands and feet. The boat was fixed at an angle between the pull of the whirlpool and the taut vine that was no longer retracting into the tower.

Drago and Batal came together, creating a shield between them and the others. Danu was in the middle, hackles up, head and shoulders down. Batal drew his sword and Drago did the same. The stick-like man kept his pace and neared the *Aeolus*, his head twisted with a lone bulging eye staring as his upside-down slithering continued. When he was only meters away, he slowed and stopped within reach of the hull.

"By the gods, it reeks," Batal whispered. "It's more lesion than human. If it's not dead, it should be."

"I speak your tongue, Batal of Skye Stone. If you'd like to keep it, listen," hissed the monk as he threw onto the deck an opaque sack he'd been carrying on his stomach. "Your weapons. All of them."

"How do you know my name?"

"The man without sores?" He spat a mass of green into the sea. "All know of the 'untouched.' Value rises after surviving the Trials. All would give anything to milk the seed from—"

A longbow with a nocked arrow pushed through Batal and Drago.

"Enough of this shit!" Jenna leaned in, her muscled arms

drawing back the bow string. Even her leather body armor flexed. "I'll chance the whirlpool to end this pitiful fuck!"

The braided vine dropped, the monk splashed into the water, and the *Aeolus* moved toward the pool.

"Wait!" yelled Drago toward the watching monks on the dock. "Jenna," he grunted.

She released the tension and placed her longbow on the deck. She then pointed toward the tower. "Either way, death has found us. And I'd risk the water over their rotten teeth."

Bubbles popped on the surface and the vine rose out of the depths, the monk gasping, but still clinging on. Again, the *Aeolus* was held by the taunt vine from the pull of the churning sea. Batal unrolled the large sack. The sunlight made it glow as fine blond hairs dappled on the sack's surface swayed in the breeze.

"It's made from human skin." He flipped it to look at the other side. A branded symbol, an hourglass within a circle. Extinction. "The Horde."

"Your weapons or your life," hissed the monk. "Now!"

Batal filled the sack with his short sword and bow then looked at the crew, who likewise surrendered their weapons. Amira disappeared down into the cabin.

"Hurry!" The monk's mouth leaked puss when he spoke.

She appeared with a dagger and handed it to Batal. "That is all of them."

Blubbering and sniffles sounded from the cabin behind them, followed by a muffled wailing.

The lone, bulging eye hid within lashless slits. "Another hides below." Pink-and-brown flesh pushed from his rotting lips and his tongue ran around the outside of his mouth, leaving a slimy trail. "Fear. Good."

Batal cinched the sack closed with the attached rope, also

made of hair, and threw it onto the monk's stomach. His loincloth opened as he adjusted to the extra weight; a scar and a small hole was all that remained of his genitals. He then rolled away, feet first, and scrabbled back the way he had come, like a knobby caterpillar. A wet cackling erupted. The monk's lesion-covered head drooped and his bulging eye focused on the crew of the *Aeolus*. "We eat all that is unnecessary! You'll see!"

The braided vine creaked into motion, and the *Aeolus* moved toward the tower and the waiting monks.

"That's no loincloth," Drago stated. "Water beads off its surface. It's made of skin, like the sack."

"Jenna, light the cooking stone and place a spoon in the flame," Amira whispered. "Be quick, and bring me the spoon when it's red."

Jenna ducked and moved toward the cabin as the *Aeolus* crept toward the dock. Amira stepped to Batal's back, hidden by her son's size, and loosened the straps on his armor.

"Hold still, both of you," she ordered. "Keep your eyes on the monks."

Drago's eyes stayed fixed on the coming dock.

Batal's jaw flexed as the blade his mother had hidden peeled random chunks off his back around his spine. His eyes wild, as muted growls eked out from behind pursed lips.

Jenna crawled toward Amira, a bright-red spoon held by a thick cloth, which she handed to Amira before rejoining the others.

"I love you, my son. Brace yourself for the worst of it." She pressed the spoon to the small wounds she'd made with the knife.

Sizzling sounds and the stink of burning blood filled Batal's nostrils. This time, it was his own. His knees buckled. Drago's left arm wrapped around Batal's waist, pulling him up hard against his side.

"Finished." Amira whispered to Batal as she tossed the spoon and knife over the rail out of the monk's line of sight.

Jenna passed Amira a cup as the bow tapped the dock.

"Stern line," one of the monks said.

As Jenna went to the stern of the starboard hull, Amira surreptitiously poured the cup's contents on Batal's back. "Sea water," she whispered as she washed away the blood, then refastened the straps of his armor.

Batal watched the ash-caked monks tie the *Aeolus* to the dock. *Ours is the lone vessel still seaworthy*, he thought as the pieces of destroyed vessels swirling round and round the maelstrom filled his mind. Battered ships with no sign of their crews.

The stench of death came in waves with the changing breeze, or was it the stench of a terrible life? The morning sun shone bright and lit the Emerald Towers and the surrounding sea. Schools of brilliant colored fish radiated near the end of the dock, where ancient pipes entered the water.

"We'll leave this place," Batal growled to Drago. "This won't be our end."

The monks drew long white daggers that hung on their sides. A lengthy green plank—a woven mat of vines stretched across a lashed frame of bones—thumped against the hull.

A monk then stepped forward. Muddy braids sprang from patches of healthy skin around his head; swirled together, they ended at the back of his neck in a ball of whitish clay. Bloodshot eyes set in yellow sockets stared at the crew, shifting from left to right, Drago to Amira. Danu, now leaning hard into Batal's leg, was silent.

"I'm Baba. I'm whole. We have so much to show you, my

friends." His mouth opened and closed like a snake trying to eat something too large for his unhinged jaws. "Such wonders await!"

The armed monks formed lines on each side of the plank.

"Please, there is no need for armor." Baba turned toward a small doorway that lead deeper into the tower. A young girl sprang from the opening with a stack of "loincloths" in her arms. Her skin above and below her opaque wrap was covered in the same whitish mud as the others. Bumps pushing out pus covered much of her body. She ran up the plank and placed the loincloths on the *Aeolus*'s deck, then disappeared back into the base of the tower.

"And no need for your clothes. Hurry, so much to see, so much awaits you all," Baba stated with as much glee as a monster could. "Leave the armored wolf on the boat and bring the coward." This time the glee was gone, replaced by a predatory snarl.

Batal reached toward the stack of loincloths and held up a long piece of hide. It was thinner and more opaque than goat or cow hide. He then grabbed a different piece that was smaller. "I think this is yours," he said as he handed the longer piece to Jenna.

This continued until everyone had something to cover all of their more delicate parts. Batal bent down and rubbed Danu's ears. "I'll be back, Danu, greatest of the Spartans."

She licked his face then followed him into the cabin. Shortly Batal reappeared, dragging a kicking and screaming Stefan. Drago helped contain the boy, and it took both he and Batal to carry Stefan down the plank.

The monks surrounded them, a circle within a circle like the whirlpools spinning outside their realm. They were in terrible condition. Rotting teeth, lesions covering most of their bodies, the pus pushing out of fissures in the layer of mud. They reeked of death and decay like the Northern Horde, but worse. There was an underlying sweetness in the air, on the monks' foul breath, and soaked into the fabric of the place. Batal and his crew had no choice but to walk into the Emerald Tower and see what awaited them.

And then the screams rang out from above.

18

MOTHER OR VEAL

A thick, winding mist dropped from the sky, wrapping itself around the dozen or so Emerald Towers Batal could see from where he stood. It hung a few hundred meters above the dock that wrapped around the tower and kept the *Aeolus* from drifting into the churning whirlpool at the end of the flowing street. Batal had seen ancient images of places called "Financial Districts" and downtowns from the cities of the Before. The Emerald Towers had been part of one of those areas. Now they were anchored to the sea floor and rose into the mist, nothing more than vertical jungles and plunging coral.

From the outside, the Towers were the most beautiful human-made structures Batal had ever seen, and it was because nature had taken them over. Somehow the Varghori Monks had found them and now made a vile and evil living within them, and his crew were about to get an intimate tour of their horrors. The screaming started again. Somewhere above them, behind one of the open holes, were people in a great deal of pain. By the pitch of the sound, Batal thought they were female.

He and the others stood wrapped in the tanned flesh of... those who had chosen the vine over the whirlpool. Insects buzzed around the vine-covered walls, and the various openings pushed and pulled the most putrid of stenches. The monks found another reason to teach Batal of their ways, and their fists hammered at his midsection. Batal found himself on all fours as feet covered in sores and leaking pus thumped away at his ribcage, while Jenna, Drago, and Amira, held back by other monks, screamed for them to stop. Even Danu's muffled bark could be heard from the cabin of the *Aeolus*. Stefan, however, just stood there, crying and shaking as he had since they'd entered the Emerald Towers. *I will return the favor*, Batal thought as a heavy foot stomped on his back, smashing him into the dock.

His eyes opened to spot a shape carved deep into the wooden surface of the planks. Flecks of blue embedded deep into the grain. The head of a deerhound. Skye Stone. A piece of a fishing boat from Skye Stone. He scanned other planks of the dock. Saffron crocuses were carved in multiple planks, others a circle with an hourglass inside. The monks were placing the planks like trophies. Greasy hands then wrapped around Batal's biceps and jerked him to his feet.

One of the monks laughed and slapped Amira across the face.

Batal broke free, smashed his elbow into the nearest mud-caked jaw, then brought his knee into the nothingness that was the crotch of the monk who had struck his mother. He landed a punch into something soft and wet before again finding himself under a pile of human filth.

"Enough playtime!" Baba shouted and the monks rolled off Batal. The screaming from within the tower ceased. "You disappoint me, Guardian of Skye Stone." He poked at Batal's naked back, fresh blood and clear fluid followed each prod. "Not so pure. Not untouched. Very disappointing. So be it, as we have other uses for you. Ash!"

Monks pushed the others in line with Batal and stretching out their limbs, pulling the crew's arms and legs wide. Jenna head-butted one of the monks, sending him stumbling off the dock and into the sea. Baba simply laughed, and the other monks chimed in as the flailing form was sucked toward the swirling pool.

"Watch!" Baba cried. "Morning is the best!"

Seconds later the monk entered the maelstrom and was torn into pieces before his body made it a full rotation. The upper ring of the whirlpool turned pink for a moment, then returned to white foam and chop.

"You sick fuck," Batal mumbled and a knuckly fist struck him beneath his right eye. "Kill every fucking one of—"

"The old one!" commanded Baba.

Amira was dragged, kicking and yelling, to the edge of the dock.

"OK!" Batal yelled, head down. "OK. I won't resist anymore."

Baba waved a hand, and the monks pulled Amira back from the edge.

"Ash." Baba said again as he moved toward them.

A monk brought a heavy sack and placed it on the planks in front of Batal. His thick hands rolled down the hide revealing the contents: a pile of white powder with bone fragments mixed in. The ash of those captives the monks had burned. The monk then centered his smooth crotch over the sack and relieved himself. Another monk stepped up and did the same, and another until a pool of urine sloshed over the rolled edges.

Baba knelt in front of the sack and stirred the contents. Ash mixed with the urine and formed a gray sludge

"I'm Baba, I'm whole." He then stood, lifted his loin cloth, took hold of his penis, and added to the sack. Finished, he motioned with his hands and four monks ran to the sack, filled their hands and began smearing the contents over Batal's body, then moved on to Drago, Jenna, Amira, and finally to Stefan, who shivered uncontrollably as they did so.

"STOP!" Baba walked up to Stefan's shaking form, running his hands over the young man's soft belly.

He then spoke in a language Batal had never heard before, and the monks took Stefan into the inner depths of the tower. Stefan didn't resist, his sobbing growing faint once they passed through the opening.

Batal met Jenna's hard stare, her skin already turning the same whitish-gray shade of the bone and piss as the warm breeze dried the mud. Drago's darker skin turned the ash the color of almonds, and the flash of a summer harvest moved through Batal's thoughts. His mother and her blade had saved him from one fate, but the next one could be worse. The monks then herded them toward a ladder woven into the vines on the tower's exterior. Bones as rungs, vines as the rails, it soared up into the mist.

Baba went first, pausing to look down once he was a few meters above them. "Batal, you first, then the rest."

Batal hated that this retched thing knew his name. This sack of flesh with the lone cock and balls. Batal grabbed the rung and did his best to not look up, sure that was why Baba had him go next. The ladder was surprisingly strong and stout. It flexed and vibrated with the addition of those below him, but now carried the weight of his crew and the dozen or so monks following.

Five meters up, the ladder passed planks lashed together and fastened to the wall, landings that lead to the openings. Baba kept climbing and Batal thought he heard the whimpering of Stefan from somewhere within the tower. Batal slowed his climb to listen, but the earlier wailing from farther above resumed, drowning out anything else. They passed another landing connecting more openings, and then another until the screaming from inside filled Batal's ears. Finally, Baba stopped and slid from the ladder to a lashed plank landing.

They weren't as high as the top of Skye Stone's wall, but they were definitely up there and the landing was less than a meter wide. *Third level, high ceilings*, Batal noted. *If the openings on the seaside were clear and they got a good run, we could clear the dock if we dove out—maybe.* Batal kept one hand on the ladder rung until the other grabbed a handful of smaller vines covering the wall. He then stepped off the ladder, shoulder brushing the vines, and walked toward the opening. A buzzing grew as he neared the entrance. Jenna and the rest were right behind. Baba slipped through the opening. The screaming resumed and took on a rhythm. Ratty-braids popped out of the opening, his bloodshot eyes fixing on Batal.

"Come, come. One is ready!"

Batal reached the opening, stepped over the vines, and marched inside. He took a few more steps then stopped.

"Close your eyes tight for a moment, then open them," Baba hissed, his voice changing with each new location. Batal did as he was instructed.

On cue, a short scream blasted from the center of the room like a Zaeafranian sheneb. Batal thought of covering his ears, hating anything that reminded him of those stupid fucking trumpets, but he kept his hands at his sides. *No weakness. They feed off it*, he thought, and then it stopped as quickly as it had started.

"They like it dark. They like it cool." Each word dripped out of Baba's mouth.

The monk's foul breath then reached Batal's face. *He's right there, but I can't see anything.* Behind him, he heard Jenna and Drago enter, coughing and fighting the putrid air. Batal's lungs had finally accepted it. During the Trials on Zaeafran, he had smelled far worse...though maybe not. A layer of loathing dissolved for Queen Zasar and his mother. *I am stronger, but am I strong enough?* He opened his eyes.

Soft light flowed from the openings along the walls—brighter from the east and turning to a warm glow to the west. The windows lit the edges of a large rectangular room with high ceilings and concrete floors that were pocked, cracked, and showed the iron bars that had made them last. Baba's silhouette moved a few meters ahead, and the center of the room was filled with—stalls? Batal focused; yes, they were smaller, but similar to the old horse stalls on Skye Stone now used for seed storage.

"Isn't she beautiful?" Baba asked.

Batal looked back at Jenna and Drago. All were shadows backlit by the morning light, but they remained still. Amira stood to one side of Drago and was turned so the light caught her profile. She was staring out the far opening toward the churning whirlpool far below. Her eyes squinting, body leaning toward the opening. *What do you see, Mother?*

A shriek pierced his ears. This time Batal covered them and moved toward the nearest stall where Baba stood, hands on hips, his head tilted down. Moisture hung in the air and carried a heavy dose of body odor and feces. Yet still he walked forward while his eyes continued to adjust to the dim light. Standing next to the monk, Batal forced himself to look down and see what living creature could make such a sound and emit such a stench.

Baba beamed with pride. "Yes. Yes, she is beautiful," he said, answering his own question.

Do not scream, show nothing, Batal thought, even though every part of him wanted to flee from the aberration beneath him, the one looking into his eyes. "We eat all that is unnecessary! You'll see!" the monk had hollered, and the living proof of that statement let out another wail as the crown of a wrinkled, pointy skull appeared between the two stubs of her legs. Batal swallowed hard, forcing bile down his throat. *Focus. Baba is watching, waiting to see weakness, trying to instill fear.* Another wail as shoulders covered in dark purple lesions emerged.

"An arm!" Baba howled. "A good sign!"

A bony hand attached to a jointed twig unfolded. The other side of its shoulder ended with a puckered pit. The torso slipped through and stopped in sync with the wailing. Its "mother" lay strapped to a single plank at the waist and across her forehead, surrounded by wood-slatted fencing. An animal's stall. Her arms and legs had been removed with jagged scars as proof. Bald, filthy, and barely human. A bucket sat on the floor beneath it, catching what the body couldn't hold in. Batal watched in masked horror while Baba cheered on the grand finale, waiting to discover the newborn's gender. The monks in the back of the room grunted in unison. Batal stared and did his best to remain stoic.

A final scream and Baba reached into the pen, holding a sharp piece of bone. The umbilical cord dropped and the unencumbered placenta splashed into the bucket. Holding the boy high in the air by its only leg, he yelled "Veal!" A monk then ran up, grabbed the child, and disappeared through a nearby opening. "I'm Baba. Only I'm whole!"

Batal turned to the monk, his chest pressing into Baba's ash-caked face. "If it were female?" Monks moved in behind him, but Baba held up a hand and met Batal's gaze.

"All limbs?"

"Sure." Spit shot from Batal's mouth. "Every fucking limb you poisonous freaks can have." His forehead was pressed down against Baba's putrid braids, eyes looking into the bloodshot pools that stared up at him. Pure evil.

"Another wife." Baba stepped back, made a grand sweeping gesture that ended with one hand hovering above the birthing pen and the other pointing to a smaller pen with a lid. Inside that pen looked to be a small bald girl, curled up on a bed of dried vines, the whites of her eyes locked in Batal's direction.

"Fucking monster!" Batal's hands shot up and wrapped around the back of Baba's head as his knee rose. He pulled the foul mass downward until head and knee met with a wet crack.

A sharp pain hammered in the back of his head and shot through Batal's eyes. The ceiling spun and darkness followed.

19
A GUARDIAN RISES

A sound floated in and out of the blackness, followed by a thumping drum while a crushing weight attacked Batal from all sides. Warm sludge slid down next to his spine, then the sound again; it was everywhere and it was nowhere. His body tingled; was he upside down? Maybe sideways instead, or just numb. The drum pounding in his ears slowed. Then voices.

"Wake him, rotate their cages. All must watch."

Cold water shocked his body. "Sea water," Batal uttered, the salt burning the back of his head and stinging his lips. Ash and water loosened his blood-caked eyelids—

"Be strong, my son." The whisper came from his side. "Steady yourself. Hope is close."

Another wave of water splashed across Batal's body, and musk replaced the iron filling his nostrils.

Grunting sounded and Batal found himself on his back, like a turtle in the sun. Sunlight sparked, burned, and finally retreated into the square openings it came from.

"Steady." Amira's voice brushed his right ear.

Batal looked through steel bars that made up the foundation of the concrete structure. He was on his back, trapped inside some kind of crate, his opaque loincloth bunched around his waist. His knees on each side of his head, he stared through his feet at Baba's bruised and broken nose, then spotted a group of monks with a splayed body hanging behind them in the shadows. Each of Batal's arms were wrapped around his calves and hung lifeless near his face.

Batal's heart drummed in his ears while his lungs searched for air. Splashing sounded on both sides of him as wooden buckets thudded on the floor. Moans and the sputtering of Drago and Jenna's voices echoed all around. Straining his neck against his knee, Batal made out two small crates to his left, and he supposed his mother was in one on his right. Danu must still be on the *Aeolus*, but where is the fifth crate? Where is Stefan?

Monks removed the woven screens from the windows behind Baba and light poured through the shadows. Late morning? *Focus, Batal. Wits are life.* He drew a mental line from where the sun hit the concrete and followed it out the opening. Early afternoon. He relaxed, giving into the unnatural bends and pressure on his body, and took his first deep breath since he'd woken up. Low tide. Definitely low tide.

The body hanging between the monks and the light was Stefan. His arms and legs were tied to a circular frame like a wheel made of dried vine and steel. It reminded Batal of an ancient sketch among his father's belongings, something he'd called the "Vitruvian Man." Except Stefan was fat and upside down. His bloated purple face was close to unrecognizable, but it was Stefan, and based on the situation, Batal prayed he was already dead.

Baba held the same knife he had used to cut the "veal's" umbilical. Grabbing the rim of the wheel, he spun it. Round and round Stefan turned, until he finally stopped. Baba's bone blade slashed horizontally then vertically across Stefan's body, as if drawing a cross. Pink lines ran from Stefan's pubic bone to his sternum and another from side to side across his belly button. Baba shifted to the side, arms folded, and turned toward Batal and the crates.

Murmurs sounded from the crates. Drago spat, his breath heaving and sucking with the effort. Jenna growled, coughed and wheezed as she tried to feed her lungs. Amira was silent, knotted in a ball and facing Stefan. Batal screamed, without a sound leaving his lips. *I will not die like this. Fear. They feed on fear.*

Baba jumped toward the steel wheel, grabbing it from the side with both hands. Stefan's eyes opened wide, massive white disks set in a purple ball, just before Baba's feet left the ground and he spun the wheel with all his might. The cross cut into Stefan's skin turned red, becoming a blurring circle that flung crimson and greenish fluid onto the crates and their contents as Stefan screamed and pleaded for Baba to stop. The wheel slowed. Stefan's purple face ticked by, the momentum slinging him like something rolling down a hill with speed then crawling uphill only to speed back down again. Stefan, sobbing, stopped spinning when he was again upside down, choking on the blood and bile pouring from his stomach.

Monks whispered from behind the wheel and Baba's head bobbed from side to side as he approached the contraption again, the screams and whimpers of Stefan going unnoticed. Poking and prodding the incisions, Baba pushed on the surrounding fat. Content with what he saw, he jumped off the ground and spun the wheel again, leaping to the side. Gurgling, Stefan's mouth produced frothy pink bubbles that floated through the air, carried on the breeze from the spinning wheel. Entrails exploded through the incision and spun like a horrific windmill inside the room. Intestines and organs slapped the floor and slid across the ceiling high above until the gore acted like a brake and the wheel came to a sticky stop.

Short, quick breaths pushed from Batal's contorted mouth. Baba dropped to his knees and slid through what was left of Stefan, coming to sit in front of Batal's crate. He pushed his broken face against the iron bars, his putrid breath filling Batal's space.

"Show nothing," Amira whispered.

Baba and Batal turned in unison to stare in her direction.

Feral screams filled the room. Jenna's crate began to rock and bounce with Drago joining her.

Baba's eyes flicked to the others, then back to Batal. A shiny, bony finger moved to his mouth, and he licked it as he watched the bouncing crates, a smile just about to break through. "Fine. They can go next," he whispered to Batal. "And don't think I forgot about that hound. A delicacy enjoyed alive." He brushed the back of his hand over his forearm. "Skin a piece, eat a piece."

Batal released everything. His bowels and bladder added to the stench, with the little air he could muster, he cried, screamed, and wailed over his mother's pleading.

"Take me," Amira then cried, barely able to muster anything above a whisper.

Baba's ragged teeth shined and his eyes reflected the changing sunlight. The bone blade sliced the vine woven around the end of Batal's crate. He motioned to the monks holding the iron cage to ensure Batal had the perfect view of what was left of Stefan as they dumped his body on the cold floor—twisted, bruised, and folded into a rectangular heap.

"Down! Get it down and processed!" Baba yelled with glee as he pointed at the remnants of Stefan.

Two of the monks dragged the body away while two more scraped up the entrails and slopped them into one of the empty buckets.

"Sweet meats! I want sweet meats!" Baba hissed to the monks with the bucket as they departed. He again laid next to Batal's slowly stretching form. He motioned to the remaining three monks still holding the other crates. Quickly, they approached him, coming to stand in a circle. Placing bloodied lips near Batal's ear, he whispered, "No longer 'untouched,' just feedstock like the rest—veal. I'm Baba, only I'm whole. I'm about to cut off your cock and balls and eat them in front of your mother, you sniveling cowa—"

Blood poured from Baba's mouth. Batal pulled Baba's own bone blade out of his throat, then rolled onto his back and, using Baba's body as a shield, spun on the cold floor as he slashed at the back of the standing monk's heels. Two fell, reaching for their sliced Achilles, while the other limped toward the exit. Batal pushed Baba to the side and swung his prickly arm toward the nearest throat. The tip of the razor-sharp bone caught enough flesh to take care of the monk.

"Behind you," Jenna puffed.

Batal rolled away, hearing the point of a sword strike the concrete behind him. He staggered to his tingling feet. Outside the tower, shouting erupted, followed by a fading bellow and a splash. He lunged toward the sword-wielding monk, a growing pool of blood gathering at his feet. Batal missed and was now out of position and defenseless. The monk placed weight on his injured foot, it gave way and he crumpled to the ground. Batal spun back around and drove his blade through the monk's chest.

Barking rose from the dock.

"Danu!" Batal slid toward the crates, cut the vine on each end, and pulled out Jenna, Drago, and Amira as the feeling rushed back to his limbs in pins and needles.

Distant shouts echoed outside. Drago pulled himself toward an opening. "The dock is clear, but monks are coming from the other towers!"

"Sun," Amira said. "Low tide was coming. The whirlpool was slowing with the leaving tide." She panted, gulping in breaths. "I saw it out the opening."

Jenna stood, swaying on her feet and bending down to grab a bone-sword. "If there's a wind, if it's low tide, we can fill the sail. Break out of the whirlpool." She spat something red. "Leave this fucking hellhole. If Amira's right."

"They're using the vines from above!" Drago yelled. "And below!"

"Go!" Batal ran toward the birthing stalls. "I'm sorry," he whispered to the tragic abomination inside.

The eyes attached to the stumps turned glossy, the face nodded, and he hoped he read the movement of her lips: "Please." He'd remember it that way at least. Batal drove the bone blade into her heart, then moved to the next stall, the one with the lid, slashed the vine, and threw off the top.

"Now, Batal!" Drago screamed from the opening where he and the others were moving through. "Leave her, we don't have time!"

Batal reached in and pulled out the slight, bald, and ash-caked form. "Hold on to my neck." He had no idea if she understood a word he'd said but swung her around his shoulder anyway. Thin, surprisingly powerful arms clamped around his neck, feet digging into his waist. *Guess she does*, he thought, then ran for the opening.

"Down!" Drago bellowed.

The light blinded Batal, but his ears were true and the shattering tips of arrowheads were enough for him to slide onto the hanging walkway, keeping the girl and his back to the tower.

"What the fuck good is down? Shooting from above!" Batal looked to the dock far below. The monks had left the *Aeolus* alone and were now crawling up the vines and ladders. "The flow has slowed, so current isn't as strong. Must be low tide, just as Mother said." The monks were closing in from all directions. "Hold on, little one. Don't let go, no matter what." The tiny arms tightened around his neck. He looked to Jenna, who had rolled into a ball, covering her face. More arrowheads clanked against the vine-covered concrete. "Jenna! You're the strongest. Help Mother."

Batal then sprang to his feet, took a lone powerful stride, and launched off the walkway. "Now!"

Jenna grabbed Amira—"I'm sorry!"—and tossed her as far as she could, then leaped with Drago at her side.

Batal hit the warm, flowing sea. The current was nothing like it had been earlier, but the *Aeolus* was approaching quickly. Batal kicked and paddled toward the center of the stern, where the swimming deck touched the sea between the twin hulls. The girl held steady, loosening her grip each time he coughed. "Reach!"

Releasing his neck, her hands grabbed the wooden platform first, while her thin body was pulled underneath it. Batal clamped onto the rail on the side, wrapped his arm under her shoulders, and pulled them both up and onto the deck.

"Line!" Drago sputtered.

He and Jenna had reached Amira but were too far out. Danu barked, scratched, and pawed at the cabin door.

No time. Batal sprinted across the deck, slid around the corner of the starboard hull, and ran toward the bow line. He slammed into the rail, grabbed the coiled line, and threw it in front of them like he used to cast his fishing net. Drago got a hand on it, passed it to Jenna, who tied it off like a big loop around them all and started to pull the trio toward the boat.

A high-pitched scream sounded.

Batal spun toward the girl, who was now standing near the cabin door.

A monk stood on the dock below, his ebony skin showing through the gray ash. A bundle of weapons and leather armor in his arms. He tossed them onto the *Aeolus*. "We were all something else once. For my queen. For Zaeafran."

A dozen pink tips erupted from his body. The monk sank to the dock, arrow shafts covering his back and legs, propping him up like a marionette.

"Down!" Batal motioned with hands.

The little one crawled down the steps to the cabin, unafraid of the beast barking and pawing at the door.

Batal began to hunt through the sack. *Bow, bow, leather*— "FUCK!" *Sword.* He ran to the front of the boat, hacked through the thick vine holding it against the dock, then ran to the stern where a thicker vine was attached. The bow of the *Aeolus* started to creep away from the floating deck toward the pull of the whirlpool. The *zip* and *whoosh* of an arrow passed his ear. Another even closer. The vine frayed, then snapped as monks poured from the lowest level of the tower and ran for the boat, skidding to a stop at the edge of the dock. Arrows aimed from above by raggedy arms remained nocked.

Smiling bastards. Knowing they would collect the pieces later, Batal thought. *Not a single arrow wasted.*

"Help!"

Oh shit. Batal ran to the starboard bow, grabbed the line he'd cast out, and pulled. Jenna and Drago were working it from the other end with Amira facing backward behind them.

"Ladder!" Jenna cried.

Batal tied the line to the nearest cleat, grabbed the rope ladder, hooked it onto the side of the hull, and let it unroll. Jenna untied the loop and emerged first, then stumbled down toward the captain's wheel. Amira's head appeared with a push from Drago below. Batal grabbed his uncle's outstretched hand and pulled him onto the deck.

"Sail! We have wind," Jenna cried.

"Now?" Batal answered.

"Yes!"

Panting and heaving, Batal and Drago pulled the mainsail line. The Scottish deerhound symbol of Skye Stone slowly appeared, a meter at a time, until the sail filled, and the *Aeolus* pulled hard to port and away from danger. The whirlpool was lazy, turning with little force and slowing with low tide. Death and debris spun within its mass, moving farther and farther from its center. A macabre merry-go-round.

"Are we safe?" Batal asked Jenna as he stepped toward the cabin door.

Jenna's hands shook, but they held the wheel steady. She nodded, exhaled, and looked down toward the small girl untying the vine from the handle of the cabin door. "Terrified. Never been so afraid." Jenna's voice quaked. "You saved us. Again." Her eyes fell on Batal. “Like Amira said, one would come at the end, unmarked and fearless. One to lead us against the growing Horde, against the darkness. A bread-scarfing fisherman.”

“Not sure about Mother’s mystic ramblings,” Batal replied with a forced smile. “I was scared. Pissed and shit myself in front of everyone.” He then held up a finger. “On purpose. Was a planned ‘save the day’ kind of shit.’”

“Happy to have you in the club.” Drago laughed and sat hard on the chest beside the cabin door, still twisting and stretching his back. “Thought that was the end.”

A high-pitched, joyful squeal, pulled their attention toward the cabin. Danu sprang from the open door and began licking the ash off the little one’s face.

20
CHILD OF THE GURKHAS

The *Aeolus* sliced through another dawn of endless swells. Rising and falling in rhythm with each breath. Batal stood behind the tied-off captain's wheel. A hot wind rushed over his damp scalp as he looked to the chart clipped to the cabin door and back to the sea, hoping the depths marked were accurate. The menacing Emerald Towers were far behind them with no new landmass in sight. He unrolled Skye Stone's latest map-in-progress. A sketched skull with sharp teeth now sat next to the Towers. Batal erased another section.

"Most of India has been taken by the sea. The Bay of Bengal is now an extension of the Arabian Sea..." he mumbled, tracing a finger toward the Hiroshima Archipelago. "No gulfs or bays. No land, definitely no South China Sea. Just sea."

A blanket moved on the bench behind him and two thin arms appeared. Amira stretched and yawned. "Even with your mumbling, there's no better place to sleep. Rocked by the loving embrace of the sea." She rolled on her side to face Batal and snuggled the blanket around her.

A gray tail slapped at Batal's ankles from under the bench then disappeared.

A toothy grin grew on his mother's face. "You know what's required."

"She's holding true but watch the line. Wheel's a bit slick, been slipping southeast." Batal slipped off his sandals and tiptoed toward the bow.

He returned a few moments later. "Mother. Mother," he whispered. Scabs now covered much of her face, her arms, and even her eyelids. *She is strong*, Batal thought as he placed a hand on a clear patch of skin.

"The sea is so peaceful here." Her bright eyes showed again as the tail below the bench returned, thumping against Batal's shins.

He knelt on the deck and placed a large piece of dried fish opposite the magical tail. Danu's head slid from her cave, coming to rest within striking distance of the fish, which disappeared in a blur of a pink tongue and gray fur.

"Love you, Mother." Batal reached for a bottle wedged behind her, pulled out the cork with his teeth, then placed it in her hand. "Weeks have passed. Still no sign of land. Plateaus, mountain ranges, and shorelines should be everywhere according to the map." He swept his hand across the horizon. "All gone."

Amira sat up with a groan. "Maps and charts are of the old world until we change them to the new. Why do you think we use charcoal?" She took a sip from the bottle. "When one of us returns, everywhere we've been and all we've observed will be written in the Book. It remains the most precious of all things to Skye Stone. It's where we started, where we're going, and how we get there. The Earth heals herself by shedding much of her old skin to insure there is energy for the new. Water is her ultimate elixir."

"Four centuries of quakes leveled old countries, oceans covered continents, and that which started it all still falls from the sky erasing all with its flames and poisonous reach," Batal complained. "I hate them for it. I hate them all." He sat and leaned against the edge of the bench. Danu's muzzle wiggled under his hand and started flipping it in the air. "OK, girl," he said as he started to rub her head and ears.

"Not all the ancestors where evil," Amira explained. "Many tried to turn their leaders to hope and peace. You need to read the early volumes of the Book. For now, keep recording our journey in words and drawings. You have a talent for it. It will help when the time comes."

"When what time comes—?"

Amira rested her hand on his shoulder. "And our crew? The Towers were far worse than any of us could have imagined. The Varghori Monks are..." She wiped at her eyes and returned her hand to Batal's shoulder. "Barely human. Following a similar path to the Horde."

The captain's wheel continued to jiggle back and forth, the line holding the boat's course. Batal spoke of the pain of the others with his mother. It was his way of releasing the horrors, and she knew it. "Jenna is below with the little one. The girl won't leave her side. Jenna is strong, but laughs less, and guzzles spirits as water. I think less with each passing hour, but few jugs are left. The little one is quiet. Her eyes seem less haunted, her body is growing stronger, but I have yet to hear a word cross her lips."

Nodding, Amira took a deep breath. "Not so little, but we'll save that for later. My brother? How is your uncle, Drago?"

Batal took a moment, listening to his slumbering uncle atop the cabin roof. The sound of warthogs in battle was all that came to mind, and Batal had only seen a warthog once on one of the spice trader ships in Skye Stone. Still, Drago's snoring was legendary.

"Relieved." Batal cranked his head so he could see his mother. "It terrified me. Watching Stefan being torn apart, unable to move, barely enough air to breathe. Drago showed no fear, but there was something else—"

"Helplessness. Nothing worse than a Guardian dying without striking a blow or at least falling with a shield or sword in hand. Yes, my son, relieved to not leave this world trapped in a cage. You gave him that gift." She leaned down, kissed his cheek. "And how is Batal? Fighter of a giant octopus and cockless monks?"

"Lusca. I want it written as 'fighter of lusca and slayer of cockless monks.'" A smile turned into laughter, then ended with tears. "I may have saved, Jenna, even helped us escape"—he rubbed his eyes—"but not all of us. Vlad and Stefan are dead. And how many of Queen Zasar's people have fallen to the Horde since we fled?"

"Some of us burn bright and fast, others slow and steady," his mother replied. "Honor their life-gift to you, Batal. Pay tribute to their history and spirit." She looked out toward the breaking sunlight streaking through puffy clouds. "There are bigger wheels turning in the sky. Our fate spins upon them and takes us to the Hiroshima Archipelago. But we may have one more stop before we get there."

Batal looked to the endless sea. "Where?"

"I think the girl is from Jiuhua." Amira slid over, allowing

Danu to jump up and curl up next to her, squeezing into what space there was between Amira and the rail.

"Jiuhua?" Batal stood, unrolled his map again, and moved toward his mother. He lifted Danu to make room, then sat down, laying the dog's head and front legs across his lap.

"Here." Amira pointed at a spot in the southeast corner of what the old world chart had named China. "Isle of Jiuhua." She stood and shuffled toward the port side of the *Aeolus*. "There," she said as she pointed to the distant horizon.

Danu dropped her front paws to the deck, stretched, and padded her way forward until her rear end slid off the bench and she joined Amira at the rail. Batal grabbed the spyglass.

Leaning into the rail, he scanned the horizon. "Nothing out there. Water, not even a shadow... Wait. Holy shit!"

Amira smacked his arm. "Keep those words for your friends. Just like your uncle, like your father."

"Sorry." He handed over the spyglass. "Not much to see from here."

"Wait until we're closer. Once, it was only a small area with many peaks that formed a great mountain." Amira returned the spyglass. "Will the line keep the wheel true?"

Batal shrugged. "Has so far, with a tweak every hour. Wind's slow, but steady."

"Monitor it from below. Wake Drago and Jenna, and bring the little one. It's time."

"For what?"

Amira moved back to the bench. "To hear her story. She speaks the Common Tongue."

Batal waited with Danu, both still staring at the tiny, shimmering pyramid in the distance. "How do you know the little one speaks the Common Tongue?"

"She listens now."

Batal turned to look at one of the cabin's small portholes. A freshly scrubbed face with only a few sores on almond skin peered back through brooding brown eyes. Eyes that understood, eyes with wisdom, eyes without fear.

~

The morning sun filtered through the curtains of the cabin. *Same material as the sail*, Batal thought. His father's design moved beyond the wood and included everything. Curtains could patch the sail; hatches, tables, and even cabinet doors could patch the hull. Everything had a purpose beyond its immediate use. He felt a kinship with the *Aeolus*. She was family and his father's soul was a part of it.

They sat in a circle around the central table on the built-in bench that curved around it like a giant horseshoe of pillows and cushions. Batal felt the pride of craftsmanship and design permeate him. Pillows made of sail cloth and stuffing that floats. *Father thought of everything. Everything except staying alive.*

Jenna sat straight, even rigid, orange stubble covering her pale scalp. Drago leaned against her like a drunk on a post. The little one sat between them, with Danu under her feet.

Danu. Always the ultimate mother to us all, knowing who was the most vulnerable at the moment. As if she could tell she played in Batal's thoughts, Danu let out a couple of playful yips. The fear had passed for now. Loving silence being shared between those who had survived the terrible. Relief. Yes, relief filled them after days of swimming in the guilt of survivors. It was more. Batal knew what family felt like. His eyes fell to the little one who met his gaze and held it. Yes, family.

"Tashi. Tashi of Jiuhua. Twelve winters old. I know, I am quite small for my age." She reached toward the center of the table, placing her hand there, palm down, still staring at Batal.

He slid his broad hand across and placed it on top of hers. "Batal Spartan."

She then looked to Amira.

A toothy grin appeared. "Amira Spartan." She placed her wrinkled hand on Batal's.

Drago straightened, leaned toward the table. "Drago. Uncle... Drago Spartan."

All eyes fell to Jenna. There was still a haunted soul in there. Batal could see it, feel it and it made sense. She had been the closest to Vlad and Stefan, and he knew she would carry the burden of their deaths more than the others. The greatest of warriors always did. It was why Drago couldn't speak of Batal's father without rage or tears and nothing in between.

An elbow thudded against the oak slab followed by a thick forearm and a powerful hand, laid on top of the others. "Jenna Ceallach. Guardian of Skye Stone."

Tashi wiggled, rocking to her right, her legs folded under her, and she fell into Drago with a giggle.

A gray muzzle appeared from beneath the table, followed by two long front legs, a lean back, and finally a tail. She then turned in circles far bigger than the bench allowed until the correct area was properly prepared, and without a sound, she dropped into it.

"Danu Spartan." Tashi wrapped her free arm around the Scottish deerhound. "Noble, brave, and beautiful." She grabbed a paw and placed it on Jenna's hand. "I thank you for saving my life." She then bowed and raised her head. "I thank you for sacrificing that which can never be replaced"—she bowed again—"

and I grieve for those who traveled beyond us." Tashi leaned over the table, kissed the pile of hands. "We are forever family and I am always in your debt." She pulled her small hand from the bottom and the others, even Danu, took back theirs.

Batal's stare never left Tashi's. Something passed between them. *I know you*, he thought. The crate. He spun his mind back to the Emerald Towers, the cockless and vile monks, pure evil of Baba, and the crates. There were many crates, and he only thought of one. That which held the girl covered in ash and filth. Tashi.

"They will be close." Tashi stood on the bench and reached her arms toward Batal.

Without a pause, he grabbed her and placed her on the floor next to the cabin door. For the first time, he noticed the early beginnings of more radiation lesions on her arms and neck.

"They?" Jenna slid around the table to join Batal as he scanned the horizon through the starboard portholes, the towering Isle of Jiuhua taking shape ahead.

"The Horde follows, they always do, with spies everywhere. Baba spoke of Batal, the ultimate gift for the King of the Horde, alive if untouched, dead if not. Soon they will attack." Tashi pointed toward the bow. "Jiuhua is ready. My Gurkhas stand with Batal of Skye Stone, the 'Untouched,' and son of Seb. Your father's travels fill our history books, and he was loved by many."

"I would like to read them someday," Batal said as he looked down.

Tashi then turned to Amira. "You saved his life. Crude, but the cuts were effective. Baba underestimated Batal once he thought him vulnerable, like the rest of us."

"A mother does as she believes. Your Gurkhas?" Amira asked. "You are Tashi Gurung. Daughter of Chief Gurung."

"Father died. Slain by the King of the Horde the day they took me. Weeks before I was traded to the Varghori Monks... four seasons past."

"They stuffed you in that crate for a year?" Batal's voice trailed off. "Traded for what?"

"Breeding livestock. The human kind." Tashi swallowed hard. "But a little humanity is left in the monks, thank the gods, and I was in and out of the crate, depending on Baba's mood. I knew 'someone' would come before I was of age to replace the Mother." Tashi wrapped her arms around his waist. "You gave her peace. You set her free," she whispered.

"Skyward!" Jenna and Drago said as one as they moved out of the cabin, Danu on their heels, barking, hackles up.

A flaming sphere emerged from the ring of clouds protecting Jiuhua's towering peak. Arching up and out toward the approaching *Aeolus* until it splashed into the sea.

Tashi and Batal joined the others while Amira remained in thought, watching the two pointing toward the sky.

"Firing at us?" Batal unlashed the line holding the wheel and took over as he tried to quiet Danu's barking.

Jenna loosened the line of the mainsail, releasing the wind and slowing the boat's progress. "A warning?"

A fiery glow exited the clouds. This time the flaming sphere arched west, toward the open sea.

"The first one was to get our attention, the second, a warning." Tashi pointed off the starboard hull. "There! Follow the path of the fire." She placed a hand on Danu's shoulder. "You've caught their putrid scent."

Batal grabbed the spyglass, pictured a line from Jiuhua to where the fiery sphere skipped over the rolling swell and disappeared, and adjusted based on the position of the *Aeolus*. "Nothing. Just empty sea out to and beyond the horizon."

"Closer." Tashi moved to Batal's side. "Where the sea rises and falls the most. The shadow."

He angled the spyglass down a bit and scanned a darker area that seemed to rise and fall as a massive chest. "A shimmer. Debris?"

Drago climbed on top of the cabin and Batal passed up the spyglass. "Two hundred meters out, a dark patch. I think I saw a reflection."

Batal made way as Tashi pushed her way forward. "Careful," he warned.

"I want them to see me." She moved with an uncanny speed to the bow. "We're in the range of the catapults on the peak."

Batal examined Jiuhua from the ocean to the clouds. *Gotta be a thousand meters up.*

"Horde Fleet!" Drago slid off the cabin roof and onto the deck. "Painted as the sea, sails down, and they're watching us. Caught a reflection off their scopes. Even their masts are the color of the sky. Tricky bastards!"

"How could they be here already? They went around the Emerald Towers." Jenna grabbed the line to the mainsail and tied it off. "Hold on. I hope Tashi's Gurkhas don't blow us out of the water!"

"It's worse than camouflage." Drago handed the spyglass to Jenna. "It's what they've camouflaged."

Batal took the wheel, allowing Jenna to go to the rail. "That's not possible," she muttered.

"What, Jenna?" Batal asked. "What's not possible?"

"I count six. Six multi-hulled craft with forty-meter masts."

She turned toward Batal and Drago. "We just lost our greatest advantage. They've copied the *Aeolus*."

"Maybe they have." Batal looked toward the small girl standing at the bow of the port hull. "But we've made an ally. Anyone who keeps the Horde's fastest boats from raising their sails? Now, those are friends I want to have."

Amira left the cabin, climbing until she stood on the top step. "We must go to Jiuhua. The winds and sea are with us, and a secret path to the Hiroshima Archipelago awaits."

"We are safe from the catapults. My people have seen me," Tashi reported. She looked over at Amira. "And yes, baker, Guardian, seer, and mother of the untouched, a strong current exists just beneath the surface near Jiuhua that can carry a vessel to the Archipelago at great speed. But only one vessel can make the journey, and few survive."

"If you're torn apart by the sea"—Drago's muscled shoulder rose and fell—"Kaminari can't kill you in combat."

Batal nodded. "Perfect. We go to Jiuhua and test fate once more. And you, Uncle, forget to whom you speak." Batal folded his arms and gave Jenna the look.

She rolled her eyes. "Fine. Untouched One, slayer of a giant octopus—'

"Lusca," Batal corrected. "Slayer of luscas."

"Right, and shitter of his pants, dumbass who knows not the difference between a birthmark and a lesion."

"Enough, children." Amira admonished as she pointed toward the mountain of stone rising into the clouds with the sea lapping at its base. "Welcome to Jiuhua."

"There, to the west of the lone pine," Tashi instructed Jenna. "There is a gate to the fortified harbor."

Jenna spun the wheel, and the *Aeolus* made its way to the harbor.

In the distance, six similarly shaped vessels raised their sails, each emblazoned with a blood red hourglass within a circle. Keeping out of the range of the Gurkha catapults, they moved on a parallel path toward a strange ribbon of motion on the ocean's surface—a ribbon that started just offshore of Jiuhua and ran northwest as far as the eye could see.

21
I AM THE EGG MAN

Batal had never seen anything as magnificent as what stood before him. Craftsmanship so fine that everything grand and beautiful in Skye Stone paled in comparison. Even the *Aeolus* and her curving perfection of woodgrain running and climbing into the shape of twin-hulled vessel was a distant second. Jiuhua was sand, trees, and stone, and its people had mastered the materials in ways one not skilled in the arts could understand only if standing before the end product.

The harbor lay on the only accessible area, the west side of the isle. It was carved into the rock, and a perfectly weighted section of the walled bay acted like a portcullis that fell into the ocean. Tashi pointed to the gate's jagged-stone top, which remained below the surface as the *Aeolus* entered. The Gurkhas controlled the depth at which the gate submerged to ensure their lighter vessels, which drafted shallow, could pass and enemies ships would sink after their hulls were gouged on the stone. Pure white sands filled the space between the boat dock and the towering mountain. Tashi claimed Jiuhua's glass blowers were unmatched in items of art and war and the sacred white sands of Jiuhua were the reason.

A tower rose on the outside of the steep mountainside up and into the clouds. According to Tashi, it was over a thousand meters tall. From the protected harbor, it looked like the mountain. Built of thick stone that followed the mountain's face, the occasional tree even grew from the tower's side. Catapult chambers were dug into the stone and hidden behind blinds. They were scattered from bottom to top and could reach great distances; the biggest was placed on top and often hidden by clouds. Within the tower, hundreds of homes, shops, and gardens drank in the light that ran through the center of the tower from its open top. Veins of glass infused with stone dust to hide their luster ran down the sides and glowed from within.

It was similar in concept to the tower at the center of Skye Stone, Batal was sure, but he would not see the inside of this tower. His fate was that of the Guardian, and the only one who could travel the path to the Hiroshima Archipelago. Whatever the hell that meant.

Within moments of their arrival, Drago had organized another training session for him with a small group of Jiuhua's elite and eldest Gurkhas that required him to wear another loincloth. Drago took great satisfaction in the details.

The Gurkhas crafted their armor of fibers from the trees spun with a glass-like filament; it was kept flexible by adding another material that was sacred and secret. Batal's initial guess was a copper filament, put after closer inspection of the armor, he bet it was spider silk, but the Gurkhas kept their secrets. Before the training session began, the tallest of the Gurkhas spent the first fifteen minutes measuring Batal like a tailor from back home in Skye Stone. Tashi stood nearby, writing on a paper each number he spoke. Done measuring, the Gurkha lifted Batal off the ground, grunted a few times, and he called out a final number to Tashi.

"A type of armor," Tashi explained. "For your journey to the archipelago." Batal then spent the next few hours having the shit kicked out of him by four smiling faces, including the toughest of them—the tailor. With each strike came a lesson, another with each hold or lock, and by the end of the third hour, Batal's beatings turned into a friendly payback, and he'd always smile while returning the favor. The locals' curved knives reminded him of the Zaeafranian's khopesh swords, but on a smaller scale and equally deadly. They had left them in the sand, however; another lesson for another time.

Toward the end of the training, Tashi appeared from within the mountain, through a rotating door that Batal didn't even notice until it was closed. He lowered his hands and started to bow, and the four Gurkhas surrounding him charged. Laughing as they tackled him and landed half-hearted punches, kicks, and various holds that under combat circumstances would likely end his life.

Tashi waited for the warriors to unravel and for each of the bruised and reddened faces to form a line in front of her, with Batal rising last, spitting sand with a bright smile stretching across his perfectly weathered face. "I see your introduction to the 'basics' is going well," she said.

"Only way to learn is to do." He spit out a bit of blood and wiped the sand from his mouth. "Your Gurkhas' way of striking and grappling are effective."

"Each fighting form is an art, an arrow in your quiver. Your scabs are healing quickly. Amira is cunning. Soon your skin will be as intended—untouched." She walked around the line. "You have a patch of mottled skin on your lower back? Fire?"

"I don't know. I've always had—"

This time Batal caught the turning stone door as it opened. Amira approached with a stack of bluish clothes as the opening once again disappeared. *Fucking brilliant*, Batal thought. *Fucking brilliant.*

"Fire," Amira said as she handed him the stack. "Fire from the Horde."

He took the clothing; it resembled the texture of the thin, but effective armor of the Gurkhas. "Fire from the Horde? You've never spoke of this before."

Tashi's eyes widened and she looked at Amira in awe. "A carrier? You or his father?"

"First day of the siege, his uncle, Drago. Second day, his father," she replied, her face taking on a distant look, as if summoning visions long past. "It was the third day. I wore the carrier with Batal nestled on my back under its armored shell. One of the Horde smashed an oil-flamer on my back. Without the carrier—"

"I wouldn't have the greatest mother in existence," Batal said as he dropped the clothes on the sand and wrapped his arms around her. "And a beautiful scar to remind me."

"You both are very fortunate. Be careful with these." Tashi picked up the clothes, brushing off the sand before handing them back to Batal. "Your journey requires them."

"Is it time?" Amira asked, still leaning against her son and running her fingers across the smooth, glass-like fabric.

Tashi nodded as the stone door swung open behind them.

A muscular woman appeared, holding the front end of a

gurney on which a two-and-a-half meter clear cylinder with a pointed head lay strapped. A second later, a man entered carrying the end where the cylinder ended in three curved fins fixed around a bowed bottom. It reminded Batal of the rare missile that fell from the sky and didn't explode. Instead, it would bob in the sea and wait for the brave few of Skye Stone charged with towing such missiles toward the current flowing west to the dead zone. Some of the volunteers never returned, but all knew why when a mushroom cloud climbed into the sky.

Batal stepped out of the way, and the gurney traveled down the path and toward the harbor where Drago and Jenna were loading fresh supplies onto the *Aeolus* under Danu's "supervision." Batal watched the glass missile's progress for a moment, then glanced down at the stack of bluish clothes in his hands.

"You've got to be kidding. Tashi? Mother?" He then placed the clothing into Tashi's arms, his hands up in front of him. "No, no, no way am I getting into that deathtrap—"

"It's the only way. The Horde lies in wait, and the *Aeolus* is no longer the fastest boat." She pushed the clothes back into Batal's hand. "You will travel unseen, and only you can go. The Akiro clan chooses Batal; Kaminari Akiro chooses you. Without the Akiro clan, there is little hope. The Horde will spread, and the island nations will fall."

"Is there anyone, anywhere who doesn't know of the Quest of the Untouched?" he grumbled as he shot Amira a glance. But then he saw the ribbon in the sea—a current that ripped toward the Hiroshima Archipelago. Batal knew if he and the others could see it, so could the Horde vessels, and there they'd sit, just outside the current. Half of their boats on each side, sea anchors out, waiting for the *Aeolus* to make its run, enter the current, and let fate choose. But they were waiting for a boat, not a man in a glass tube. The egg man.

Batal caught sight of Danu's furry mass charging off the ramp to the dock, chasing one of the Gurkha's mastiffs, yipping and barking. All play bows and bluster. Jenna lifting far more than any human should be capable of while Drago counted and cleaned. *They would do anything for him*, Batal thought. *And I for them. So be it; the egg it is.*

He grabbed the clothing. "Thank you, Tashi."

"Socks, too?" Batal held two shiny blue tubes in the air.

Tashi, Drago, Jenna, Amira, and Danu stood in an arc around him. They had covered the dock under their feet with a mat made of some type of animal hair. Danu sniffed at it relentlessly, so Batal bet they had spun it from the brushings of the mastiffs.

Tashi looked to Amira and rolled her eyes. "Yes, Batal, everything. The full head mask, the long-sleeved shirt, the pants with stirrups, the gloves, and the socks. That scar on your back, the one left when fire melted every layer of your skin. That could happen to any part of your body not covered with this material."

Drago rubbed Batal's chest. "I like it, and the color should help you blend into the water."

"Agreed." Jenna stated with a nod. "Only wish it came with a belt. Accentuate those big hips of yours."

An uncomfortable silence followed. Batal read the concern on their faces even as they did their best to keep it light. Batal twirled, his shiny, tight shirt shimmering in the light. "Don't worry. I'll be fine, what could go wrong when wearing this outfit?"

Batal's laughter broke out first and he dropped to the mat, Jenna and Drago were next to join, then Amira and Tashi gave in. Eyes watering, Batal pushed off his knees and stood upright, slipped on the head mask and tucked it into the opening on his shirt. He then pulled the socks over his feet and slid the gloves over his thick hands. Everything fit perfectly in all the right places and the openings somehow sealed closed.

"Wow, that's amazing!" He held up his arms, the gloves disappeared into the sleeves of his shirt.

"Static charge." Tashi said. "The material working with your skin, which is just a wrapper for a squishy battery."

"Tashi, I'll take your word for it." Batal moved his fingers and ran in place. "Amazing."

A few meters away, Gurkhas had lashed the glass missile-like vessel to the *Aeolus*'s stern by tying two lines across the expanse of the twin hulls with the vessel's pointed top aligned with the bow and the curved fins with the stern. When ready, Drago would cut the lines and the vessel would roll to the center and fall into the water like a stone. Or at least that's how Tashi explained it.

The group moved to the *Aeolus*, hiked up the ramp, and stood next to the glass vessel at the stern.

"Not enough room for us all," Amira said as she hugged her son. "I will see you soon. Know that I am all right." She walked toward the *Aeolus*'s cabin and waited for Danu at the steps.

Jenna smacked Batal on the back. "What she said. Only you could pull off this look. Blue brings out the highlights in your eyes."

"They're brown."

"Still." Jenna then took her position behind the captain's wheel.

Danu wedged herself between Batal's legs and used the top of her head to lock herself into place under Batal's crotch.

"Sorry, girl. You can't come with me this time." He lifted a leg to free himself from her grip, then bent down and placed a hand on each side of her furry face. "I got this. I've been through worse." He glanced up to Tashi, who raised an eyebrow. He kissed the deerhound's muzzle and Danu slinked toward the cabin and Amira.

Drago reached to the end of the vessel, just below the base of the three fins and unscrewed a thick glass cover the width of Batal's shoulders. The underside of the lid was curved and hollowed out in the exact shape of the top of Batal's head. Inside the glass missile was a chamber shaped as if they drilled it out with a triangular blade: wide at the top and skinny at the bottom.

Batal's breaths came shallow and fast.

"Slow down. Focus on each breath," Tashi said as she placed a hand on the nose of the vessel. "It's much stronger than you can imagine." She moved to the curved fins. "The speed of the current is nothing like you have ever experienced at sea. Created when the world shifted, the mountains fell, and the water rose. These fins will turn like a propeller on the old world ships but driven by the water itself. They will keep you in its path, But"—she clutched his sleeve—"the fins spin the entire vessel at tremendous speeds. This material allows your body to stay in the center while the walls of the turning glass move unhampered without creating heat, though the cool water takes care of most of it. The color of the suit will shield you from eyes above the surface. The glass is shaped and weighted precisely to your body, you'll sink and stay at ten meters below the surface. The Horde expects a boat with a vast sail bearing the symbol of Skye Stone. But this vessel should give you a chance. Now get in. Breathe easy and you will have enough air to reach the archipelago."

"By the gods!" Drago clapped his hands together. "Better than the screamers at the wall. You, my nephew, will shit yourself again, which"—he held up two fingers—"will put you in the Spartan lead!"

"I love you too, Uncle." Batal meant it. He then saw the look in Drago's eyes: fear, fear for the nephew he had treated as a son.

Tashi handed him a palm-sized glass mass with an iron nub in the center. "Thank you again, Batal. I will not forget."

"You felt like family. I could not leave that feeling behind, but I'm not through with the monks. We'll save that talk for another day." He looked at the object she'd given him. It fit perfectly in his hand, the nub facing out. "What the hell is this?"

"Goes in the pocket above your navel." She then made a slight slapping motion. "Your exit. The current will drop you close to the Akiro clan's harbor. When the current slows, the fins will slow with it." She pointed at the pocket. "Hit the glass and the vessel will 'release' you."

Batal held up the small object. "This?" He then pointed at the thick glass. "Will break that?"

A mischievous smile lit Tashi's face. "Special, just for you."

He slipped the object into the pocket, hugged Tashi, and slid feet first into the vessel. Drago brushed a sticky compound onto the threads of the glass cover.

Batal stuck out his head. "Are you sure this holds enough air? And how will the Akiro clan know I am coming?"

"Just enough air based on our measurements. You'll get a little sleepy by the end, but the journey is much shorter this time of year. And my Gurkhas have been sending messages in smaller vessels for days. The last one left this morning before the Horde ships moved closer. The Akiro clan is expecting you." She then motioned to Drago, who positioned the lid over the opening.

"Moved closer? Wait!" He waved a hand at Drago. "How many horde ships? How many have done this before?"

Tashi looked to the sky, her hand rubbing the side of her face. "Maybe two ships? Many have made the journey. Never at this time of the year, though, but we knew you would come. The Untouched can make it."

Of course, Batal thought. *Everyone but me knows what I'm doing* He managed a smile and even a chuckle. He wiggled his hips, made sure his hands could reach the "magic iron nub" in its special silky pocket. *I feel like a cork.*

Drago spun the lid until the threads tightened and the compound oozed out.

No, that was the cork. Batal gave him a thumbs-up and focused on his breathing as Tashi had instructed while the glass began to fog.

Within minutes, the *Aeolus* was underway. Drago's stout form appeared in Batal's view not long after, though with an eerie halo around him. So Batal wiped the surface in front of his eyes, the material from the gloves leaving tiny stripes of condensation. Drago then cut the lashings, and the vessel rolled to the center of the slack. Batal remained on his back, the cylinder spinning around him with little effect. *I can do this, just another screamer. Just another wall to go up.*

Fire lit the sky over the *Aeolus* as the mightiest of the Jiuhua catapults cleared a path, all to play up the idea of a ship making a mad dash. Then the nose of the glass vessel dropped into the sea, sinking like a rock. Batal glimpsed the twisting duel rudders of the *Aeolus* as it disappeared overhead; back to Jiuhua, he prayed. Toward the horizon the surface flashed and pieces spread. Pressure built, his ears and eyes aching. *I will implode in a fucking glass egg*, Batal thought as the black consumed his foggy view.

The cylinder slowed its descent, then stopped and rose back toward the surface for a few seconds, into a hazy light, before hovering. Batal wiped at the glass around his face again and caught a glimpse of what lay ahead of him, beyond his feet. The ocean's surface rolled five or six meters above him. Burning debris cast shadows above, legs and arms flailing among them, people churning up a frothy mix of bubbles and blood.

"It's not the *Aeolus*, it can't be," he whispered over and over as he sat helpless, swaying back and forth, inching toward those fighting for their lives. Beyond them, duel rudders lay directly ahead, each fastened behind a double-hulled vessel that blended into the ocean. Those ships he was sure belonged to the Horde, but he couldn't see enough to count them from below.

Under the shadow of wreckage, a four-legged mass, still and sinking as a leaf falls from a tree. "No! I'll kill every fucking last one of you!" Batal's forehead slammed into the glass, his gloved hands wiping as far toward his feet as he could reach. The shape drifted into the filtered sunlight and rotated as it sunk.

"Dressed and roasted!" Each breath a burst. "Fucking deer carcass. She's OK, she's alive." *Control yourself, easy...* A long, finned predatory shadow rose from the depths. Jaws wide, teeth forward, it snatched the tiny carcass and both flew from sight, as if shot out of cannon. Perhaps sucked into the mouth of a bigger, more massive predator? Toward the shadows of a canyon? Batal's imagination reeled as the curved fins behind his head began to turn. "Oh shit."

He glimpsed what lay ahead. The cylinder was moving closer to it. A city—a vast city like the ones in the Book. With a thousand times the number of the Emerald Towers but hidden beneath the sea.

The area he'd wiped clean of condensation turned faster and faster, until it blurred into a stripe and Batal's glass egg turned opaque in the fading light. He focused on each breath, in and out. "Like the screamers along the wall, just another—"

His head pressed hard into the concave glass molded to its shape, his spine compressed, blood filled his face, pounded in his ears, and Batal disappeared into what Tashi and her people called the Rogue Torrent.

22

DREAMS, NIGHTMARES, CANNA, & GINGKO

The spinning glass surface beneath Batal cleared of condensation, while everything above him grew thick with it. His body grazed the glass cylinder, but he got used to it and no longer attempted to stop it. He gave in to the movement and trusted his shiny new suit to keep his skin from rubbing off. He rotated around, face looking outward into the depths. Rushing over the tops of buildings, some towering along the sides of the flow with their coral tops kissing the surface.

Whales entered and exited with great force while other forms of sea life were torn and shredded in the Torrent's flow. The speed was stunning, turning everything into blurs at the edges of his vision—some objects appearing as big as a triton or maybe whales that chose not to enter. *It had to hurt even the biggest and strongest of creatures*, he thought as another beast entered up ahead and was twirled into a frothy pulp.

And here I sit, carried in a glass egg toward a woman I have not seen since I was a boy. It hit him, rushing in like his surroundings. *I am not a boy, nor a young man or fisherman. I am a Guardian. A killer...and all in less than a few seasons' time.* He let the thought pass, disperse like the frothy pink pulp. He did what he'd had to. *Would you've let Danu be kicked to death? Let Jenna die in the bowels of a giant octopus?* "Lusca," he whispered to the voice in his head. "Slayer of luscas." *What of Tashi and the rest of your family? Let the cockless monks butcher and feast upon them? 'I am Baba, I am whole.' One day, I will remove the end of that sentence. See, you are a Guardian of those you love.*

The magical glass egg moved hard to the left, and Batal's body pressed against the side until the cylinder straightened out again.

Kaminari Akiro, warrior and seeker of the Untouched. Now why would she choose you to partner? This voice was familiar, one of the earliest memories torn from his childhood. *The opportunity to kill the Untouched and end this senseless quest to father children resistant to the radiation of this world?* "A large man..." Batal mumbled. "Angry, yelling at father in the market, even Father looked scared, said nothing, but moved so he stood between us." The voice intruded into his thoughts again. *How many will die along the way? And for what? Whelps free of lesions to feed the Varghori Monks or slave out to the Horde King?*

The bottom of the current exploded and a vast shadowy form entered the flow. Batal stared downward at the black mass only a meter or so below him. It rose, and for a moment, seemed to touch the glass but stopped. The filtered light from overhead accentuated the rubbery surface. It rotated, the glass cylinder passing it by, meter by meter. A dorsal fin larger than Batal and with a bite mark passed by and an eye the size of Batal's head appeared and remained. He placed his hands, palm down, on the glass to each side.

"You are the triton from the before. When laughter sounded from each end of the *Aeolus*. When brothers quarreled and smiles came without cause." Batal placed his face on the glass, the material of his hood scratchy and rough, but the cool glass was blissful, and the eye of the triton kind. The eye closed, and the triton dropped to the edge of the flow. Then, just when it appeared to be leaving, it shot back up and slammed into the glass.

Batal's eyes opened, he was on his back again, the visible skin around his face matched the bluish hood. Light filtered in from above. His hands were wrapped around his neck, his chest burned, and the inside of the glass cylinder spun end to end and up and down. "Pocket," he sputtered and fumbled around, clawing at his stomach, sucking in but nothing filled his lungs. He no longer controlled his hands, and a numbness consumed him.

A shadow crossed the surface of the water, then grew bigger and bigger. The glass of Batal's vessel shattered, and the sea pulled him down. A pale form approached from above, arms outstretched, her silver hair flowing, eyes as bright and green as they were when she was a child. His lungs burned with incoming saltwater.

But I have seen you at my end and that is enough, Batal thought. *That is enough.*

"Listen, Batal Spartan of Skye Stone and don't speak, for it will hurt," a familiar female voice whispered close to Batal's ear. "Don't open your eyes. The bandage will block out most of the light, but keep them shut. Within a few hours the pain and pressure will fade, and your lungs and throat will burn no more. The straps on your arms and legs are part of the ceremony before combat. My choice, my clan's rules."

Every part of him ached, thumped, or was just numb. Whatever he was lying on, it was damn soft for the parts he could feel. Besides, where was he going to go, anyway? So, he laid there and listened to the woman who had saved his life. The last vision before he gave in to the sea. Kaminari Akiro. Her voice had changed from their childhood. Deeper, powerful, and yet he heard the emotion in the whispers. She still cared for him, even after all these years.

"You are far more handsome than I remember," she said. "Excellent muscle tone and that cute mushy part around your belly is gone."

"I was seven," Batal croaked.

"See. Hurts." She sat down near the bed. "All this way, just to die in my care or at the end of my sword. Strange, I never thought you'd come, or at least, I didn't think you'd make it." She leaned closer. "Thirteen hundred kilometers. You travelled thirteen hundred kilometers in a fucking glass egg with fins, in only six hours. Tashi is a wonder. The oldest twelve-year-old I've ever met."

She laughed. Batal remembered that most; Kaminari laughed easy and often. Would she laugh when standing before him, before combat?

"Bet she never told you what the Gurkhas call it? The current. The Rogue Torrent!" She slapped her legs. "Your little egg was traveling at over two hundred and sixteen kilometers per hour! Best estimate was five-and-half hours of oxygen. You went six. I'm impressed with the man version of you, Batal. Why would anyone do such a thing? "

"You," Batal replied, swallowing the little spit he could make. "You sent for me."

"I said the only name I could think of when forced to decide. Warrior or not, every member of the Akiro clan must partner."

Maybe, Batal thought, but there was more in her voice; the words rang hollow. Warrior-speak to instill fear and not show weakness. Just like the Guardians...he hoped.

"My name was there, when no other would rise." His throat felt better already, even the burn with each breath was subsiding.

A chair screeched across the floor, then Kaminari's voice came from above now. "Hopeless. We will meet at sunrise with weapons of choice. I will not submit. One of us will die. Someone will come to remove your straps and bandages."

"What about the clan rules?" Batal asked.

"I wanted to see you first. On my terms, there are no rules, but you will be sore for quite some time." Her laughter then faded. "Batal, you should have stayed a fisherman. I will kill you tomorrow."

And she was gone.

Batal woke to the gentle pull of the bandage leaving his eyes. A slight form moved from strap to strap until he was free to sit up.

"Who are you?" he asked, rubbing the sleep from his eyes. "It's dark. What time is it?"

"I am Itō-sensei or Sensei. I am the lead scholar for the Archipelago." He placed another pillow behind Batal's back. "And you must be Spartan-san, Akiro-san's choice for partnering. We have heard much of your quest." He turned a dial on a nearby lamp and the flame grew tall and bright. "The sun will soon announce itself. Your match is still a few hours away."

He was small of frame, but Itō carried weight. Batal couldn't see an ounce of fat on the man's bare torso, which was roped with sinewy muscle and covered from the base of his neck to his waist in black tattoos turned gray from too much time in the sun. He wore loose black pants with brilliant daggers hanging on each hip. The tattoos partially concealed them, but judging by the number of lesions on Itō's arms and sides, Batal guessed he was in his forties.

"It's an honor to meet you, Itō." He noticed a frown forming on the man's face. "Itō-*sensei*." The frown vanished and a smile appeared.

"Though the Archipelago swells with new arrivals from the remaining isles, we choose to hold on to a few of the old ways. Use surnames with 'san' at the end unless instructed otherwise. Easy and always respectful."

"Sensei." Batal swung his legs over the edge of the bed, then realized he was naked under the sheet and lumped it in his lap. "Lead scholar of what?" But he knew before he asked: Itō-sensei was a warrior scholar, a Senshi.

"Teacher and student of the fighting arts. Chosen leader of the Archipelago."

Batal slid off the bed, dropped the sheet, half-bowed, picked it up to cover himself and finished the bow. Itō-sensei doubled over, hands on his knees, the kind of laughter drumming out of him that Batal would expect from a man three times his size. Batal liked him immediately.

"No bowing, that tradition died centuries ago. But thank you for the effort." He extended a hand, which was inked to the tips of his fingers. "Welcome to the Hiroshima Archipelago."

Batal shook the offered hand. "Thank you. I hope to be around for a while."

"Yes, don't we all. Akiro-san will have much to say in that matter. Soon you will prepare for the event, but first let us talk of your travels. Sit." Itō-sensei pulled out the chair next to the bed and sat. "The Northern Horde is pushing south. New vessels, increased numbers, using weapons and warcraft never seen before." He slunk back, hands behind his head. "You should know, Queen Zasar has held Zaeafran." He then looked at the smooth wood floor. "At a substantial cost to her forces."

"I felt she still lived, thank the gods,." Batal said. Aunt Zasar was not one to die easily.

"Which ones?" Itō-sensei asked, "Which gods?"

"All that would listen. She is a General Queen. Acts for the people and not the one. I believe...she means well for the new world."

Itō-sensei nodded, then stared through Batal.

"Itō-sensei?"

The Senshi master shook off the thoughts distracting him. "You went through the Trials. I can see it in your eyes. Not an easy task, as many die sparring or succumb, having lost the will to continue. All the Archipelago's Senshi enter and we lose many, just as the Guardians and the rest of the clans who send their people."

"May I ask a more personal question, Itō-sensei?"

He nodded.

"Kaminari is an Akiro and you are an Itō, but your ancestors are from the Archipelago and hers are from a northern land." Batal adjusted his position. "I only knew her as a young girl for a few days when your trade ships were at the port in Skye Stone. Where—"

"The island once known as Greenland. Her people fled the coming Horde. Few made it. Our leader, Akiro-sensei, found her in a small boat hiding under the bodies of her slain family. Gave her his name and trained her as his own. And you both share something far more than childhood memories. The Horde King who killed your father murdered her family only weeks later."

A small child floating through the ocean in a small boat filled with the dead bodies of those she'd loved, Batal thought of the monks and the crates. "How long? How long was she out there?"

"Akiro-san doesn't know. But based on her story and the amount of food and water she ate and drank after, maybe three weeks."

Batal sat there, taking in the horrors of another's tale of survival. To stand after all around you are slain before your eyes. What type of person survives? *A Senshi*, he thought. "How good is Akiro-san?"

"As Senshi?" Itō-sensei's hands came together in his lap. "None more deadly, none more honorable."

He then straightened and leaned toward Batal. "Now tell me of the Horde. Every detail, and after you have finished, I will feed you, give you armor, and let you choose your weapons."

"I will tell you of many things, Sensei. I will tell you of a great hero who killed a mighty lusca!" Batal raised his hands high in the air, embracing the art of storytelling. "But first, the attack on Skye Stone. The Horde rose into sky and rained down upon our village..."

~

Roast chicken, eggs prepared in ways Batal didn't know existed, and the wine! Red, white, grape, rice, berries of varieties only a trading nation could acquire. Robed in fine silk, he sat in a great hall with the glow of dawn filling the windows that ran from the floors of fine-sanded wood to stone and more wood high in the vaulted ceiling. Another stunning display of craftsmanship, and even more of a people who found it important to create such beauty. He reached for another clay mug of wine. *If I die today*, he pondered, *it will be with a full stomach and a light heart, or a drunk head...same thing.* Then he tipped back the mug.

"That may not be a sound tactic. Didn't you learn from Queen Zasar or Drago a bit about the art of strategy?" Itō-sensei asked from tall double-doors at the end of the great hall, a grin on his face.

"Join me, Sensei!" Batal said much louder than intended. "Yes, I've learned much over these past months. Taught by mothers, warriors, uncles and aunts—and deerhounds, the greatest of all!" A belch escaped somewhere in the middle. "And one cannot forget the lusca! Or gutted friends in crates and cockless monks...except one monk had one, but only one! Only Baba can be whole!"

Itō-sensei nodded as he stepped to one side.

A group of Senshi then entered. Each was bald, bare-chested, and covered in tattoos with silver daggers that matched Itō-sensei's hanging at their hips.

Batal stumbled to his feet, got caught between the bench and table, but finally stood facing the warriors and assumed one of the many fighting stances he had learned during his quest. "Ooh, this is rather silky," he said as he twisted and wiggled in his robe, his butt sticking out, swaying back and forth. "Yes, silky indeed. Can I have this, Sensei?"

"Yes, young Guardian, drunken warrior of Skye Stone, you may keep the robe, and these Senshi are here to take you to choose armor and weapons." His hand moved to his hip, head easing side-to-side. "This is tradition. You honor the Senshi and yourself by allowing them to guide you."

Batal straightened. "Yes, Sensei." He started to bow but fought the urge. "I am sorry, Itō-sensei. I mean no disrespect." His head dropped. "I don't know what to do. I can't kill Akiro-san, or even try to kill her, and I rather like being alive."

"The rules of combat are simple. The one who chooses the partner must submit"—Sensei raised his hands, palms up—"or someone must die."

"What kind of rules are those?" Batal proclaimed more than asked.

"Under normal conditions, the one choosing wants the union. The combat is ceremonial only," Itō-sensei explained. "Submitting is the act of giving oneself to the other. You find yourself in another Trial. Different, but the same. You will know what to do based on who you are. Now go choose your armor and weapons and try not to die on this day, Batal of Skye Stone, Untouched, and a man I respect. A good man with an honorable soul." As he turned to leave, he paused and instructed one of the Senshi, "Strong tea, lots of tea."

The warriors led Batal through a long corridor filled with sketches of Senshi through the ages in centuries of battles. Each hung on a wall panel fashioned of wood and white paper. Batal recognized the Spice Islands, Skye Stone, and even the Emerald Towers. He stopped in front of a grand mural that covered ten panels. "Beautiful," he whispered, studying the group of islands. Each sketch showed extensive walls around the islands' edges and within trees blossomed in gardens, and there were temples and clusters of homes and shops. Outside the walls, each island had a protected harbor with the entrances facing inward toward the other islands. Each a stunning fortress, beautiful and sad.

"Gone." One of the Senshi pointed at a smaller island at the top of the group. Above the tattoos covering her breasts was a single red symbol inked at the base of her collarbone. She pointed to another of the islands. "Gone." And another, "Gone." Another Senshi, this one with a blue symbol inked above his naval moved to the mural, waited for the first to nod, then preceded to spread both hands over the lower islands in the group. "Gone."

Batal pointed to the lone island in the center of the group. "Hiroshima?"

The Senshi with the red mark, who he assumed was the highest ranking of the group, nodded. "Home and all that remains." Her tattooed hands moved across the islands around Hiroshima. "Horde."

Her tattoos contained the shape of the uppermost island, almost like the old maps Batal had read as a child that showed the height and depths of mountains and hills with rings and lines. Each Senshi wore the markings of their home islands and its people. *And they all live on Hiroshima now. Even the mighty Akiro clan is being decimated by the Horde.*

The Senshi's hands moved over the tattoos covering her chest and stomach. "Red canna flowers." And then each arm. "Gingko trees." Her muscles flexed as her hands formed a single fist. "Hope and power."

Each of the Senshi had the same markings on their arms, beautiful gingko trees that reached around with their elegant branches, roots twisting and turning into beautiful knotwork that reminded Batal of home. They started down the hall again, and he followed them in silence. *So much lost and still their hope prevails.*

They arrived at a small square door, maybe a meter and half tall and wide. The wood had been sanded to a glass finish, and there were three iron cylinders protruding from the center. The ranking Senshi pushed the cylinders like keys in a memorized order until all three slid into the face, disappearing into the wood. She then placed both hands in the center of the door. The other Senshi followed suit, one after the other.

"One, two, push." The door slid ajar, revealing a three-meter tunnel of wood that gave way to stone and finally opened up into a cave carved out of a mountainside that was lit by the light of the tunnel. Lamps blazed and Batal watched the cave grow. *Thirty meters? Maybe more to reach its smooth domed ceiling.* In the center were racks of armor: steel, chain mail, plate, the black pants of the Senshi, and even a woven material that reminded Batal of the clothes he'd received in Jiuhua. And leather, too. "Skye Stone? Guardian armor?"

The Senshi nodded as one. "Trade with all the isles," a new voice stated.

Batal grabbed the tanned leather pants and boots from the rack, then pointed at a cave wall where every imaginable weapon leaned against the stone. "And that one. I want that one. And a pair of scissors..."

23

MORE DUST, MORE BLOOD, PEACE

Drums pounded on the other side of the massive doors. The doors' wooden surfaces had been sanded to the feel of glass, and each was at least four meters high and five meters wide. *Everything here is beautiful*, Batal thought as he studied the ironwork of the heavy, plated hinges on each side. The crack between the two slabs of wood barely showed, almost a perfect fit. The bass rumbled through his feet each time a drum thumped and a rhythmic chant began—muffled, but building from what he guessed to be hundreds of voices. The Senshi stood at his back, forming a protective arc, but it was obvious they were there to ensure he remained when the doors opened.

"Control your fear and focus your will," the Senshi with the red mark advised. "Canna and Gingko."

"Canna and Gingko," Batal whispered back. "Hope."

Steel slid across wood on the other side of the doors. The drums and the chanting fell silent, and the doors swung open without a sound, revealing a dark tunnel with light at the far end, coming from what looked to be a ring of sorts.

"You must travel alone from this point forward," the Senshi said. "May your warrior spirit be victorious or find its way to your next life."

Batal took a deep breath and walked toward the light. The doors swung closed and someone slid the bolt across, but he kept walking, focused on the task at hand and spinning his weapon—a wooden staff—with both hands. When he reached the opening, the only sound came from his bare feet on the corridor's planks. Stepping through the threshold, he looked upon an oval floor covered in a fine white silt. *Possibly ground shells*, he thought. *Like the Trials.* The floor was enclosed by a stone wall at least twice Batal's height and perfectly smooth. He slid a foot across the silt and smooth wooden planks appeared.

Looking up, darkness consumed all above the stone. Lanterns with iron tops cast a warm flicker on the ring from just below the darkness. Batal took a few more paces into the space, and the door slid closed behind him, leaving him in the ring. *Alone*, he thought, *and wanting nothing more than to hear Danu's paws running to my side.* Another entrance sat directly across the ring from him. Almost like a black eye, cold and menacing. The echoes of stone on stone cracked and ground from overhead, sounding like those at the wheat mill his mother bartered flour from. A crescent of bright light poured down from above, cleaving the darkness as it grew bigger.

Faces were lit above the stone wall. Row upon row of stoic Senshi, who looked down into the ring from their perches. The drums resumed their pounding beat, causing Batal to bounce with the ground, a haze of white powder rising from the floor and creating a hanging mist below his knees.

And the chanting started again. A rhythmic bass released between booms of the drums. Batal opened himself to it, bathed in the ridiculousness of it all. *Am I a pit fighter now?* He widened his stance and placed his weapon between his feet, folding his arms over it as he waited for the "chooser" to finish this silly game.

A shadow appeared in the opening on the other side—or had it always been there? The menacing eye no longer looked black but a smoky gray. There was a figure standing just beyond the light, watching. It was the shape of armor and power.

Kaminari Akiro stepped into the ring, and the drums hammered and the chants melded to a roar. Her eyes blazed green from behind a matte black helmet with two wings protruding from the sides. Black chain mail, slim and fitted, covered her from neck to boot with openings under her arms to ensure she could swing the Senshi broadsword attached at her waist, left of her hip. A small, half-moon shield hung on her left hand. Many of the Horde carried this style of shield to keep their sword hand swinging to its full range. But it was the short sword—a tantō—hanging at her right side that spoke of finality. A finishing tool of an artist dealing death.

"I've made a terrible mistake. Misjudged the girl I knew so long ago." Batal looked to his bare feet and wished he had brought the boots of his homeland, which were still sitting in the armory; his leather pants were nothing more than light armor for archers who hid behind walls. He shook his head and tapped his staff on the wood planks beneath the silt. *Fuck. She will kill me here and all will end because a boy with a crush chose a stick over a sword. I will have failed. My quest over and the Untouched will lose most of his perfect limbs and ruin a ruggedly handsome face.* He looked at his bare torso: muscled with only a handful of scars, the perfect canvas for her sword work. He then turned his attention to the magnificent Akiro-san and smiled, finding humor is unfounded arrogance. Her silver braids were wrapped into a single plait that hung from the back of her helmet. She was stunning and chilling, beautiful and deadly. *I'm a fool, but a fool who'll die at the hands of perfection.* "So be it," he whispered. "I'm tired of running and fighting."

The mist reached his waist before the drums and roar stopped as one, allowing the powder to sift back to the ground.

Someone somewhere spoke in one of the ancient tongues. It sounded like one of the beautiful Ryukyuan languages, but Batal wasn't sure. He bowed his head as he listened because it felt right. After a few minutes, the shared common tongue replaced it, explaining the contest's only rules: the chooser must surrender, yield, submit, or concede to the chosen—or one must die. He glanced again at Akiro-san and was relatively certain a concession from this chooser was not in the offering. *I will not land a single damaging blow, but I will defend myself with honor. Ice and smoke.* He repeated Drago's words in his head as he slid his foot through the fine white powder.

A metal clang bounced off stone and rose through the open ceiling high above the combatants. Akiro-san glided across the ring, skating on the hard soles of her boots. Batal slid to the side, staff above his head, and blocked the first strike from her broadsword. The oak staff took it well, and he used the momentum to spin and bring down his weapon at the back of her ankles.

Kaminari jumped over the staff and slammed her shield into Batal's back, sending him into the stone wall. *Fine*, he thought as something wet ran down his shoulder blade. Charging, staff low and to his right, he sprinted toward the wall as she moved to attack, dragging the staff as he ran. A cloud of white filled the surrounding space. Batal jumped, pushed off the stone, and swung the staff at her raised shield. A thunderous crack and Akiro-san rolled, sprang to her feet, and threw her bent shield to the side.

Moving around the edge of the ring, scraping the stones with her chain mail, she picked up her pace and Batal followed, keeping his distance. She lowered her sword, dragging it through the silt and within seconds, the ring was a blur of white smoke. Batal moved to the center where the air was clear, turning around and around trying to catch a glimpse of her in the thick cloud.

A flash of steel and shadow. He swung the staff late and blood ran down his chest, then she was back in the smoke. The Senshi above gazed on in utter silence. A mistake. Sunlight reflected off steel nearby, and before she could attack, Batal estimated her location and threw the staff end over end into the dust. Metal thunked on stone. More dust rose high as a dented helmet with one wing remaining flew from the white cloud. Batal ducked, and it rattled off the stone behind him.

"Fight me!"

The tantō flew from the cloud next, catching Batal on the side of his thigh with the hilt. Painful, but bloodless.

He dropped to his knees, picked up the tantō in time to block the slicing broadsword falling toward his chest. The force sent the short sword skidding towards the wall.

Kaminari straddled his chest, the blade of her sword against his throat. "I ask you again, why would anyone do such a thing?" he grunted as he felt the blade slice a layer of skin. "You stood for me once. Without asking, you could've let them beat me senseless." Her green eyes bore into his, the pale skin, the single braided mass of silver hanging to the side of her neck. "I love you," he whispered, the air hissing from his windpipe.

Her face softened. The blade remained close, but no longer touched his skin. "You what?"

"The first time I saw you. On the Akiro trade ship. You sat at the bow as you always did, long before we met face-to-face." He swallowed hard, took a deep breath. "I've loved you since the first time I saw you. I know that now. I can't and will never lay a hand to you...well, except for the staff I threw, but that was an accident."

She continued to stare at Batal.

"Kill me," he continued. "But I won't hurt you, even if I could."

She tossed her sword to the side. "Damn you, Batal Spartan." She pushed off his bleeding chest, offered a hand, and pulled him to his bloody feet. "The hell with it. I yield to Spartan-san. The ceremony is over. We are partnered for the remaining days we have." She turned back to Batal, then kissed him hard and deep. "They may be short, though, unless we stitch you up."

Batal swayed, blood running from his chest. "Wait, we're what?"

"The people of the Hiroshima Archipelago and the people of Skye Stone are bonded in friendship and family, and we will fight our enemies as one." The words of Itō-sensei's echoed off the stone walls from his place among the gathered Senshi. Cheers followed, the doors to the ring opened and Senshi flooded in and carried Batal and Kaminari out of the ring on their shoulders.

Batal sat up, fists ready to fly and head on a swivel. Each breath huffed, his heart pounding. Steam poured from an open door a few meters from the bed where he lay, a sheet lying across his waist. Kaminari exited the steam, striking as always, wrapped in a sheer fabric, each defined muscle highlighted beneath it. Her damp, silver hair hung just past her shoulders and her bright green eyes looked down toward his waist.

She squinted. "Still there and better than expected. You enjoyed your sponge bath, by the way."

Batal pulled back the sheet partially covering the parts he thought he had just lost to Baba in something worse than a nightmare. His thigh ached, but was only a bruise. Batal ran his fingers across his chest; the wound already cleaned and stitched by talented hands. "Did you do this? And did we"—red found his cheeks as his mouth tripped over the words—"join as one?"

"Yes, and sadly no." Kaminari sat next to him. "You lost quite a bit of blood and have been sleeping for a few hours. I mended your wounds without a sound from Spartan-san." She then placed her hand on his cheek. "Itō-sensei told me of the Emerald Towers, and the rest of your journey. He felt I should know." She brought her other hand to his face, her wrap falling to the bed. "I'm sorry." Her lips moved close, brushing his with each word. "We need each other. Just as you needed me to fight for you as a boy. I know I needed you then, too, needed to know someone cared for me when few did." She kissed him, slid the sheet to the side, and pushed her wrap off the bed.

"We've all...we've all had our own evils to overcome." Batal tried to adjust what was happening below his waist.

"I know you, Batal Spartan of Skye Stone. I've always known

who you were, even as a boy. You're good to a fault, but I see in your eyes you've found the fighter, the Guardian. He will be needed in the times now upon us."

Batal's mind sifted through thoughts and feelings coming as a storm. "I've lost friends but have been given far more than was taken. You are Untouched? You even kept your beautiful hair." His eyes scanned her body, lingering in areas, but seeing not a single lesion. Overwhelmed, he felt the world spinning...

"You and I are the only ones, and it's why I have no tattoos." Kaminari's fingertips pressed against his lips. She placed her hand above the stitches on his chest and pushed him to the bed. She placed a knee on each side of his hips. "Be at peace, let your wounds heal, and I'll do the rest."

She placed him inside her. Batal cleared his mind, opened his heart, and gave it to her.

24

ELPIS, SPIRIT OF HOPE

The stone wall surrounding Hiroshima was without fault. Not very tall, but wide and defended by ballistae, bows, and what Itō-sensei called "dragon's breath." Batal called it acid mist, and anyone touched by it would die poorly according to the stories. His wounds healed, he had found a peacefulness with Kaminari that strengthened him, and he was desperate to keep it. Many months had passed since he almost died traveling the Rogue Torrent. Tashi sent messages from Jiuhua carried in a stunning array of glass containers. Drago, Jenna, Amira, and Danu had traveled back to the Kingdom of Zaeafran to help rebuild what the Horde destroyed there and were now back in Skye Stone. Stranger, though, was the news the Horde had vanished. They hadn't been spotted anywhere since they had chased the *Aeolus* to Jiuhua. The Clans of the Northern Spice Islands had also disappeared with them. No trace of where they went or if they were alive. Queen Zasar's warriors could not find a single soul to the north to tell of what happened. They were simply gone.

Batal finished his dawn training and began his morning run. As his bare feet tapped the stone, he noticed again that he had yet to find a standing seam; just a smooth surface like everything else in the Archipelago. Craftsman warriors that could build, farm, stitch wounds, ferment the best drinks, and offer friendship and love without expectations. The Akiro Clan and its Senshi were indeed powerful allies. Small groups and families had even started returning to their islands to rebuild their villages.

He passed the home he shared with Kaminari and caught the moment the rising sun touched her from behind as she worked in the garden, her backlit silhouette showing, hidden under her loose wrap, the growing life created the first time they shared a bed. It was unheard of to create life so quickly and easily. The legend of the Untouched grew, and with it the pressure of a child entering the new world free of lesions. Hope was spreading among the Free Isles. Pregnancies were far shorter in the new world; in the old world, women gave birth after nine months, but then people lived into their seventies, even eighties. *It was hard to imagine, but they didn't live with radiation as we do*, Batal thought.

"Mother bless you, Batal," greeted the Senshi with the red mark.

"Mother bless you, Senshi," he responded and kept his pace. Once you were no longer a visitor, "Batal-san" became just "Batal"; the only person treated differently was Itō-sensei. But for the Senshi, names weren't used unless they were partnered. Though he missed his friends and family, he felt at home with Kaminari and her people. Almost one of them. It was Danu he could not live much longer without. He needed the deerhound.

When he learned how the "torrents" worked and that more were found each year, he hoped to bring Danu to the Archipelago; but right now it was too risky, too dangerous. Still, he worked with the local craftsmen on new designs to safely travel the high-speed rivers of the oceans. They estimated most of the torrents averaged one hundred seventy-five kilometers per hour, but during certain times of the year, up to three hundred kilometers per hour had been recorded. Many had died conducting the research as some torrents ran through submerged buildings, where the glass carriers clipped steel and concrete.

He adjusted his breathing so he could continue running for a few more laps. He did his best thinking while pushing himself further. *If most the torrents changed direction at dawn and dusk, with the proper vessel we could cover thousands of kilometers before the switch. It would change every—*

He came to a stop. Below, in the great Akiro Open Lands, two small children laughed and screamed. Each held a string connected to the ends of a rectangular windsail that flew high above the wall. They sat atop sacs of flour on a flat dolly with small wooden wheels, which was being sluggishly pulled by the handheld windsail across the grass of the small park.

"That's it." Batal smacked the stone rail on the interior side of the wall. "By the gods, that's it!"

Two Senshi approached. "What is it?" one of them asked. "Are you OK, Batal?"

He pointed to the kite. "I know how we can use the torrents. How we can connect ourselves to the other isles!"

Batal stood before a large wall of slate. Holding chalk in both hands, he sketched a giant sphere with a line through the center. Where the line broke the sphere, a bite had been taken from the circle, giving the end of the line some amount of space around its tip. The Archipelago's elders, which included the leaders from each of the repopulating islands, had come back to see what the Untouched had designed to harness the power of the torrents. They sat a few meters away from Batal along the bottom row of a small auditorium. Kaminari chose a row behind them, writing, then erasing, and writing more. She needed the extra room to spread out her papers and for her swelling belly. Batal had insisted she be there, not only because she was the greatest of the Senshi, but also she was gifted in mathematics, which was one of his weaknesses. Besides, he drew power having her near. Adding a few lines from the sides of the sphere to a large rectangle below it, he nodded. "Good enough." He then turned to the elders and Itō-sensei.

As he stood and waited, the elders whispered back and forth to Itō-sensei, who sat in the center of the row and said nothing; he just listened to each elder, his hands cupped about his ears to make it easier. Finally, the elders sat still, and Itō-sensei lowered his hands to address Batal.

"Before we speak of designs, Batal-san, we would like to know the purpose of such vessels."

Batal turned back to the slate wall, wrote PURPOSE next to the sketch, underlined it, and then jotted down a list:

1- High-speed trade routes

2- Form a defensive coalition with allies, Senshi transport

3- Evacuation

"These are the key purposes," he said, "but there are many more."

Itō-sensei sat straight. "Please continue."

"Our concept is simple," Batal grabbed a pointed stick and used it to point at the various parts of his diagram. "This is the outer shell of the sphere, made of wood and smooth as glass." He indicated the line running through the sphere's center. "A rod parallel to the ocean's surface to hold the sail lines and allow the shell to spin on the surface." Batal switched the pointer to his left hand so he could draw another circle the size of the shell and a second smaller circle within it, then continued the line across the center. "The interior sphere is the cabin of our vessel and is fixed to the rod, holding it stationary. We use sea water to fill the void between them and to act as a cooling agent."

More whispers erupted from each side of Itō-sensei, who sat quietly until they stopped. He then tipped his head to the side and narrowed his eyes. "How will a sail be much faster than any other vessel? The torrents are five to ten meters below the surface and little movement outside the 'ribbon effect' occurs above them."

"The sail is not for the wind." Batal drew a squiggly line near the bottom of the sphere with the lines to the rectangle below it. "The sail is an ocean-sail. For the water rushing through the torrent. Instead of the dangerous pods used by Jiuhua, this vessel will be pulled from below and spin across the surface while those inside remain seated." He shaded the area around the rod and the crescent cutouts. "These are crafted of glass and can be opened for air flow and access. Tashi of Jiuhua can have her glass blower start as soon as we are ready."

Itō-sensei turned in his seat to look at Kaminari. "Will this work?"

She pushed her papers to the side. "With our unmatched craftsmanship with wood, and sea water between the spheres, I see no reason it won't. The torrents themselves would act as a rudder. The speed of their current's narrow flow makes it nearly impossible for the ocean-sail to leave it once it is deployed and the surface vessel will skin the surface until the ocean-sail reaches the torrent's end. We can calibrate the sail by using different weighted materials so we reach the proper depth." She raised her eyebrows. "The beginning of the voyage could be exciting, but with time that too can be managed."

"Why not just use this ocean-sail on our current vessels?" Itō-sensei asked.

Kaminari reach for one of her pages and scanned it. "It would pull down the bow. If that doesn't sink it, the speed will be compromised. A spinning sphere presents the least resistance, least friction."

An elder whispered into Itō-sensei's ear. He nodded. "If we need to exit the torrent in the middle, before its end point?"

"Batal-san and I have struggled with just that for the past few days."

Batal watched from the slate wall and reveled in the way she had paused for effect. Kaminari had them right where she wanted them.

"Or at least until the master of the ballistae had a simple suggestion."

"Which was?" Itō-sensei asked.

"Add a release for one of the lines at the rod's tips."

There were nods of agreement from the elders as Itō-sensei rolled his eyes at Batal in shared amusement. *The simplicity of it was laughable, but effective*, Batal thought. *A sail is only a sail if the ends are connected to something; release one and it collapses.*

"How many passengers can one of these vessels fit?" Itō-sensei asked, bringing the group back on topic.

"Depends on how big we build them." Batal looked to Kaminari. "One person or a hundred? The Archipelago has enough craftsman to construct them in only a few days if we pull them from their other duties."

Itō-sensei then spoke with the Elders, who didn't whisper back. Once that was completed, he returned his attention to Batal and Kaminari. "You both have one chance to prove your design. In one hour, we'll provide you with twenty of our finest craftsmen. Meet them in the shipyard. You have two days. On the third, you ride the Rogue Torrent again, Batal-san, Untouched and father-to-be." Itō-sensei and the elders then left the room.

Batal collapsed in a chair next to Kaminari. "Went better than expected, but holy shit. Why the haste? More important, why am I the test subject?"

"Your insane idea, your design." Her hands rested on her belly. "Who else would go? The believer or the naysayer. Do you believe in our work?"

"I do. Forget the list, rapid Guardian and Senshi transport is the key." He leaned over and wrapped his arms around her and her belly. "Wow, she's getting big. Won't be long now."

"She?" Kaminari's lips tickled his ear. "You've never called our baby that before."

Batal kissed her neck, grabbed her earlobe between his lips, and pulled back lightly. "I know, but I know it's a girl, and she'll be just like her mother. The new world needs more of that."

"Let's hope we make it that long. Sensei and the elders know the Horde will come, and this time, they will not ride behind a tsunami. They may *be* the tsunami."

"Why else would they withdraw from all the Free Isles?" Batal looked to the wall of slate and his sketches. "They are amassing for a final blow. We need these to work." His smile returned, his eyes lighting with their usual hint of mischief. "But first"—he looked to the nearest skylight and gauged the sun's position—"we have thirty-two minutes to name this wondrous vessel of ours."

~

Dusk came to the Archipelago. The ribbon of water shimmering toward the horizon faded for a few moments.

"It's changing," Batal said as he hung his head over the gunwale of an Akiro trade vessel sitting five kilometers from the harbor. In the distance, lamps lit the outer wall of Hiroshima and a glow grew brighter within the wall as homes filled with waking families and the bars and restaurants opened the doors.

He pointed. "There. The current flows toward the city." Subtle, but a slight ripple moved toward the island. Batal kissed Kaminari. "It will work." He looked at the beautiful, bobbing wooden sphere that was tied off to the side of the boat. The sphere's sail lay folded on top of its outer shell, a line from each side secured to rod ends on each side of the sphere. "I wish we had the glass but leaving the access holes open guarantees a quick exit if needed. Carving her name was a nice touch. *Elpis*, spirit of hope. And by watching it from the ship, you can tell if the outer shell is turning."

Kaminari nodded and continued to take in the *Elpis*'s beauty. "It's perfect. Glass or no glass, the water should remain between the two spheres as long as the outside shell spins the way it should. From our position, the test run is five kilometers to where it drops near the harbor. Two days to build, and we could have finished two in the same amount of time." She placed her hands on her extended belly, again, "Show them what it can do"—she kissed him—"and then come home."

"It's going to be fine." Batal kissed her damp cheek, then bent down and kissed her belly. "Love you. Back in a flash!"

He climbed over the side of the boat, slid into the closest of the two openings around each rod end of the *Elpis*. Once inside Batal reached out to give a thumbs-up, then sat in the chair fixed to the inner hull and waited. The inside rocked back and forth, the weight of the passenger and the fixed chair keeping in properly aligned. A deckhand untied the line holding the *Elpis* to the escort ship, then reached out with a pole to push the sail over the front of the vessel and then used to pole to push the *Elpis* toward the surface ribbon. Not long after it was placed in the sea, the ocean-sail was pulled by the tide toward the Rogue Torrent.

The chair was cold, but it fit snugly against his back and the cushioned headrest was a nice touch. The *Elpis* bobbed, rose, and fell with the sea. Inside, beyond the up and down of the swell, only a slight rocking motion of the interior shell. *The balance was perfect*, Batal thought.

"She's turning!" bellowed one of the crew.

Muffled or not, Batal heard that and grabbed the sides of his chair.

The *Elpis* surged ahead, smooth and only a slight slap as she rolled and skipped behind her ocean-sail. A few minutes passed, and the sphere slowed its progress, soon coming to a stop. *Damn it. Line or sail must have broke.* Batal untied his belt strap and pushed out of the chair. He stood, grabbed the rod that passed through the center, and looked through the opening through the two shells he had only moments ago crawled through.

"Holy shit. It works!" he shouted as he spotted the harbor, which was now only a hundred meters away.

At close to midnight and within an hour of the successful test run, Batal and Kaminari returned to the shipyard, where the ship artisans had gathered with Itō-sensei and ten Senshi, who were also the finest engineers on the Archipelago. Itō-sensei carried a leather tube filled with rolled maps and charts over his shoulder, while each of the engineers had a copy of the design plans for the *Elpis* and a pad of freshly made paper that still warm from the stone press they had come from. And raw materials were already staged, so all was in readiness.

"Improvements?" Itō-sensei asked.

"We don't need the glass over the openings," Batal replied. "The spinning outer shell keeps the seawater from spilling in and the air flow is good for the passengers." Batal looked to the notes he had made while waiting to be picked up. "Add five meters of the rubberized line developed for ballista levers to the ends of the line connecting to the sail. It will ease the launch by stretching instead of jerking." He shrugged. "That's all I have so far."

Kaminari then referred to her notes. "Increase the sail ratio by 20 percent and the *Elpis* vessels will travel at the full currents speed of Torrents." She flipped over a few pages. "Scale the sphere to fit fifty people. About ten times the size of the trial *Elpis*. It'll be cramped, but efficient. Fasten a canister with a sealed lid for the toilet. Any bigger and the ocean-sail will not fit in the torrent."

The engineers nodded in understanding, then split off into assigned groups.

"Why are we starting at midnight, Itō-sensei?" Batal asked. "Surely we can begin in the—"

"Our lookouts spotted the Horde," he replied. "A fleet is massing a week's sailing north of Sicily."

"Skye Stone is less than a day from Sicily." Batal looked out at the teams already cutting and shaping the materials. "I must go. I can take the prototype, as it only needs a few adjustments."

Kaminari's eyes narrowed. "Just you alone?"

Batal placed a hand on her belly. "You're too close. Our daughter will come soon, and this is far too dangerous—"

"You speak for me now, Great Untouched of Skye Stone? We are partnered and you are not the only warrior in this family." Then she noticed Itō-sensei was being very quiet. "There is more, isn't there? What aren't you telling us?"

"There is another fleet a week's sail northwest of the Archipelago. I fear the Horde aims to destroy us all in one massive assault." Itō-Sensei folded his arms. "The sails of the clans from the northern Spice Islands are with them. Our lookouts could not count the numbers of ships, but the fleet is vast and covers much of the ocean. All the Free Isles have been warned to prepare the best they can."

"We can fight them off. Our walls will hold, and our weapons are powerful," Batal said. "But I must try to get to Skye Stone." He took Kaminari's hand. "All of us."

"The Varghori Monks are on the Horde's ships that sail toward Sicily and Skye Stone," Itō-sensei continued. "It is said that the 'Baba' you spoke of is aboard the Horde King's flagship.

The choice is yours, Batal-san and Kaminari-san, but the Senshi cannot leave the Archipelago defenseless." He turned toward the shipyard. "If we can build enough *Elpis* vessels, we can evacuate the Gurkhas on Jiuhua." He pulled a rolled chart out of his canister and handed it to Batal and Kaminari.

They unrolled it, each holding a side. It was a chart of the new world, with the names of the oceans, seas, waterways, and trade routes through and around the Free Isles. But there were a dozen thin red lines of varying lengths on the chart. Each had a moon on one end and the sun on the other with an arrow next to it.

"Torrents?" Batal guessed.

"This is one of the oldest charts handed down through our people from the beginning of the new world. Some torrents have disappeared while others are new, some still change directions at dusk and dawn and others don't, but most are unknown to all but a few." He pointed to one of the red lines, which arched up from the northern island of the Hiroshima Archipelago toward the lands of the Northern Horde and back to the north side of Sicily. "This is the Shinigami Torrent. It is the oldest and travels through the most dangerous oceans of the new world."

"My family has another fishing boat near the Sicily harbor that I can borrow. It's being cared for by old friends of my father."

"We will make the adjustments to the *Elpis*," Kaminari said as she pointed at the sun with an arrow aiming toward Sicily, "and leave in the morning. Together."

"Then it's decided." Itō-sensei hugged Kaminari. He shook Batal's hand. "A boat will leave in three hours to tow the *Elpis* into the Shinigami Torrent."

25
ARK OF THE UNTOUCHED

Batal stood on the deck of an Akiro attack boat—a small boat that looked larger than it was due its heavy sails—anchored at the northern point of the Hiroshima Archipelago, 9,900 kilometers from Skye Stone. The *Elpis* bobbed against the attack boat's hull. Fifty meters away, the Shinigami Torrent tore across the sea toward the northwest horizon. No ribbon, this was a raging river even on the surface, and ten meters below was the center of its power.

He handed armor, bows, swords, and provisions to Kaminari through the port access in the middle of the *Elpis*. Finally, Batal slid through a meter-long iron rod, just in case they needed to repair the main rod. She then stored everything behind the two seats set in the center of the sphere. A small deck had been built to create a flat surface that would keep any water below their feet. The *Elpis*'s blue-green paint blended perfectly with the angry ocean, and like the Horde catamarans, blended into the sea's surface as well.

As Batal watched Kaminari working inside their creation, he did his best to keep the dark thoughts from taking over. Again he had a sense of helplessness, as he had when Stefan was slaughtered before him.

The Senshi with the red mark handed Batal a thick folded cloth wrapped in a heavy line. "Mother bless you, Batal and Kaminari."

"Thank you, Senshi, and Mother bless you." He took the spare sail and passed it through the iron supports to the waiting hands inside. Kaminari then stacked it on top of a small box of food and drinks.

She touched the red mark at the base of her collarbone. "Eiko."

"It is an honor, Eiko." Batal looked out to the raging current. "I hope to see you again."

Eiko took his hand and eased him into the *Elpis*. He and Kaminari then waved through the access space and the line released, allowing the dawn tide to pull the wooden sphere toward the Shinigami Torrent. Batal moved through the supports on the port side while Kaminari did the same at starboard. Sitting on the iron bars, they checked the lines connected to the rod ends, counted to three, and tossed the lines and ocean-sail into the sea. They then slid back inside and quickly found their seats.

"I estimate thirty-five to forty-eight hours to Sicily," Kaminari said as she adjusted her loose shirt around her belly.

Batal grabbed the sides of his chair. "Based on the surface flow, only thirty-five, if we have time to detach the sail before the torrent reverses at dusk." He grabbed her hand while the other kept gripping the seat's frame. "Going to be fine. We're just about to travel three hundred kilometers per hour in a wooden ball in the middle of the ocean on a torrent named after the god of death." He then leaned in and kissed her as if it may be their last. "What could go wrong?"

Laughter filled the sphere as it flew from the Archipelago, skipping and spinning over the sea's surface.

Batal pointed toward the iron supports of the outer shell, which rotated into a barely visible blur. "That looks fast. Keep your hands away, but the view is almost clear."

After a few hours, the *Elpis* smoothed her track, skimming more and skipping less across the rolling surface. Batal stood, feet wide, and grabbed the curved rail added to the interior shell. He worked his way a few steps and opened the toilet canister lashed to the rail.

Kaminari grinned. "Already? And I'm the pregnant—" She grabbed her stomach. "She's kicking like a Senshi this morning. Knows we're moving." She shook her head as she watched Batal relieve himself. "Don't stand. Sit."

"Much better." He closed his eyes for a moment, then exhaled and stood. "Seal works. No splashing, but no hand washing for a day or so."

"I love you." Her bright eyes softened, the green looking more like the ocean. "Maybe since I first saw you, but definitely after you fell in love with me."

Batal returned to his seat. "Finally, you admit it was love at first sight!"

"I've always thought it, so seemed time to admit it. What are the chances we make it all the way? According to the chart, we pass just offshore of the Horde's lands and through the troubled waters filled with... Wait! I forget I'm with the great slayer of lusca!" Kaminari's laughter once again filled the space and ended with her holding her belly. "Now *I* need to pee."

"Let me help you." Batal stood and helped steady her at the rail, knowing she didn't need it but was allowing him to feel useful all the same.

He looked out the access porthole. The sail line strained against the pull of the torrent. Swells ten meters tall rolled on each side of them, kept at bay by the racing current on the surface. "It's protecting us from the angry ocean. Maybe *shinigami* doesn't mean 'god of death.'"

Kaminari worked her way back along the rail. "In the common tongue, 'death spirit' is more accurate."

In the distance, just outside of the torrent's path, dozens of suckered arms broke through the surface.

"Lusca," Batal whispered, hoping they couldn't hear him or see the spinning blue sphere. The appendages slammed into the ocean, again and again, but were quickly left far behind.

Kaminari kept a safe distance from the starboard opening but continued to track the rocky isles in the distance. "They were on my side, too. I think they were feeding off the things dying in the torrent. But that means... The Bern. We're already passing through the Bern?"

Building-size stones rose high out of the ocean and stood against pounding waves. The *Elpis* streaked between them as it was pulled along the meandering path of the Shinigami Torrent.

Batal had both hands on the wooden shell. "The inner sphere is warming." Steam appeared from the openings. "We must use the buckets to add water between them when we transition. We still have a few hours till dusk." He looked across to Kaminari, who watched out the other opening. "How fast are we going?"

"Faster than we think. It's only going to take us one transition. If it goes smoothly, we release one of the lines, use the small paddles to push us out of the torrent, pull in the sail, then wait for dusk to hitch a ride to Sicily." Kaminari wrapped her arms around the baby inside her. "We'll be a bobbing target for ten hours."

Batal pulled the chart out of a pocket on the wall. "Will we? The chart shows a sun and a full moon. The torrents change direction when the moon is out. Tonight is a new moon, so the sky will remain dark. Perhaps the torrent will transition, or it may just slow and keep its direction." Batal looked toward the sky. "Or maybe, like the tides, it will become more powerful, using the sun and the moon as one. Either way, we'll be fine. Best case, we go faster, or worst case, we bob around a bit till dawn. The *Elpis* is virtually invisible." *I hope.*

The largest of the volcanic stone Isles of the Bern soon came into view only a few hundred meters off the port side, the rising steam from between the shells lending an ominous touch. Then the towering masts of rocking ships appeared as the torrent swung wide and provided a view to the back side of the isle. One of the Horde fleets was anchored off the isle's rocky shore, many of the ships facing the *Elpis*'s path.

"Oh fuck... Seats and straps!" Batal helped Kaminari to her seat and looped the shoulder straps over each arm. A whistling sound filled the sphere. Batal dropped in his seat and reached back for a shoulder strap. Raining balls of fire splashed all around them, knocking the *Elpis* hard to the starboard. Batal smashed against the wall and slid to the deck, blood seeping from his nose and mouth. Splashing sounded from behind as they drifted clear of the fleet and out of its range.

"For fuck's sake," Batal leaned against the inner wall, hands cupped over his face.

The *Elpis* steadied herself and found a smooth track once again.

Kaminari pulled her arms out of the harness and crawled out of her seat, opened a trunk bolted to the deck behind them, and pulled out a medic's sack. She moved Batal's hands from his face. "I can see this is a habit for you." She used the water sloshing up around the edges of the deck to wash away the blood.

"Since I was a boy," Batal replied, bloody bubbles popping from his nostrils. "I tend to bleed a lot."

"Still too beautiful, but you're slowing taking care of that, one scar at a time." Studying the damage, she nodded. "Just a nosebleed. Hold this on it for a few minutes. And thank you for strapping me in. Your daughter is getting in the way now and wants out."

Batal reached over to place his hand on her thigh. "What a pair we make."

"Indeed. Untouched by lesions only. Bruises, blood, and lumps? That's our thing." She lifted herself back into her chair. "Looks like we'll need to bail out a bit of water, too. We can use it to top off between the spheres, so no need to hang outside if we don't have to."

"Agreed." He pulled the cloth away from his nose. The bleeding had stopped. "Must have been the fleet heading toward Jiuhua and the Archipelago." His head dropped. "More masts than I could count, and if they didn't know of the Shinigami Torrent before, they sure have some questions now. We must reach Skye Stone."

The Elpis skimmed the ocean at a breathtaking pace. Kaminari slept while Batal tightened every lashing, checked every lid, and scanned every inch of the inside of the *Elpis* as the minutes passed and the hour of dusk and the 'transition' approached. He drank one of the berry wines he had stowed with the food, then popped up a piece of the deck and bailed out the few inches of water with the wine container, dumping it carefully through the opening between the spheres, topping off the natural coolant between them. The ends of the rod outside the shells continued to hold the lines to the ocean-sail, the lines looked strong with little fraying and the interior shell remained securely fastened to the rod casing without any stress cracks, though the casing was hot.

It was the rate the outer shell looked to be turning that made Batal uncomfortable. The iron supports were now fans blowing hot air into the interior. Air heated by the radiating exterior shell of the *Elpis*. How much could it take before the lines would weaken from the heat or snap from the shear speed of the torrent? The sun was almost past the horizon, so Batal nudged Kaminari awake to help with transition if it happened.

She rubbed her eyes, stretched, and took his hand. "Well, now comes the fun part."

They stood silent as they listened for a change in the sea, each with their hands on the inner shell, trying to feel any disturbance. The sun was gone, and the black night of a new moon had taken over. Their speed seemed to increase, judging by the rising heat of the air blowing in, but there was little more they could do but wait.

"Thank the gods, no transition," Kaminari said after several more minutes. "I'll take the watch so you can get some rest. This journey was quicker than we could have dreamed." She shook her head. "Your design is brilliant, Batal. I'm so proud of you."

A soft snoring sounded from below. Batal already lay on the deck, a shirt piled under his head, fast asleep. He looked like the boy fisherman, sleeping on a warm beach after a big catch.

"Sleep, my love, and know that you are all I dreamed you would be. Sleep and ready yourself for what comes next," she whispered before returning her gaze to the darkness and rushing sea. "Death Spirit, hold your vengeance for those deserving and take us to Batal's people."

26
RUNNING FROM THE DEATH SPIRIT

"Batal!"

He was running through sand, the stench of the Horde filling every part of him. Kaminari fell behind, the weight and mass of the baby holding her back like a dragging anchor on a fast ship. Batal turned and faced the Horde King, urging his love to stand and run, but she remained on the ground, a heap of pale skin and silver hair, a thick bolt from the king's crossbow pinning her in place.

"Batal!"

He woke with a start, Kaminari shaking him, "North!" She shifted to the port side access, the filtered light of dawn casting on her face.

A caged beast, Batal thought as he watched her and he rose to his feet, shaking off another nightmare that had followed him into the daylight. He stumbled over to her, where he could share her view. There he saw Horde ships of all shapes and sizes stretched out five kilometers ahead of them and heading toward the Shinigami Torrent.

"So many," she whispered. "Of course they knew of the torrent's existence. It's on their doorstep, after all." The faint shadow from the black cliffs of the Horde lands sat on the far horizon. "We're leaving them behind, though. They'll never catch the *Elpis*, that is if their ships survive at all."

Then Batal spotted it: a massive black barge with towering masts and stained sails emblazoned with the blood-red hourglass in a circle. "The Horde King." The barge moved through the farthest ships in the fleet, parting them like a shark through a school of fish. The *Elpis* raced above the torrent, almost hovering above the surface. Soon they would be ahead of the Horde Fleet and putting distance between them. As they passed the king's barge, they spotted a long string of black spheres being towed behind it.

"No. It's not possible!" Batal screamed as the *Elpis* overtook the fleet.

The smell of heat and burning hair, then smoke, blew into the sphere. The starboard line snapped, and seconds later the port line followed. The *Elpis* slowed to a crawl, keeping pace with the surface current.

"Sail!" Batal cried. But Kaminari already had the storage chest open and was handing him the extra sail. He started to unwind the line wrapped in layers.

"They've released their spheres," Kaminari reported. "Hurry! They're floating toward the torrent."

"Fuck!" Batal cursed as he burned his hand on the end of the rod. He grabbed the empty wine container then tossed it to Kaminari, "Pull up the decking, cool it with water!" He reached to the wall and tore off the leather pocket, tossed the chart on the seats behind him, and filled the pocket with seawater from under the deck.

Steam poured off each end of the rods ends until Batal tied off the sail line and slipped out the portside access. He then threw the second sail line across the top toward Kaminari's side.

She caught it and began tying it off.

"The spheres are in the torrent, building speed. Hurry, Kaminari."

The sail slid down into the surface current and sank below. She finished the knot slid back through the starboard access seconds before, the sail ripped the *Elpis* along, throwing them hard into the seats.

"Are you OK?" Batal asked.

"Back's a bit fucked, but yes, I'm good," she replied. "Can you see the Horde's spheres?"

Batal grabbed the rail, pulled himself out of his seat and held his face as close as he could to the spinning supports of the access hole.

"We have a lead, but just a few kilometers. Hopefully the *Elpis* is faster. The Horde's vessels are at least ten times our size." A turn in the torrent gave him a brief glimpse of the Horde's numbers before it straightened out again. "A dozen or so spheres, close together."

"They could have five hundred fighters chasing us," Kaminari guessed. "We need to find another way to get to Skye Stone—"

"The shimmering ribbon!" Batal jumped behind the chairs, grabbed the dripping chart off the deck, and unrolled it, placing a jar of food on each side to keep it flat. "We shared our waters with Sicily, and they with us. We also sold our catch in their markets if we were closer to their port than ours."

"Please get to where you're going, Batal. We are here"—her

finger touched near the end of the thin red line—"so we have minutes until we become a bobbing target with five hundred of the Horde coming to practice their aim."

"There." He indicated a point just beyond the end of the Shinigami Torrent. "It's there, off the port side it trails away, toward Skye Stone. I know it's there. We used it to get back from the Sicily Market, a gentle current. A shimmering ribbon on the surface, right to our harbor! It must be a torrent, so we just need to get to it."

Kaminari was off the deck and unpacking her sword. "Hand me the paddles."

Batal unlashed the paddles and handed her one. She placed the round end on the deck with the paddle end at eye level. With two quick cuts, a perfect *V*-shaped chunk of the end fell to the deck. "The other." After she repeated the cuts with the second paddle, she placed them together and lashed them tight, lining up the *V* notches. "It will take all of your strength."

"What are you going to do?" he asked Kaminari.

She unlatched the replacement iron rod from the deck. "Take care of the supports."

Batal pushed his face dangerously close to the spinning supports. "I can see Sicily. Almost there!" Behind them, the Horde's spheres were only a hundred meters away and closing. "How are they closing on us—oh shit, we're slowing!" A ripple appeared off the port as the *Elpis* came to a stop. "That's it! Batal, move back—now!"

Kaminari threw the repair rod into the spinning supports. The iron bar flew into the sphere and stuck in the wood, making the sphere drop to the left side, the shells resting on the rod.

Batal pushed the paddles through the access hole, the *V*-shaped chunk catching the sail line. Quickly, he turned his back to the front of the *Elpis* and pulled as hard as he could. Kaminari joined him, both pushing off the seat with their feet, using the interior shell as the fulcrum point.

The sail pulled to the port and caught the edge of the torrent and then exited the flow, flinging the *Elpis* up and away from the ocean's surface until it splashed down, skipping and spinning across the waves. Behind them, the Horde vessels flew by, still following the Shinigami Torrent toward the Sicily harbor. Batal and Kaminari watched their sail move toward a shimmering ribbon. A few seconds passed, and then the damaged *Elpis* was speeding toward Skye Stone. To the northwest, flaming orbs flew from Sicily, wave after wave until it disappeared from view.

"We did it!" Batal said as he watched Skye Stone come into focus. He and Kaminari embraced. "We made it."

She then dropped to her knees, clutching her stomach. "Not now, please not now."

He helped her into the chair and put the straps around her shoulders. "Contraction?"

"Maybe, I'm not sure. I've never done this before."

Smoke crept in from the damaged portside access. The exterior shell spinning directly on the rod.

He grabbed her tantō. "The surface ribbon ends right outside the entrance to Skye Stone's harbor, so this will be close." The stone wall of the break came into view, and in the protected harbor, the *Aeolus* sat at the far end of the spit, safe and undamaged. He'd done this a hundred times before, but only using the surface current. As the sphere flew toward the harbor entrance, the steel door off the beach sprang open. Guardians streamed out, swords drawn, bows leveled, as Batal cut the ocean-sail's line.

The *Elpis* spun across the calm surface, slowing with every turn, until it rolled up onto the beach and stopped.

Batal's hands popped up out of the sphere and waved at the approaching guardians. "It's Batal! Don't shoot me!"

"Prove it," boomed a deep voice from the beach. "Show your face or we burn that thing to the ground!"

It was a voice Batal recognized. "Uncle Drago!" He threw out their armor and weapons first, then slid through the undamaged starboard access and helped out Kaminari.

Jenna and Drago ran to them. Drago placing an arm around Kaminari's back, helping her through the iron door and into Skye Stone as Jenna watched their backs, bow at the ready.

"You don't waste time!" Drago said with a grin. "Batal the father? Who would have thought?" He spotted Batal picking up their gear before he followed them inside the gates. "Good to see you still have the family armor and weapons. Amira will be pleased."

Shafts then splintered off the surrounding stone. Horde warriors floated down from the sky, their mottled sails rippling in the breeze. Jenna slid in front of the open gate, shielding Kaminari and Drago, and had loosed three arrows by the time Batal had unraveled his bow. Three dead Horde warriors slammed into the ground.

"You'd better put that on." Jenna pointed to the armor he had let fall to the ground in his haste.

"Where's Danu?" Batal asked in a panic.

"On the *Aeolus*. Your hound is a bit banged up, but she's safe and will be damn happy to see you. Lots has happened since you left us." She looked to Drago. "I'm moving her to the south pier. It's safer, and the Horde will focus here." Jenna then sprinted toward the *Aeolus* as more chutes opened high above the wall.

"Come on! Dress when we get to Amira," Drago yelled. "She's at the pub. It's the only section of Skye Stone besides the harbor that we still hold."

Batal grabbed Kaminari, and they headed toward the pub on the south side of the city. "How are the contractions?" he asked.

"Bearable, but just," she replied through gritted teeth. She swallowed hard. "She's coming, Batal."

"We'll make it, all of us." He looked to Drago. "The Horde Fleet is here. We passed them before Sicily. More ships that I could count."

"They've been hitting us for weeks using the catapults and sails to get over the wall," his uncle reported. "We've evacuated anyone who couldn't fight and now the Guardians are leaving." Drago grunted. "The Horde's numbers are endless. Like an infestation, we kill hundreds and hundreds more replace them."

At Kaminari's instruction, Batal slid her chain mail over her head, which was lighter than he thought, and placed her bow over her shoulder. "Now you look like the Senshi I remember," he said as he wrapped the belt with her, her sword and tantō loosely under her belly. "You sure you want all of it?"

"Not dying here. Yes."

"You're not dying, either," Drago said, pointing at the leather armor still under Batal's arm. Batal slipped the leather vest over his skin, took off his boots, dropped his pants around his ankles, kicked them off, and slid on the leather ones.

He smelled the Horde soldier before the sword in a filthy hand slashed at his chest and tore the leather armor. Kaminari stuck her short sword through the warrior's ear and he fell.

Batal dropped the ruined leather vest to the ground, slid his bow over his shoulder, and attached his sword to his belt. Blood seeped from his chest as he pulled his boot back on. "I'm OK, but I think I should have worn your sparkly chain mail, Uncle. The leather is not working for me anymore."

Drago picked up Kaminari and jogged toward the stone building that housed the city's pub. "Hurry, Batal. She's very close." He then hammered on the thick wooden slab door. "Amira, I have Batal."

Latches clicked and scraped then the door creaked open. "Come in, come in," Amira said, closing and securing the door once everyone was inside.

"Why are you all still here?" Batal asked. "You could have left days ago."

"We knew you were coming. Received word from Tashi and Itō-sensei. You arrived just in time." Amira moved a few paces back from the door and made a bed out of seat cushions and table cloths. "Quickly, move Kaminari here. It's time.

27

A PERFECT SPARTAN

An ax slammed into the other side of the door, a piece of its crescent blade breaking through. The stench of death and shit filtered through the gap as the sound of stomping boots stopped on the other side.

Batal held a firm hand across Kaminari's mouth. His eyes burned red, tears sliding down his cheeks. Her light chain mail dug into the wound on his bare chest, but he wrapped his arms around her, his olive skin contrasting against her silver hair, and pressed his lips to her ear.

"You must push with all you have, my love," he whispered.

Drago threw a thick wooden table against the door then grunted while pushing a towering shelf across the stone floor until it slammed into the table. He followed that with stools, crates, sacks of vegetables, and anything else he could find. He reached into a crate at his feet, pulled out a bottle of clear spirits, ripped the cork out with his teeth, and guzzled half its contents in a single motion.

"They're coming, Batal," he said as he wiped his mouth. "The Horde is here. Their stench is everywhere, so they're searching for another entrance." His deep baritone never rose above a whisper.

Amira knelt between Kaminari's legs, adjusting the armor to make way for the new arrival. "I can see the head." She pushed outward on her knees. "A shoulder—"

"For the GODS!" Drago hollered as feces-tipped arrowheads pierced the front door, splitting a shelf inches from his face. He reached behind his back, unsheathed a stained blade, and pushed against the barricade. "I cannot hold them back much longer."

"You are Senshi," Batal whispered to Kaminari. "The greatest I have ever known. I will not leave you here. Push or we all die."

"Batal!" Drago screamed from the door. Foul hands reached around the barricade. Fingers missing, pus, blood-and-shit covered, the hands grabbed and pulled at anything within reach. Drago sliced off one, then another. A scrape sounded each time the barricade inched across the stone floor. "Hurry! I will not die cowering in a fucking tavern!"

Kaminari bit down onto Batal's fingers. Muscles rippled across her exposed stomach, the chain mail sliding further down her sides.

"She's out," Amira said as she cleared the baby girl's mouth and massaged the infant's back. A sputtering cry sounded. "This is going to hurt. Batal, hold Kaminari tight." She then set the baby down, cut the cord, and reached into Kaminari. "It's detached—"

Batal stepped out from behind Kaminari, sword drawn before he fully reached his feet, and cut through the "man" squeezing between the opening door and the barricade. A scream from behind him cut through the Horde's grunts as they battered at the door.

"Placenta's out. It's whole." Amira applied a bandage fashioned from a torn tablecloth between Kaminari's legs and helped the pale woman to her feet. "It's OK," she told Batal. "We were prepared for this possibility. I will carry her from here." His mother reached down and placed the crying baby in an armored pouch, then gently slung it over her shoulders and grabbed her bow and quiver.

Kaminari, pale and drenched in sweat, swayed while pulling her armor around her chest and attaching it once again. "I am ready." Her striking green eyes locked on Amira's. "If I fall, her name is Chiyo Akiro Spartan." She took a deep breath, slipped a bow and quiver onto her back, and attached her short sword, her tantō on to her side and left her broadsword.

Drago and Batal grunted, still pushing against the furniture barricade while swinging their swords, creating two wet piles of hands, arms, and other parts at their feet.

"The back door is clear," Amira whispered. "Now is the time."

Drago turned to Batal, another arrowhead bursting through the wood in front of his face. "We hold here for as long as we can then use the walls and tight paths to fight our way out and to the *Aeolus*. South pier should be open."

Batal nodded. "Jenna will be there. She's never let us down." He hacked off another arm. "Go, Kaminari. Take Mother and Chiyo—" An iron spearpoint erupted through the splintering wood next to Batal's groin.

"I won't leave you!" Kaminari growled.

"Protect Mother and Chiyo. We will see you at the *Aeolus*."

The barricade moved another inch, and Batal kicked his heal into the floor. "I love you. Now save our child."

Amira and Kaminari then disappeared into the shadows.

The door shook violently. Batal and Drago fell back a step from the barricade then threw their bodies against the moving mass of furniture and crates. Armored heads appeared, wiggling through the growing opening. *They are only men*, Batal thought. *Evil, stinking, filthy brutes, but men all the same.* He brought down his sword with a quick powerful motion. A shit-encrusted helmet clanked off the stone, the head inside rolling out.

Again, the barricade shook, forcing Drago to his knees. But then he was up again, throwing himself against the barrier, but it continued to move.

"Alleyway!" Batal grunted. "Bottleneck at the iron gate."

Drago nodded, then mouthed "Three, two—"

The crates, shelf, table, and door exploded. Batal's chest hit his knees, his body half bent and light as a feather as stones set in the floor passed beneath him. *How carefully each is placed*, he thought. Drago tumbled next to him, twisting, yelling at the shadow that stood on the other side of the room, filling the doorway. Both men skidded on the stone floor, stopping near the back door of the tavern. Batal staggered to his feet, stumbled forward, and grabbed his sword off the floor. His bow was gone. An arrow hummed by his left ear and clanked against the stone wall behind him.

Across the room, the shadow ducked, turned, and entered what was left of the doorway.

Batal froze. "What the fuck—?"

Another figure blew through the door behind them. "Get Down!" screamed Kaminari.

Batal hit the cool stone. Arrows zipped overhead.

A roar consumed the tavern, and the shadow fell back.

"Run!" Kaminari was exiting out the back of the tavern behind a staggering Drago.

The shadow was coming toward them and others had joined it. Batal rolled up off the stone and sprinted toward the door. Sun lit his face as he crashed into the wall of the alleyway, turned, and headed toward the iron gate. Crossbow bolts shattered on the wall behind him. Drago ran and limped ahead of Kaminari, who ran sideways, her bow focused in Batal's direction. Blood trailed down the inside of her thighs. She stopped to lean into her pull.

"Left!" she shouted.

Batal moved left, arm grating against the stone wall as her arrow zipped past his eye and something thudded on the path behind him.

"Right!"

Batal cut right and pushed off the stone wall, gaining speed. Two arrows flashed by, only a second apart. Another roar sounded from behind, the wailing fading as he ran. Kaminari dropped to a knee, bow falling from her shaking hand. Batal slowed his charge, dipped, and slammed her midsection with his left shoulder as he grabbed the bow with his right hand.

Both screamed in pain, but Batal ran with her over his shoulder, heart pounding. Twenty meters ahead, Drago reached the iron gate set into the mammoth south wall of Skye Stone. The Guardians and their powerful deerhounds were gone.

Holding his arm close to his side, Drago kicked the small gate open and pushed through, holding it open from the outside. "Run! Run, Batal!"

An arrow tore through Batal's side and broke against the wall. He and Kaminari fell through the gate and tumbled onto the gravel. Waves lapped at the foundation of the towering stone fortress. Drago slammed the gate shut and wedged a stout, bleached log gifted by the high tide into the stone surrounding the door. Shafts hammered the other side.

"It won't hold for long." Drago lifted an unconscious Kaminari off the ground and slung her over his shoulder. "Don't look back, Batal. Just get your ass up. The end of the spit's within sight. Where's the *Aeolus*?"

Batal straightened and grabbed the flapping flesh at his side, then looked at his bloody hand and reached down for Kaminari's bow. "It'll be there! Go!"

The iron gate's hinges screeched, the plating stretching outward. A deep bellow boomed from the other side. Another thunderous impact and the gate rattled, a second protrusion appearing below the first.

"There!" Batal yelled, pointing at the towering mast of the *Aeolus* that had appeared from behind the breakwater. "Jenna has come!" He unslung the quiver dangling from Kaminari's back. "We'll need time. Just get her to the boat."

Drago strained forward along the narrow stone spit. "Make them count!"

"I will." Batal turned, dropped to one knee, and nocked an arrow. Voices sounded from behind him, but he focused on the iron gate that was rattling like a loose tooth.

"Steady, my son. On your left," Amira said from behind him.

The gate's upper hinge flew into air.

"Mother, where's Chiyo?" Batal drew back the bow.

"Drago can carry them both, I cannot."

"Please get to the *Aeolus*. We both don't need to die."

Amira's small feet twisted into the ground behind him and

she released a controlled breath. From over his left shoulder, an arrowhead and the curving wood of a drawn bow appeared.

"Do not worry about your mother," she replied. "She has the best shield a Guardian could ask for. A bit bloody, and lacking his armor, but a nice shield all the same." Grit entered her voice. "We're all getting on that boat."

Metal on metal echoed as the iron gate flew through the air like a leaf and tore into the gravel only meters in front of Batal and Amira. Two rotted forms moved out of the shadows of Skye-Stone.

Amira's bow drew back further. "Wait, Batal. Hold for what leads them."

Batal tried to pull in a breath, his lungs burning, hands shaking. *Blood*, he thought. *I am losing too much. But steady yourself, all depends on this moment.* He exhaled slowly and drew back his bow until the base of the arrowhead touched wood.

A massive hand emerged from the shadowy hole and grabbed the stone doorway. Another hand grasped the other side. Grunting sounded and the arched stone surrounding where the iron gate had once stood birthed the biggest man Batal had ever seen.

"It cannot be," Amira whispered. "The Horde King lives."

Amira and Batal loosed their first and second arrows before the beast stood fully upright. An inhuman roar followed. It must have been three meters tall and the width of two men and carried a crossbow as big as Batal. He nocked another arrow and released. The beast grabbed one of the Horde and held up the squealing man as a shield, then charged toward their position.

"Go, Mother. The king's armor is too thick!" The pair of them turned and ran down the spit, with Batal staying between

Amira and the Horde as they poured out of the gateway, following their king.

Spears, arrows, and stones rained around Amira and Batal. The *Aeolus* was at the end of the spit, and Drago looked to be loading Kaminari and Chiyo onboard. The narrow stone path made a hard right twenty meters away, and then it was another thirty meters to the *Aeolus*. But his mother was slowing. She dropped her bow and kept running. Behind them, the smaller of the Horde gained ground as their King loped behind them.

We won't make it, Batal thought. *The turn will make us easier targets for the Horde.* They headed right, the *Aeolus* already drifting off the spit on the receding tide, ready to flee. A tall, armored figure holding a longbow appeared on the end of the spit, red stubble glowing on top of her head. Arrows flew in rapid succession.

"Jenna!" Batal turned and loosed a shot as he ran. His target dropped and some of the Horde stumbled over the body and fell, but more kept running. As spears raked around them, Amira reached the end of the spit. Jenna grabbed her and threw her toward the *Aeolus*. Drago caught his sister's hand, clinging to her while she hung against the side. Jenna loosed what remained in her quiver, downing the closest of the chasing Horde. She then turned, took two powerful strides, and launched onto the boat.

Batal shot his last arrow at the Horde King to little effect and then jumped from the edge of the spit, crashing over the ship's gunwale and sprawling onto the deck in a heap.

"Pull in Amira!" Jenna yelled to a battered and exhausted Drago. "There's no wind inside the break, just the current!"

Drago was half stretched over the side, holding onto Amira's arm with both hands as her legs skimmed the water's surface. Batal got to his feet, swaying with the boat's movements, and staggered toward Drago. The *Aeolus*, the dual-hulled catamaran, was pulling away on the tide, but her distance from the end of the spit was only twenty meters.

Movement from the spit caught Batal's eye. The Horde King stood with his giant crossbow aimed in his direction. Even from the growing distance the king's eyes remained locked on Batal, black bottomless spheres that covered half his face. *He's not human, he can't be.*

"I'm losing her! Help me, Batal!" Drago yelled.

Batal knelt next to his uncle, but kept his eyes on the spit. The Horde King shook his head, a sharp toothy smile taking up the rest of his face as he adjusted his aim, tracking the *Aeolus* with a bolt the size of an oak branch aimed at Batal.

Batal leaned over to grab his mother's arm.

The Horde King's crossbow moved from Batal, angled up to adjust for the growing distance, and then he loosed the weapon's thick bolt.

Amira fell slack, the force of the bolt ripping her out of Drago's grip, pinning her lifeless form to the hull while the *Aeolus* picked up speed. She then slid off and disappeared beneath the sea.

"No!" Batal screamed. "No!"

Batal crumpled to the deck. Hundreds of arrows from the Horde filled the air only to slip harmlessly into the waters behind them. The rocky spit had become a writhing mass of filthy arms and legs. From a distance, it looked like a colony of ants. Then the Horde was gone, and so was Skye Stone.

Jenna tied off the wheel so she could help Drago and Batal to their feet. "I'm sorry." She then put her arms around them, and they all three wept.

Finally, Batal stepped back. "Kaminari and Chiyo?"

"Safe and sound below deck," Drago replied, tears flowing. "Both exhausted and weak, but sleeping soundly. Chiyo is a perfect Spartan. Lesion free."

Batal moved toward the stern and the hatch to the cabin below. "It's not your fault, Uncle Drago."

Drago collapsed against a storage locker, bought his hands to his face, and cried for his sister.

"You saved us, Jenna. You could've sailed to safety," Batal said. "If such a thing exists."

"No." Jenna stepped over to the wheel and sat at the helm. "I couldn't."

Batal opened the hatch and sat on the steps. "Danu! Danu!" he cried.

A heavily bandaged deerhound limped out of the cabin and came to sit on Batal's lap, where she licked his face, yipping and happy.

"Mother is gone." Batal wrapped his arms around Danu. "We've lost it all, girl. We've lost Mother and Skye Stone to the Horde." He kissed her muzzle and turned toward Jenna on the wheel. "The Great Unknown. That is where we find a safe harbor, train an army, build a fleet, and take back Skye Stone from the fucking Horde."

Batal then rose and went over to the cleat that held the line for the red sail.

"For Amira! For Skye Stone!" Jenna yelled.

Batal released the line and the vast red-waxed cloth unrolled from the top of the mast and caught the wind. The sail with the noble face of the Scottish deerhound pulled them southeast toward the Great Unknown.

SEA SHANTY (SONG & PRAYER)

Oh, we'd be all right if the wind was in our sails
We'd be all right if the wind was in our sails
We'd be all right if the wind was in our sails
And we'll all hang on behind...

And we'll ro-o-oll the old Aeolus *along!*
We'll ro-o-oll the old Aeolus *along!*
We'll ro-o-oll the old Aeolus *along!*
And we'll all hang on behind!

Oh, we'd be all right if we make it out the bay
We'd be all right if we make it out the bay
We'd be all right if we make it out the bay
And we'll all hang on behind...

And we'll ro-o-oll the old Aeolus *along!*
We'll ro-o-oll the old Aeolus *along!*

We'll ro-o-oll the old Aeolus *along!*
And we'll all hang on behind!

Now, another cup of wine wouldn't do us any harm
Oh, another cup of wine wouldn't do us any harm
Woah, another cup of wine wouldn't do us any harm
And we'll all hang on behind...

And we'll ro-o-oll the old Aeolus *along!*
We'll ro-o-oll the old Aeolus *along!*
We'll ro-o-oll the old Aeolus *along!*
And we'll all hang on behind!

Oh, we'd be all right if the wind was in our sails
We'd be all right if the wind was in our sails
We'd be all right if the wind was in our sails
And we'll all hang on behind...

And we'll ro-o-oll the old Aeolus *along!*
We'll ro-o-oll the old Aeolus *along!*
We'll ro-o-oll the old Aeolus *along!*
And we'll all hang on behind!

And we'll ro-o-oll the old Aeolus *along!*
We'll ro-o-oll the old Aeolus *along!*
We'll ro-o-oll the old Aeolus *along!*
And we'll all hang on behind!

If you enjoyed

***Batal, Volume I of the Spartan Chronicles**,*

please leave a review to let the world know.

Independent authors need your voice as much as their own. Thank you for supporting my storyworlds.

Without you, they would not exist.

– Iain Richmond

ALSO BY IAIN RICHMOND

Darkness, Book 1 of the Oortian Wars

Beyond Terra, Tales from the Seven Worlds

Coming 2020

Rise of Spartans, Volume II of the Spartan Chronicles

Planet Stealers, Book Two of the Oortian Wars

WORLDS OF IAIN RICHMOND

Thank you for purchasing this book. Visit
www.iainrichmond.com
and sign up for my spam-free newsletter
and receive a free copy of
BEYOND TERRA, Tales from the Seven Worlds,
an anthology of short stories!

I'll let you know when new releases are in the works, give you sneak peeks at rough drafts and original storyworlds. Free, no spam and a unique view into the worlds of Iain Richmond.

ABOUT THE AUTHOR

Iain Richmond is a builder and designer of creative spaces and unique furniture from Kathmandu to San Francisco. He has worked with and learned from craftsman around the world using salvaged and reclaimed materials. From living on a 30' boat in Juneau, Alaska to building his own home (board by board, paycheck by paycheck) on his small ranch in northern California, Iain has always dreamed of a life where he could follow his true passion... writing science fiction. When he leaves his 'writing shack' on Lore Mountain, Iain visits countries and communities that inspire new characters and vast storyworlds: Nepal, Isle of Skye, SE Alaska, Malta, and Southern Utah are a few of his favorite spots. He loves life with a small footprint, wildlife, wild-lands, and the hope of a perfect world filled with tolerant people. You can still find him boxing (more of a punching bag these days), playing rugby (see punching bag), trekking, and gardening (wine or scotch in hand), but spending quiet moments with his wife (much better half) and Bernese Mountain Dog(s) still ranks at the top of his life-list.

Lightning Source UK Ltd.
Milton Keynes UK
UKHW012223021219
354640UK00001B/67/P